Courtney stopped abruptly as the scatterings of a cave-in came into view. "Oh no," she whispered, one hand to her mouth. Moving slowly, she noticed a body slumped in the hallway. "Please don't be dead," she said over and over again as she moved closer. She couldn't help but wonder which of her friends lay there, and what had happened to the other.

The closer she came, the more detail came to light. She recognized Tyler Durand as he lay on his side. His light-colored hair lay limp against his head. His skin looked unnaturally pale. At least she didn't think he was dead. It took a lot to kill a dragon. But just beyond him, a little more out of the way, lay Anwen Porter. And she wasn't moving.

Also by Karlie Lucas

TARRAGON: KEY KEEPER
TARRAGON: DRAGON BANE

THE UNKNOWN ELF

KAS

Tarragon
Dragon Mage

KARLIE LUCAS

DragonKey Press

Tarragon: Dragon Mage
© 2017 Karlie Lucas
http://www.karlielucas.com

Cover Design by Karlie Lucas

Paperback ISBN-13: 978-1-948028-06-6
Library of Congress Control Number: 2018915079

DragonKey Press
Dallas, Texas USA

PRINTED IN THE UNITED STATES OF AMERICA

To all Key Keepers and Dragon Mages alike.

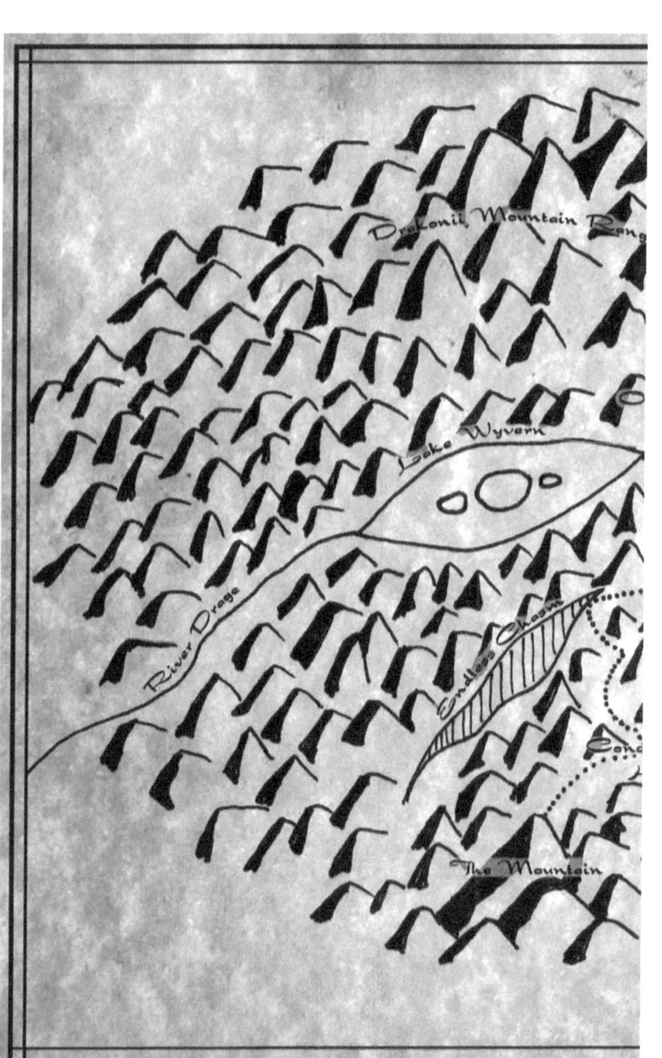

Drakonii Mountain Range
Lake Wyvern
River Drage
Endless Chasm
The Mountain

...in Range
Village of Lindwurm
Old Mill
Blausii
Concencrated Hall
...untain
N
W E
S
Bandon Desert
Copyright 2013 Karlie Loucas

Tarragon
Dragon Mage

ONE

THE LOW GROWL OF A lion filled the air as Courtney Willis gripped her spear. Slippery with sweat, her hands slid across the smooth surface of the carved weapon. Blood trickled down her cheek. She'd barely managed to avoid being mauled by the massive beast before her. Despite her fortune, the beast had still left a decent looking mark on her skin.

Next to her, the simulacrum warrior waited to strike another blow. Summoned from Vision Dust, the ghostly woman had more than proved her worth. Courtney couldn't have asked for a better companion. She only wished she knew who the woman was and where she'd come from.

The stone columns of the courtyard lay in ruins all around her, more so than they had before the battle began. Even the small amphitheater at the one end of the square had been affected by the battle. It no longer resembled the smooth-walled structure it once was. Courtney felt glad, though, that the destruction didn't go past this part of the Ruined City.

Pushing a loose strand of hair from her face, the mage hoped the Fallen was as tired as she felt. It seemed like the battle had lasted hours. In reality, it had only been about thirty or forty minutes. Still, it felt like an eternity had passed since she'd watched Tyler and Anwen race away. She just hoped they'd reached the Gates of Eternity unhindered. Even if she failed, her sacrifice would be it worth it if those two made it inside the Mountain.

The manticore let out another roar as it finished licking off one of its more painful wounds. The gash made it more difficult for the Fallen to maneuver before. The blow had almost severed one of the back leg joints above its knee. But it was stubborn and spun around on three paws. Its scorpion-tipped tail came crashing down towards the fledgling dragon mage once more.

Before the stinging tail could reach Courtney's neck, the translucent warrior blocked the blow. The clash sent out a strong gust of wind, knocking the simulacrum off her feet. For the briefest of moments, the dust composing her body scattered across the stone ground. Despite this, the ghost managed to pull herself together again in time to block another round.

Courtney cried out in pain as a sharp fragment of stone pierced through her upper arm on the left side. While her companion blocked the continued attacks, the mage pulled the fragment free. She ripped off the bottom part of her shirt to create a makeshift bandage, pulling it tight. The only good point she could see about this turn of events was that it wasn't her dominant arm.

Finished with her ministrations, Courtney hefted her spear, ready for the next attack. Feeling time was against her, she decided on a drastic course of action. Her strength was waning. The Fallen's wasn't. "Give me speed," she whispered as she drew upon her meager knowledge of dragon magic. It was a spell she didn't use often. It was quite taxing, but speed was of the essence if she was to end this once and for all.

Feeling her entire body vibrate with energy, Courtney launched herself at the manticore. Her spear thrust out to score the underside of its belly. With a yell, she thrust the point upward at the last possible second. It broke through the coarse lion skin, piercing the monster through the heart. At the same time, the dust warrior thrust her ethereal spear through its skull. It traveled clean through the bone.

Another strong blast of wind threw Courtney backwards as the energy she'd exerted rebounded. She rammed into one of the many fallen pillars, the wind knocked from her. She could only stare like a fish out of water as the massive Fallen disintegrated into dust. Another gust of wind filled the shattered arena. It blew the ashy remains down the mountain path and out over the Endless Chasm some ways away.

Heavy sobs as tearless as the desert wracked her body as she tried to process what had just happened. Courtney's chest constricted with the need for air. She hyperventilated for the first few minutes until she could calm down. She wanted to be sick, though there wasn't much to expel. All the same, she heaved several times until her mind was able to smooth over the shock and distress.

Back in control, Courtney looked around to see that only part of the manticore remained, the spiked end of its tail. Perhaps it was like the last drop of blood crystallized into stone as a trophy of conquest. Whatever the reason, she felt no desire to claim it.

Instead, she turned away from the massive stinger and looked around for the apparition. But no matter how hard she looked she couldn't see her. The woman was gone. Courtney sent a quick word of thanks towards whatever corners of the earth the spirit had scattered. For a small moment, she wondered if she'd ever see her again.

Just as she was about to assess the total damage to her body, the ground rumbled beneath her. The few remaining upright pillars fell to the ground with resounding thuds, sending dust up into the air. Courtney had to turn and cover her nose and mouth to not breathe in the fine powder.

After a minute or so, the shaking stopped, but she felt more than a little rattled by the sensation. One of the pillars could have fallen on her instead of on empty ground.

Then realization hit her like a bolt of lightning, knocking her to her knees. "Anwen! Tyler!" she gasped. Without another thought, the girl launched herself towards the long path leading towards the gates. If the Mountain quaked, more so than when the Gates had opened, something must have gone wrong.

Madame Millard surveyed those sitting before her with smug satisfaction. Their time had finally come. After feeling the quake, she'd ordered all members of the Mage Circle to gather. Surely the quake signified the unsealing of the Gates, a much-awaited event.

Once word had spread, it hadn't taken long for them to assemble. And now they all sat facing the portly woman. Knowing there were enough to fill the city hall only made her feel that much more powerful. These were her people and she knew they'd follow her no matter what the cost.

"My fellow mages," Matilda Millard began, arms raised. "Our time has come! Though it may not be in the manner we'd hoped, the Mountain has been reopened! Now is our chance to take control of Tarragon once and for all. Before the dragons are wakened from their spell-induced slumber!"

Cheers filled the air of the assembly room. Many exchanged smug smiles as dragon mages, both male and female, nodded in unison. Legends had been passed down the generations. Legends of the great battle for control of the Mountain many hundreds of years ago. Hopes had dwindled over time, but were now rekindled.

The master mage surveyed the growing excitement before her. It was easy to incite a crowd when one had the ability to manipulate matter. Some were more skilled than others. But of all those in the Mage Circle, she had the most experience and skill. And she wanted to keep it that way.

Competition was not allowed. But those closest in ability and skill were invited into the Inner Circle as a matter of respect.

Just as the master mage was about to open her mouth again, the ground shook like a galloping mare. Those mages who were standing were thrown to the ground. The others managed to maintain their seats. Exclamations of fear filled the air as the lights flickered. Never had the Village of Lindwyrm had such a quake.

Madame Millard avoided being thrown by grabbing onto the podium she stood in front of. Her eyes grew wide as the Soul Presence of one of her mages suddenly vanished from the Mountains. "No," she whispered, her knees going weak as the floor settled back to its more solid state. It wasn't possible. Her niece was too careful, too skilled to be snuffed out like a candle. It should not have happened. Not when she was up against a wannabe mage, a defenseless Keeper, and... a dragon lord.

The overweight woman gasped. Had her dreams from earlier that afternoon been true? Was Tyler Durand actually a dragon? Now that she thought about it, the idea made sense. And if Daphne had gone up against a dragon, there was a chance the girl wasn't as strong as she'd believed. Her loss meant some things had to change, though part of her loathed the idea.

"Madame Millard!" one of several mages exclaimed in alarm at her pensive expression. "Are you all right?"

The woman nodded. Her face was still pale from the realization. "I'm fine," she assured, waving off the helping hands. "There is something going on that I don't like," she admitted. "We must mobilize now, before anything else happens. I want everyone ready and waiting out on the Quad before the sun rises. No more waiting. We go to claim the Mountain on the morrow or die trying."

Massive cheers filled the room, though the mages still moved to obey. An order given by the master mage ought never be ignored.

TWO

AFTER WHAT FELT LIKE AN eternity, Courtney stepped over the threshold of the Gates and into the Front Gallery of the Mountain stronghold. Despite the damage to the courtyard below, the path and gateway were intact. It was almost as if some spell kept them from destruction. Or, perhaps, more likely, magical reinforcements she could not see with the naked eye.

Conjuring an orb of light, she noticed footsteps in the dust. They were only a little disturbed by the Mountain's quaking. Guessing the prints belonged to the other members of her party, she began to follow them. Walking pace steady for a good ten minutes, she traced their course. The going was slow as her limbs felt stiff and leaden, but she plodded on. Chances were good her friends were in worse straits than she.

Some while later, one set of prints seemed to disappear into the wall of the passageway she followed. The blond almost despaired at this unexpected dead end. But, upon closer inspection, she realized the second set of prints continued on. Their owner had doubled back, and then gone on in a different direction. She took into consideration the difference between the two sets. It was easy to discern that the individual had been in a bigger hurry the second time around.

The mage followed these newer prints with haste. They led her through a maze of stone hallways and tunnels. Just when it began to feel like she'd never find her friends, she saw something glowing ahead. It took her a moment to realize the light came from another conjured orb. Heart pounding, she ran towards it, hoping it wasn't some kind of trap. She'd had enough fighting for one day.

Courtney stopped abruptly as the scatterings of a cave-in came into view. "Oh no," she whispered, one hand to her mouth. Moving slowly, she noticed a body slumped in the hallway. "Please don't be dead," she said over and over again as she moved closer. She couldn't help but wonder which of her friends lay there, and what had happened to the other.

The closer she came, the more detail came to light. She recognized Tyler Durand as he lay on his side. His light-colored hair lay limp against his head. His skin looked unnaturally pale. At least she didn't think he was dead. It took a lot to kill a dragon. But just beyond him, a little more out of the way, lay Anwen Porter. And she wasn't moving.

The mage moved to Anwen's side. She felt relieved to see her chest rising and falling at a steady rate, even if she was covered in blood and dirt. Because of the low light, it was hard to tell what kind of damage her friend might have received. But at least she was alive. And in her clenched hand lay the master key. Courtney heaved a sigh of relief for that luck.

Moving back to Tyler's side, she dropped to her knees and shook him. He didn't respond, even after she called his name. She felt for a pulse and was gratified to feel the faint throb of circulating blood. Mustering her remaining strength, she rolled him onto his back. She then chaffed his wrists to try and warm them.

Anwen began to stir. She groaned as she opened her eyes, quickly closing them against the light. "Ow," she managed, raising one arm to cover her face. The key dropped from her hand, landing on the stone floor with a dull thud.

At the sound of Anwen's voice, Tyler also began to stir. He opened his eyes, pulling his hand free from Courtney's to try and block out the light of the orbs as well. A raging headache throbbed behind his temples. With a wave of his other hand, the light from the orbs dimmed. Then, much like a weary soldier, he moved to a sitting position.

Courtney felt tears welling up as she slumped back, the stress of the past few days finally catching up to her once more. And, unlike outside in the courtyard, this time the tears flowed. "I can't believe we're all still alive," she confessed. "I was afraid--"

"That we'd died?" Tyler finished for her. "It was a near thing."

Eyes now adjusted to the lessened light, Courtney looked around. She nodded towards the rubble around them. "What happened?"

Rolling to one side, Tyler grunted. "Long story. Can you help me with Anwen? She's pretty banged up."

Courtney moved to her friend's other side, opposite of Tyler. While she moved, Tyler placed a hand over Anwen's forehead and heart. She couldn't help but notice the resulting light from the contact seemed dull. She tried to remember if the last time he'd done this had been the same or not.

Tyler sighed in relief. When he'd split his soul, offering up half to her, he'd hoped for a miracle. And he'd gotten one. The superficial wounds remained, and one of her legs was broken, but it could have been worse. He thanked the stars for that small mercy.

Anwen tried not to wince as she shifted to a more comfortable position, deciding to just sit up. With some help, she managed to move to the wall where she could have some support. "You asked what happened," the Keeper said, looking at Courtney. "It was Daphne. She tried to kill me."

"Daphne? Daphne Millard?" Courtney stared at her, trying to understand. "But she wouldn't hurt a fly. I grew up with her. Sure, she's a pain, but she'd never do anything like that."

Anwen laughed without humor, trying not to cough. "Funny how she gave off that impression, until she began using me as a human pin cushion." She groaned in pain as Courtney jogged her leg by accident.

"Sorry," Courtney apologized and moved a bit further away.

Focusing on breathing, Anwen nodded. "It's fine. I'm okay. It just hurts. It could definitely be worse. I could still be under that pile of rock." She indicated the rubble with a twitch of her shoulder.

Tyler shook his head. "Will you ever learn to stop being so self-sacrificing?"

Courtney tried to hold back a snort but couldn't. It broke free like dammed up water. She laughed so hard it hurt and she had to roll onto her back, wiping at her eyes with dirty hands.

"I didn't think it was all that funny," Anwen retorted.

Tyler just shook his head as he moved to examine Anwen's leg. It was broken mid-thigh, exactly where Daphne had pierced the bone with her spear. "We're going to need to find something to splint that with," he noted. "I'm pretty sure I don't have enough left in me to fix it right now."

Anwen looked up as he spoke; reminded of something Daphne'd told her during their confrontation. "Tyler, is it true? What Daphne said?"

Tyler took off his shirt and started ripping it apart, using that as an excuse not to look at her. "Is what true?" Ripping one section near the bottom, his hand brushed the fallen key. Without thinking, he picked it up, pocketing it in one smooth motion.

Hesitating, Anwen bit her lip. "While taunting me, Daphne called me stupid for not realizing you were a dragon. Are you one? A dragon, that is?"

Courtney lay breathless on the floor, spent. She turned towards Tyler to see how he'd answer; knowing neither one of them had told her yet.

Nodding, Tyler moved to bind Anwen's still bleeding wounds. "Yes. It's true. I am a dragon."

Anwen held back the need to scream as he bandaged her arm. The wound ran deeper than the other three Daphne had inflicted. "Why didn't you tell me?" she asked through clenched teeth.

Tyler tied off the makeshift bandage, using his teeth to tighten the knot. "I decided you had enough on your plate. Discovering that not only are you a Key Keeper, but that there are many out there who want you dead, is a lot to handle. That's why."

Courtney nodded at Tyler's words. Whether her auburn-haired friend accepted that or not was, of course, up to her. "I know I'd be more than overwhelmed with just half of that," she commented. "I'm overwhelmed just knowing you exist."

The dragon lord ripped off another length of fabric. He used it to bind Anwen's other arm. "What else did she say?"

At his prompting, Anwen began to describe what had happened after they'd been separated. She shuddered at the recollection of the callus cruelty in the older girl's eyes. "Daphne mentioned something about being the rightful heir of the Kaida line. She said she was a direct descendent of the first Dragon Mage. What did she mean by that?"

Hearing the name Kaida, Courtney rolled back to a sitting position. She wondered how Tyler would answer that question. Having been brought up as a mage, she already knew the answer. But Anwen was different. She was an outsider, not someone who grew up in the village.

Finishing his ministrations, Tyler brushed his hands off on what remained of his clothes. "Kaida is the name of the first dragon mage," he replied. "She was the daughter of Kern Durand and Anna Magus. Kern was--is the oldest dragon in the world. Out of respect for their line, Kaida became a sort of title. It was used for the one destined to inherit the full power of the dragon mage."

"Oh." Anwen slumped to one side, hands pressed against the ground. A million questions swarmed in her mind; a million questions she dared not ask. Wasn't Tyler's last name Durand? Was he somehow related to this Kern? Or was that just a coincidence? And what about her? Her middle name was Kaida. Was that just a coincidence as well?

Tyler smiled at her. "Let's worry about that later," he said. "Right now, we need to figure out a way to get out of here and get you some better medical attention, okay?"

Returning his smile with a more hesitant one, Anwen agreed.

Courtney got to her feet, brushing off the dust. Her movements reminded her of the wounds she harbored but she didn't mention them. "Sounds good to me. And since I seem to be in the best shape, I volunteer to go find something to use as a splint." Not waiting for a response, she headed back the way she'd come, her light orb bobbing behind her.

Tyler watched her go, pursing his lips. It didn't take soul tracing to know Courtney was also hurt. He could smell the blood. He just hoped her injuries were more superficial, or they'd all be in trouble.

Anwen swooned. "Ugh, I want to be sick," she announced. The sensation reminded her of falling off the Mountain, except it wasn't from vertigo.

"You've lost a lot of blood," Tyler noted as he turned back to her. "That will make you light headed. And I don't even want to contemplate what kind of internal injuries you had when I unearthed you. That will have an effect too, even if most of those wounds have been healed. If I had the energy, I'd repair your other injuries as well. But I don't."

Tyler had to blink. Behind his closed lids, he saw the image of Anwen lying there on the ground, lifeless. Her soul energy had been almost non-existent. As such, he'd done the only thing he'd thought possible. He shuddered at the image of her pale complexion, almost waxy in color, before reopening his eyes. "As is, I don't have enough energy to do much of anything. It kind of leaves me feeling pretty useless, to be honest."

"Not useless," Anwen disagreed, pressing one hand against his arm. "No one is useless."

Tyler gave her a wan smile. "Thousands of years and it's all I can do to see straight," he chuckled.

Moving her least injured arm, Anwen pressed a hand to the side of her head. "Can I just have a day, or even a few hours when I don't feel like someone's trying to kill me?" She slid to lie fully on the ground, curling up around the dragon lord as best she could.

Still laughing, Tyler agreed. "I wouldn't mind in the least." He leaned forward to play with a strand of her hair. "A fine sight we look. Especially when you add in Courtney fighting off a creature from your darkest nightmares."

"Yeah," Anwen agreed, glad for the coolness of the stone floor against her temple. She closed her eyes.

Images flashed behind her closed lids. Daphne taunting her. Daphne cutting a lock of her hair. Daphne sprinkling the hair into the blood she'd lost. Daphne throwing powder around the room, chanting some kind of incantation.

Pushing herself up just a little, Anwen looked at her companion. "Tyler, there's something I need to tell you. It's about when Daphne trapped me in that," she glanced at the mass of earth behind her, flinching a bit as she did. "I'd almost forgotten about it."

Hearing her serious tone, Tyler sat up. "What is it?"

Struggling to recall exactly what had happened, Anwen pieced together the events for him. She was even able to recall a few of the strange words Daphne had used in her seemingly random mutterings. Why she hadn't told him earlier was beyond her. Feeling even more drained; she dropped back to the ground, clutching at her head once more. It felt like someone had set a jackhammer loose inside her skull.

Tyler remained silent as he digested what Anwen had just told him. A cold dread formed in the pit of his stomach. Finally, he looked up. "You're sure that's exactly what happened?"

"Yes," Anwen managed. The pain was becoming far worse than any she'd felt before. "More or less."

She saw the dark-clad girl gloating over her. She could feel each stab of the spear as if for the first time. The air grew thicker as she thought about it, trying to remember.

Tyler leaned closer to her, almost hesitant as he reached out a hand to touch her face. "Anwen, this is important. I need you to try and remember. What happened after Daphne completed the circle of dust?"

Grimacing, Anwen squeezed her eyes shut. The events of that encounter fragmented behind her eyes. She desperately tried to grasp them and put them back together. Her breathing became more labored the harder she tried. "I... I reached into my pocket for the key. I remembered seeing Mathias using it as a sword.... and thought about your bone knife."

Anwen paused, her chest feeling heavier and heavier. "She threw the dust on me. It burned. Then she raised her hands and--"

She tried to contain a scream as light exploded behind her closed lids, searing her mind. With one more push of pure willpower, she all but forced out the last sentence. "Then the key grew into a sword and there was a bright flash of light... And--" Her words trailed off with another grunt of pain, followed by silence as her whole body went limp.

"Anwen?" Tyler's eyes went wide. He shook her without thinking about what further damage he might inflict. "Anwen? Anwen, wake up! Come on! Don't do this to me!" Rolling her onto her back, he noticed her chest still rising and falling. He almost sat back in relief but didn't.

"We can't stay here," he said to himself. "We're going to need help though. I can't do this alone." He looked around for anything he could use to send a message.

THREE

COURTNEY RETURNED TO THE MOUNTAIN chamber to find Tyler rummaging around in the debris. She carried two pieces of wood, perfect for making a splint. She felt rather proud of herself for coaxing the wood into this form. "What are you doing?" she asked, almost causing Tyler to jump.

"Don't do that," he admonished, embarrassed that she'd managed to catch him off guard.

"Sorry," she apologized, holding out the splints.

Abandoning his search, Tyler accepted the wood shafts as he moved back to Anwen's side. He had to tear more strips from his shirt, this time from his pants, so he could tie the wooden lengths in place. "Looks like I need to get a new wardrobe," he joked.

Courtney moved closer, her light orb bobbing behind her as she knelt next to her two friends. "Is she going to be okay?" she asked, glancing at Anwen's pale face. She didn't like how her breathing sounded.

Tyler sat back after finishing the last knot. "I'm not sure," he admitted with a sigh. He closed his eyes, passing a hand over his forehead to wipe away the sweat that had accumulated there. He looked over, staring into Courtney's concerned eyes. "Have you ever heard of the Ritual of Obliteration?"

Courtney sucked in her breath, eyes going wide.

"I'll take that as a yes," Tyler said, nodding in confirmation. "I believe Daphne was trying to perform it on Anwen. She told me a few things about what Daphne did while you were gone and it sounded a lot like that ritual." Seeing the look on Courtney's face, he hastily added, "I don't think she finished. But it was likely a near thing."

Courtney felt sick inside just thinking about it. "Only the highest level mages could perform something like that," she whispered. "But why they'd want to, or why it was even created, I'll never know."

Tyler checked on Anwen, making sure she was still breathing. Reassured, he resumed his previous search. "Why do humans do many things?" he asked. "Because there are many things you creatures do that don't make sense. My guess is they devised it by accident. Then decided to write it down in case they found someone who, in their eyes, deserved it. Someone who stood in the way of their goals."

Courtney watched Tyler as he pulled out a long stone splinter from the mess of debris. "Sounds like something the Mage Circle would use," she commented, thinking about Madame Millard. "But how in the world did Daphne learn about it, let alone how to do it? From what I understand, it takes a great deal of power and concentration to do. Not to mention the right materials."

Tyler nodded as he ran his fingers down the length of the shard he'd found, searching it for impurities. "I know. I'm still trying to figure out where she could have gotten the ashes of a dragon. Were they given to her or did she steal them? The Mage Circle would guard something like that with great care. Especially since there haven't been any dragons to use for that purpose."

He grimaced at the thought, wondering if the remains had belonged to anyone he'd known. It was possible and he mourned for the potential fool they belonged to. It was likely they were from a dragon who had sided with, then been betrayed by the Circle. Or, more probable, it had been one who had fallen defending the Mountain.

Courtney looked troubled. "Goes to show you just how little I knew about her," she commented. "Makes me feel like a shallow idiot. I can't believe I lived most of my life like that, eyes closed, heart locked away where it couldn't feel. I don't want to return to that."

Tyler smiled at her comment. "I'm sure Anwen would appreciate it if you didn't. I know I would," he said as he moved to clear an area of floor with his hand. "Now, if I can just get a message out to a friend I have, we can get out of here. I don't know if Daphne was working on her own or not. Either way, we can't stay here just waiting for the rest of the mages to show up. We have to retreat. At least for now."

"Agreed," Courtney said. "What do you need me to do?"

Motioning her to stand back, Tyler knelt on the ground. "Just hope I have enough energy to send this where it needs to go, and to help drag Anwen to the Ruined City below. I don't know about you, but I doubt I have enough in me to carry her."

The dragon turned his attention back to the long shard in his hands. He spun one end into the ground like he was trying to start a fire. Filling his lungs with air, he breathed on the fragment, causing it to glow. "Like quicksilver in the Mountain's bowels, deliver my message on the wings of dragons." He released the stone. It sank into the ground the moment his fingers lost contact with the glowing surface. And then it disappeared, leaving nothing behind. Not even a hole.

Tyler swayed as a wave of dizziness filled him. He shook his head to try and dispel it. "I have a friend on the outside that can help us," he explained as he stood with an effort. He had to steady himself by reaching out for the wall.

Courtney watched him in concern as he caught himself. He'd pressed one hand against the nearest surface, .looking almost as pale as Anwen did. "Hey, you okay?"

"Probably not," Tyler answered, pushing away from the wall. "When I found Anwen, she was buried under all that rock," he pointed at the rubble pile. "And I almost lost her. I had to use a lot more energy than I'd anticipated bringing her back from the brink. So it will take a while for me to get up to full strength again."

Blinking, Courtney contemplated the mass of rubble blocking the far end of the corridor. She shook her head. She couldn't help but wonder just what the two of them had gone through while she'd been battling the Fallen outside. Whatever had happened, it made her battle suddenly feel a lot less intense than it really was.

"You said you sent a message?"

Tyler nodded as he staggered over to kneel by Anwen's side. "Like I said, I have a friend on the outside. Saved his life once. He'll help us, though it might take him a bit to get here. So it would be ideal if we can meet him half way. That way we can bypass the village and the mages. Hopefully no one has decided to come investigate why the Mountain shook tonight. But I'm not counting on that." He gave her a wry glance. "But if we can get down to the Ruined City, there's an out of the way corner where we can wait for help to arrive."

"It'll take us a bit to reach the City," Courtney said. "And we should lock the gates when we reach them. We can do that, right?"

Tyler nodded, patting his pocket. "I may not be a key keeper, but I do have the key. They'll be locked, just not sealed. We can come back once we've regrouped and healed. It's unfortunate, but we'll have to be ready for trouble. I wouldn't be surprised if the Circle has already realized we've reopened the Mountain. And since I don't know how long we've all been here, it's hard to say how long it will take for them to get here."

Courtney sighed as she moved to Anwen's side. "Let's worry about that after we get out of these tunnels," she advised. "One thing at a time or we'll never get anything done. They probably won't reach the City for a couple hours. Knowing Madame Millard, she'll want to go all out, and that will take time. Hopefully they won't set out until tomorrow."

Tyler agreed as he moved to help her lift Anwen by the shoulders, one friend on either side of the unconscious girl. Neither mage nor dragon had enough energy or strength to carry her far. Courtney's fight had taken a lot out of her. Instead, they settled on dragging her with her legs trailing behind in the dust.

After almost two hours, they managed to reach the front gallery. Breathing like an overused billows, the dragon lord leaned against the arched doorway. He tried to catch his breath with little success. Courtney did the same; leaving Anwen lying between them on the floor.

Courtney wiped sweat from her brow and took a swig of water; glad she'd managed to retrieve most of her gear. "At this rate it will take hours just to reach the City," she moaned as she stared across the long expanse before them. She didn't even want to try and guess at the size. Instead, she tossed the water bottle to Tyler, who caught it with less than usual grace.

"I'm inclined to agree," he said, taking a sip. He squinted towards the open gateway, about a kilometer away. "By that point, I believe it'll only be a couple hours from true dawn. Since we haven't seen anyone else yet, I'm hoping we won't find any unwanted visitors down there."

Courtney was too tired to nod. "Back to it then," she said, returning to her position at Anwen's side. The Master Key Keeper hadn't so much as moved while they'd rested. "Any idea how long she'll sleep?"

Shaking his head, Tyler joined her. His legs trembled as he bent to pick up Anwen's left shoulder. "Not the slightest. Let's go."

It took twenty minutes to cross the Front Gallery. They took another break just outside the massive stone gates. Tyler wearily pushed them shut and locked them with Anwen's key. They entered the courtyard with the amphitheater another twenty minutes later. Both were more than ready for another break.

They paused again after crossing the ruined courtyard where Courtney had fought the Manticore. The small alley leading to a side square had a lot more debris in it than it had only twenty-four hours earlier. It took a moment to figure out how to maneuver Anwen's limp body through the small passageway. Finally, they made it out to the courtyard where the dry fountain stood, cracked and empty.

Above them, the sky began to show the first pinks of sunrise. Fumbling in his pack, Tyler found the precious dragon mead. He allowed both Courtney and himself a single sip. With the drink burning through their veins, they managed to lift Anwen to a more upright position. Their shoulders underneath her arms, they moved forward once more. Since Anwen was the shortest of the three, her feet did not hit the ground. Instead, they dangled freely.

Though both were bone weary, with the added benefit of the liqueur, they managed to continue on. Crossing the small courtyard seemed to take forever. But, instead of heading towards the main square, Tyler directed them to an outcropping of rock. It looked like a dead end, but Courtney soon realized it was facade. Behind the rough stone sat a small open-air passage.

Stumbling for several more minutes, Tyler led Courtney down the hand-carved path. They stopped in a cave-like area. The passageway continued on, slanting downhill. Trying to be as careful as possible, Tyler and Courtney set Anwen down. Both slumped to the ground, breathless and exhausted. The effects of the dragon mead had quickly worn off.

"And now we wait," Tyler breathed as he closed his eyes.

Above them, the sky continued to grow lighter as the sun

climbed upward. Safe in their little haven, the sun did not slant down on them. An overhang of stone protruding out from the main mass kept them from the worst of the light. The shade provided a welcome shadow, perfect for sleep.

As if sensing the presence of an enemy, the Mountain rumbled. The ground shook, waking both Courtney and Tyler from a sound sleep. Still groggy, Courtney looked around. She noticed a wide strip of sunlight now bathing part of the open-air cavern floor.

"Sounds like the Circle's discovered the Gates aren't open," Tyler observed. He glanced up from his position near Anwen. "And, if I'm not mistaken, they've made their first attempt to get inside. As much good as that'll do them." He felt for the key in his pocket. Without it, no one was getting inside, sealed or not.

Courtney sat up as the ground shook again. She glanced around, half expecting the rock ledge above them to come rushing down. "You sure we're safe here?" she asked with concern.

Tyler moved to check on Anwen. She'd not once shown any kind of response to their altered surroundings. "As safe as anywhere else on the Mountain," he replied, "except for inside, that is. There are Wards here, just as there are at the outpost near the river. Short of a torrential downpour, we should be fine."

"That's reassuring," Courtney mumbled, looking skyward for any sign of clouds. The sky above, at least what she could see of it, was clear. "What about your friend? I thought you said he'd be here soon?"

"Soon to an undying is so fleeting and yet so long to one with mortal blood." He smiled with wry humor. "I'm sure my friend is taking every precaution possible given the circumstances. I did have to be rather vague in my message. Anything longer would have taken too long to get there. Sleep now and if he isn't here by sundown, we'll continue on without him."

Knowing there was nothing else he could do until help arrived, Tyler moved back to his elevated post. From there, he could see at least part way down either end of the trail.

Courtney yawned despite her nap. Life in the village seemed like a distant memory. She found it hard to imagine a time when she wasn't on the run with Anwen and Tyler. But even that time felt like a dream. "Easy for you to say," she replied, but within a few short minutes, she was asleep once more.

The Mountain continued to rumble restlessly for the rest of the day. Despite the constant vibrations, both Anwen and Courtney slept like the dead. Tyler dozed as best he could. He peered out from half closed lids every time he heard an unexpected sound. Several more hours passed in the same manner. Before long, the sun began to slide down towards the opposite side of the Drakonii Mountain Range. The shaking finally stopped altogether as the sun slid behind the horizon line.

Small camps formed in the Ruined City in the various courtyards. Half of the village's residents set out small tents and started cooking fires. They had trudged up the winding path under the guidance of Madame Millard and her husband.

Many decades before, they had taken the same path with Tyler. Only Tyler had used a different name and face back then. Madame Millard had vowed never to forget the path. And, as an elite member of the Mage Circle, she had no problem navigating the spotty trail. It was almost child's play.

Gathering the Circle had taken some time. Madame Millard knew if the Gates were open, they needed every supply possible on their end. But if the dragons had woken as well, they needed strength to subdue them. She prided herself on always being prepared.

Despite her efforts to gather only those of the Circle, a few others had joined their ranks. By the time they'd finally set out, Daphne's fiancée, Josef, had joined them. Knowing

Daphne had set out in that direction not more than a day before, he felt certain he'd find her there. Madame Millard saw no point in telling him she was dead.

It had taken almost double the usual amount of time to hike up past the Endless Chasm. Having such a large party demanded they take precautions on the narrow trail. But they'd safely staged everyone in the large clearing just past the vast drop. It was at the Consecrated Hall that the first real assault took place.

Most mortals found the confines of the obsidian walls disturbing. Under their influence, no two people felt or saw the same thing. Madame Millard led the incantations meant to mute the effects. It took a force of will to negate the unique properties of the stone. Even with the limited effects, the walls still took their toll on various members of the party. Some were halted while others merely slowed down, caught up in emotions or memories they didn't understand.

Josef found himself in a mental hell he had no way to describe, outside of the darkest of depressions. It had taken several lesser members of the Circle to finally enable him to move on. Even then, he staggered from the effects of the mind numbing vision he'd experienced. He just hoped it wasn't true.

From there, it didn't take long to arrive at the Ruined City. And Madame Millard had no difficulty identifying which direction led to the Gates. She only paused when they came upon the wreckage of the amphitheater. Shadows of the battle Courtney had fought with the Fallen still lingered. If one knew where to look. For a brief moment, the master mage thought she saw the form of a woman in some swirling dust. But she dismissed the notion. She had more important things to worry about.

Everyone in the party suffered a bout of disappointment when they arrived at the Gates. Not only were they closed, but they were also barred against them. Some grumbled, but those of the Inner Circle only looked on with grim faces. What had been opened once could be opened again.

For the rest of the day, and into the first hints of sunset, they pounded the wall with spells and incantations. But to no avail. The Mountain stood unrelenting and firm against them. The only effect their spells seemed to cause was the quaking of the ground. After deciding their attempts were getting them nowhere, they stopped.

Now, with the sun sinking lower in the sky, Josef was finally able to join the rest of the party. Not having any mage ability, he'd been assigned as lookout. He was supposed to keep watch for any possible intruders coming up the path. Ignoring orders, he rushed to join the others, hoping Daphne had been found at the Gates. He was disheartened to learn she had not, and skulked off to vent his frustration.

"We should wait until the new moon passes," Madame Millard told the Inner Circle as they met in conclave. "Just as the Dragon Moon marked the rise of our power, the new moon marks a temporary decrease in our abilities. We may have to use more conventional means to pass the Gates. And if that fails, we should seek the Keeper and take her."

All seven members of the Inner Circle agreed with the master mage's advice and the meeting soon broke up. With such plans out of the way, they all retired to their respective tents for the night.

FOUR

FOOTSTEPS SOUNDED FAINTLY ON THE winding path leading up the far side of the Mountain. At almost full sundown, Walter Watkins had made a later start than he'd planned. He still found it hard to believe he was even making this journey.

Walter received the urgent message in the early hours of the morning, far earlier than he was used to waking. The method of delivery was unlike any he'd ever encountered before. He'd been completely unprepared for the silvery orb of light that had woken him from a sound sleep. It had floated several feet above his bed, filling the room with a soft light. The light had grown in intensity until he'd fumbled out of bed.

Almost as if the object could sense he was awake, the orb descended until it was right in front of him as he sat up. Without so much as a thought of whether it would be prudent or not, Walter had taken hold of the globe with one hand. It felt warm to the touch in a rather soothing way that almost made up for interrupting his sleep.

An image of Tyler appeared in his mind, with the request for immediate assistance. The message was brief but unmistakable. He'd jumped from bed and made ready.

As expected, the highway over the Drakonii Range had teamed with an unusual amount of traffic. Both motorized and foot powered. He was glad he'd followed protocol and reconnoitered before making any plans. Unfortunately, he'd had to wait until at least some of the crowd had thinned. Once that had happened, he took the appropriate upwards side path with little notice. He went far enough up the Mountain to confirm his observations.

After managing to avoid the initial chaos, a brief period of rest became necessary. It had been an early morning and he was tired. Despite this, he'd wanted to make sure he knew where the villagers were before moving on.

Thanking every deity he knew that he hadn't been seen, Walter backtracked down the mountain road. From there, he headed back towards the city of Blaucii. Not quite within city limits, he navigated the back roads, using a more roundabout way to the other side of the mountain range. He was just glad his old truck was still up to the challenge as he bumped along.

Upon reaching the far side of the Mountain, Walter abandoned his truck. From there, he hiked around the base of the Mountain. The sun shone overhead as he delved into the hidden passage Tyler had burned into his mind with his message. With luck, no one had observed him doing so. And even if they had, he hoped they'd think he was some kind of adrenaline junky hoping to take a dive from the Mountain's peaks. The equipment he carried gave rise to the idea. His pack was bulky enough he might have a compact hang glider hidden somewhere inside.

The sound of footsteps continued as Tyler peered into the darkness. It was now full dark, though the lack of light bothered him little. He knew it was only a matter of time before the owner appeared on the path before them. Despite the hiker's attempts at stealth, the dragon could hear the scuff of boots on the stone floor. The sound had gone on for some time now, gradually growing louder as the lone traveler came closer.

Tyler looked around. Courtney was still asleep, even after a full day's rest. Anwen's condition had not changed. With a sigh, he rose to his feet. It would not be long before their visitor rounded the far bend in the path.

Moving to Courtney's side, he tapped her on one shoulder to wake her. "My friend is almost here," he said in response to her groggy inquiries. "Time to get up. We'll be moving on soon."

By the time Courtney had gotten up, the faint scuffing had grown loud enough for even her to hear it. She turned towards the sound, one hand going for her bone knife, a spell on her lips.

Seeing her action, Tyler put out a restraining hand. "It's all right," he assured her. "It's just Walter." He brought out the mead flask and took a sip before passing it to her. "Might need this for the next part."

Courtney let the warm liquid slide down her throat, further waking her up. She rummaged in her pack, taking out a stale piece of bread to munch on. Turning, she noticed a faint glow begin to show around the trail's bend.

Walter entered the small open cavern with a slight sense of misgiving. His low headlamp illuminated a rather depressing sight. Seeing Tyler, he all but rushed over. "Came as fast as I could," he said, kneeling next to his friend.

Tyler looked up from administering to Anwen. "Walter," he greeted. He moved to give the older-looking man an uncharacteristic clap on the back. "You have no idea how glad I am to see you." He fumbled a bit as he left off from the embrace. He had to catch himself from stumbling back as Walter's lamp cast deeper shadows under his eyes.

"You look like you've been through the mill," Walter commented as he looked around. He let his light shine over

Anwen, taking in the visible bandages and splint. "And your friend here looks like she's seen a lot worse." He ran a hand through his close-cropped dark hair.

Taking a moment to close his eyes, Tyler nodded. "You have no idea. But if we don't get her off the Mountain, we might have a lot worse on our hands." He looked over to Courtney, who looked a lot better than he felt. "This is Courtney. She's from the village."

Courtney nodded in greeting as she closed her pack. "Nice to meet you," she said, holding out a hand. Her makeshift bandages strained as she moved, dried blood showing at the edges of her sleeve. She couldn't help but think his skin coloring reminded her of milk chocolate.

Walter accepted the offered handshake. "Walter Watkins," he replied, "former chief medic in the Reserves." The niceties out of the way, he turned his attention back to Tyler. "So, what've we got here?" Walter's tone conveyed his professionalism. It was all business now. He knew answers to crazy questions would have to wait.

Tyler opened his eyes and looked down at Anwen. "Various lacerations, broken femur bone, possible concussion and internal injuries. I did what I could while inside the Mountain, but I don't think I got everything. And I don't have enough in me right now to finish the job. Everything else, I'll just have to tell you about later."

Walter nodded. "Now I understand why you wanted these." He pulled out a field medic-kit. He also brought out another more bulky bundle from his pack and a few collapsible poles, which he gave to Tyler. He then took out an electrolyte pack and tossed it to Courtney. "Might want to drink that, love," he said.

Taking the equipment, Tyler unrolled the bundle to reveal a durable fabric stretcher. He unfolded the poles, which reminded Courtney of tent poles. That accomplished, he slid the long shafts into the appropriate sleeves on the stretcher. His fingers moved with long familiarity, and before too long, he had the stretcher ready for use.

Meanwhile, Walter took a stethoscope from his bag and began examining his patient. He started by checking Anwen's vital signs. Seeing Tyler had finished, he threw him another electrolyte pack.

"Not a bad job with the splints and bandages," Walter commented as he checked the bandages. "Though they'll definitely need to be changed once we get down into the city. I'll be able to tell you more about things then. But for now, she seems stable enough to move."

Courtney watched as the two men carefully shifted Anwen onto the long canvas. She moved to spread a blanket over her. "How long until we reach the bottom?" she asked. She sipped on the pouch given her, cringing a bit at the taste.

Tyler looked up, trying to calculate where the moon might be hiding. His usual sense of time failed him and he shrugged. "This path's easier going but a lot longer and round about. We'll have to go single file almost the entire way down. Taking breaks, we might get down by day break?" He looked to Walter for confirmation.

The former medic nodded, calculating how long it had taken him to reach them. He added in some extra time to allow for Tyler's obvious fatigue. "Sounds about right. But the sooner we start, the sooner we get down. And if you want to be down before those mages wake up, we'd best get started now."

Tyler bent to pick up one end of the stretcher, but Courtney moved to block his way. "No way, Tyler," she admonished. "You look like you didn't sleep a wink while we waited. I'm taking the first stretch or we're not going. No arguments."

Walter looked at the spunky girl with appreciation. He felt rather glad she'd brought up the issue. His friend looked done in already. He knew Tyler would never admit it when in a state of crisis, like they were now. "Might as well let her," he said. "Looks like she means business."

Too tired to argue, Tyler stepped aside to let Courtney take his end of stretcher. He watched in resignation as

Walter took the other end. "Fine. I'll lead," he compromised and, picking up both his and Courtney's packs, he moved out.

Walter rolled his eyes but didn't comment on the arrangement. Instead, he fell in behind the dragon. He tried to move as much in sync with Courtney as possible. Tyler was obstinate most days and downright stubborn when on a mission. It was best to let him have at least this bit of helpfulness. Or they'd hear no end of it.

By the time the sun had begun to climb in the sky, the small group had reached the mouth of the alternate passage. Staying well back in the shadows, Tyler panted as he leaned against the stone wall. The stretcher's handles rested heavily in his hands. He'd insisted on taking a turn when Courtney had started to lag. But he'd been given the end with Anwen's feet so he didn't wear out as quickly.

Walter also leaned against the wall, feeling the strain from lack of sleep starting to creep in. At his insistence, they set the makeshift bed down for a quick breather. The former medic was more than happy to take a sip of the dragon mead.

Courtney, perhaps feeling the least winded of the two, peered ahead. Seeing no one in sight, she signaled the all clear. "Let's go before someone sees us."

A bit resignedly, the two men picked up the poles and pushed away from the wall to move out into the open. Tyler almost stumbled on a low bit of brush. He managed to correct himself before Anwen could slide from the canvas frame. With a quick nod to assure his partner he was fine, they continued on.

Courtney cast a quick enchantment to try and shield them from unfriendly eyes. But up against the might of the Mage Circle, she wasn't sure how effective it would be. With the whole of the Mage Circle on the Mountain, her own abilities shrank in significance. She could only hope their eyes were turned elsewhere.

Another hour's worth of steady hiking brought them to Walter's truck. Sliding the make-shift gurney into the covered back, Tyler crawled into the truck. He collapsed beside Anwen's prone body. Courtney climbed in behind him, taking up a position on the other side. Walter got into the cab after divesting himself of his gear. He stowed it in handy bins designed for the purpose. That accomplished, he downed an energy drink to stay alert on the road.

Driving as fast as he dared, Walter navigated back down the more rugged path, heading to Blaucii City. Several more hours found him rejoining the main road. Another hour after that brought them down into the city.

Bypassing the busier sections of town, Walter drove to a more rural part of the city. He finally pulled up in front of a modest home of nondescript appearance. It was perfect for a bachelor who might be too busy with other things to do any proper upkeep. Carefully, he once more made sure no one had followed them. Sure they weren't observed, he got out of the truck and unlocking the front door. Propping it open, he went back to the vehicle, rousing Tyler long enough to have him help carry Anwen inside.

Courtney had made sure Tyler at least dozed on the drive back. She had to reassure him that she'd keep an eye on their friend before he nodded off. Thankfully, nothing had happened on their trek down into the city. All the same, she was glad to exit the vehicle and get inside.

After helping transfer Anwen to the guest room, Tyler crashed on the living room couch. He was out almost as soon as his head touched the cushions. Finding a blanket in one of the cupboards, Courtney covered him and went to help Walter.

Walter had removed the makeshift bandages on Anwen's arms and leg. After examining the punctures, he cleaned out the wounds, suturing where necessary. Double checking the set of her leg, he applied a more suitable brace. He reasoned that a cast would be unnecessary. Having once been subject to Tyler's care, he had no doubt the dragon would be able to heal the rest of the injuries. Once he'd gotten enough rest.

After starting an I.V. drip, Walter noticed Courtney watching him from the doorway. "Tyler out?"

Courtney walked into the room, nodding. "Like someone flipped a light switch."

Walter nodded. "Good. Saves me the trouble of knocking him out. Probably wouldn't have ended well for either of us." He turned his attention back to the fluid line to make sure there were no kinks in the tubing. "Haven't seen him look that worn down before. Almost thought I was looking at a ghost."

"You should have made him take a shower before he crashed," Courtney said as she moved to stand by the veteran. "I'm sure you don't want your couch smelling like mountain refuse."

Walter chuckled. "I've had worse," he admitted. "Though I'm sure you wouldn't mind the use of the facilities yourself. They're just down the hall. Take your time, okay? When you're done, we can look at what you've done to your arm. Don't think I didn't notice that."

Courtney smiled for the first time in several days. "Thanks." With a bit of a backward wave, she left the room. Walter watched her leave, wondering just what had happened on the Mountain.

FIVE

CLOUDS CAST HALF SHADOWS ON the closed curtains as they moved across the sky. Anwen Porter opened her eyes to see the distorted images behind the thin fabric. She shifted her gaze to look up at the ceiling, one she didn't recognize. It was smooth and painted a sort of creamy beige, though she wasn't sure about the color.

Looking down, she realized she was tucked under a heavy quilt. Various aches and pains began to surface as her mind registered that she was awake. She winced as she tried to roll over, a bandage pressing into her flesh where it pushed against a pillow. "Ow."

"That's a good sign," an unfamiliar voice commented as someone shifted in the shadows.

Anwen looked around, trying to discern who was sitting next to the bed. Despite her efforts, she didn't have enough strength to lift herself from the mattress. "Who's there?"

Walter flipped on a small bedside lamp, bathing the room in soft light. It threw Walter's face into shadowy existence. "Name's Walter," he introduced. "I'm a friend of Tyler's."

Heart pounding from the unexpected turn of events, Anwen tried to calm herself. Nothing made sense. The last thing she remembered was lying inside the Mountain, Tyler leaning over her. Then there had been that searing pain. But part of her felt rational enough to question the validity of this strange man's claim. At least she could try and catalogue him in her mind before saying anything else.

He didn't look like the dangerous type, but then most people seldom did. At least not to her, but she was learning. His short hair was dark but showed slight signs of gray, particularly around the temples. Though older, maybe in his late thirties or early forties, Walter looked fit with darker skin. And he had an honest face that had seen its share of chaos.

Deciding to play on the side of caution, Anwen moved back into the position she'd woken up in. The past week had taught her caution. Despite what her eyes and gut told her, she would play things safe. "Walter? He never mentioned you."

The veteran chuckled as he leaned back in his chair. He'd let her have her fill of curiosity and found her pretended disinterest amusing. "Not surprised. He doesn't tell most folks about me. Likes to keep private about most things, if you know what I mean."

"I'd noticed that," Anwen said, rolling her eyes. She put one hand to her head to brush away some loose hair but stopped as she felt the pull of the I.V. tubing. "Where am I? What happened?" One thing she definitely sure of was that she was not in a hospital. She'd been in several during her younger years. And this place definitely didn't qualify as one. She could see stacked boxes and crates against the far wall. There were other various odds and ends she couldn't identify due to the low light. She also thought she saw the doors to a closet. The idea wasn't exactly a comforting one.

Walter stood from his chair, taking out his stethoscope. "Mind breathing in and out for me, nice and slow?" He pressed the appropriate end of the instrument against her chest. "I'll answer any questions you might have so long as you try to cooperate. I know it's hard but trust me. I'm not here to hurt you."

Keeping a wary eye, Anwen did as instructed, breathing in and out as slowly as she could. "How about we start with where I am and what happened?" she asked between breaths.

Having finished checking her heart and lungs, Walter reached for something out of view. "Your lungs sound good, which is a nice change. Had some fluid in them earlier. To be honest, I'm a bit surprised you woke up before Tyler. You've both been out for about three days now, give or take."

Anwen almost sat up in shock, despite her lack of strength, but Walter pressed her back down. "None of that now," he admonished. "You've been through quite a lot lately. I don't know all the details, but it sounds like you had a time up there in the mountains. Be glad you're safe and out of danger for now. To answer the first question, you're here in Blaucii."

Anwen looked around the room as if that could tell her the truth of the matter. The boxes and oddments gave no such answers and she gave up on the attempt. "Blaucii?"

"You betcha," Walter replied. He pulled out a blood pressure cuff, which he strapped around her arm. "Got you all stored away at my place. Pretty sure no one will find you here. I'm not exactly in one of those more popular areas," he explained. He took the other end of the blood pressure cuff and began pumping the inflation bulb. He then pressed the stethoscope's chest piece just under the cuff.

The sensation of having her circulation being cut off by the blood pressure cuff was not pleasant. As such, Anwen refrained from immediately asking any other questions. Instead, she tried to think back to the last events she could remember. Outside of seeing Tyler's face, the images were all a blur. They shattered the moment she tried to recall them.

A flash of light filled Anwen's eyes and she thought she saw Tyler in dragon form, swooping down to catch her. Air seemed to rush past her as she fell. Her surroundings were so blurred she wasn't sure where she was. At least she couldn't feel any pain.

Don't worry. I've got you, Tyler said in her mind. *I won't ever let you go.*

He was holding her close to his chest as she dangle from his massive hand. The claws almost reminded her of a bird's cage, folding around her like a buffer. In reality, she knew there was no way he could have held her any differently. At least not in that form. His hands were far too big for anything else.

Anwen couldn't help but notice the many scales of his body as his wings unfurled, breaking their fall. The scales were a little rough, like seashells worn by the ocean's waves. Their silver coloring was almost blue. She felt sure she'd seen them before.

Tyler stretched his long neck as he raced upwards. In only a matter of moments, they were breaking through a series of storm clouds. A rainbow sparkled overhead as he banked to skim over the dark mass of water vapor below.

Ahead, a massive mountain protruded through the clouds. Tyler moved towards the peak, gaining momentum. Within what seemed like a blink of an eye, they were landing on a flat shelf. Anwen stood, Tyler beside her. But despite the obvious difference in size, she felt no smaller than usual than when he stood in mortal form.

Unlike last time she'd seen this place, no white dragon stood to meet them. Instead, the same old man she'd seen in her dreams so many times before stood to greet them. His robes billowed out with a breeze she could not feel. Perhaps she couldn't feel it because Tyler sheltered her from the wind. Either way, it made for an impressive sight.

"Well met, Fair Little Dragon, Keeper of the Keys," the aged man greeted, hands folded in front of him. He wore a long Eastern-style robe of white, trimmed with white gold or silver. "You have done well. The Great Gates have been opened and the seal has been broken. But your task is not yet done."

Anwen felt her heart sink. All she wanted to do was rest. Her entire being felt worn down on an atomic level. "There's more?" She looked at him with incredulous eyes, pleading for her suffering to end.

The Nurrim smiled with compassion. "I know you are weary, and rest you will have, once your further tasks have been completed. The Mountain has been unsealed, but Tarragon yet sleeps. You must wake the dragons and release them from their cold halls of stone. You must do this to restore order to our world. If you do not, I fear the consequences will be severe."

Tears pricked at the corners of Anwen's eyes as she tried to comprehend what was being asked of her. "But how am I supposed to do that? I haven't had a clue about what I've been doing this entire time! What makes you think I can figure this out? I still don't even know who I am, let alone anything about my origins!"

The Nurrim somehow stood right in front of her. There had been a sizable distance between them only moments before. He cupped her chin with one hand, gently tilting her face so he could look into her eyes. "The road to discovery is never easy, Little One. You will find the answers when you are ready for them. Heed the blood that flows through you, for you are more than a mortal, and dragon blood runs in your veins."

Blue lightning crackled up from the clouds, making the sky look like broken glass. The brilliant flash of light blinded Anwen and she had to cover her eyes with one hand. Her ears rang from the colossal crash of the resulting thunder.

Courtney felt as though she hadn't truly enjoyed herself in years. After having slept a solid twenty hours, she'd taken the liberty of enjoying the Jacuzzi tub. She'd felt as if ten years' worth of grime and stress had washed away with the running water. It was nice to feel clean again. Even after the initial shower. There was something to be said for a good soak in a tub with water jets.

Walter had been the perfect host, providing all kinds of distractions. He'd even taken time out from attending to Anwen and Tyler to look over her own wounds. None had been serious. She felt she could have taken care of them herself, but he'd insisted. And, thanks to his help, she felt as good as new.

It was after their third day with Walter that Anwen first woke, though she hadn't been awake long. Courtney went to her room to check on things while Walter finished his examination. Anwen had already succumbed to sleep before he'd finished. It was heartening to learn her vital signs remained strong.

The mage stood in the doorway, watching as he put away his equipment. "They've both been asleep for a long time," she commented. Tyler had almost become a permanent feature in the living room. He hadn't so much as moved since crashing there.

Walter looked up from what he was doing. "Morning," he greeted. "Sleep makes for one of the best cures. When they're ready, I'm sure they'll both be back to normal." He finished packing away his equipment and put it to one side, standing to stretch.

Courtney moved so Walter could exit the room. She then followed him into the kitchen. "You never told me how you and Tyler met," she pointed out. She took up a perch on one of several bar stools lining the kitchen island, waiting for his answer.

From across the counter, Walter poured himself a mug of coffee. He nodded as he poured a second mug. "You're right. I wondered how long it would take you to ask." He pushed the second cup towards her. "Cream and sugar?"

"Yes, please," Courtney said. She accepted the coffee, adding in cream and sugar. She then picked up a spoon to stir her drink, noticing he didn't add anything to his cup.

Walter walked around the island and took up a stool next to hers. He rested one elbow on top of the counter. His kitchen was modestly sized, with plenty of room for puttering about. If there was one thing he loved, it was cooking. In contrast, the dining area was crowded with various camping and survival gear.

He scratched at the stubble on his chin, not having bothered to shave in several days. "Let's see. That was about twenty years ago now? Give or take," he chuckled. "I was just starting out with the Reserve, basic training you see. The upper ups sent us all out on a survival course in the nearby desert to see how we'd do."

Walter somehow managed to survive three days in what felt like blistering heat. In reality, the weather of the southern end of the Bandon Desert had been fairly mild. But to those not used to the hotter climates, it felt much hotter than it really was.

A sandstorm had formed, separating him from the rest of his mates. It came out of nowhere, cutting right across their camp. Walter had been out in search of water. One moment he'd been collecting cactus juice, the next, he was being flung around like a rag doll in a dirt devil. He'd hit into multiple rock formations before falling down into some sort of gully. Somehow, he'd managed to roll into a slight recess that protected him from the rest of the raging wind.

The storm had lasted for several hours. By the time the wind finally died down, the sun had already set. Walter tried to roll free of the protecting overhang, only to find he was paralyzed by pain. Being thrown by the wind had done his body no favors and he felt it. Gasping for breath, he'd finally passed out. He woke much later to the sound of multiple buzzards waiting for his death.

Groaning, he tried to wave the birds away, but could barely lift his arms. Licking dry lips, he found the soft skin had cracked and was bleeding. Unable to move, he sobbed dry tears. But his strong will refused to give in. Someone had to come looking for him. He refused to believe the others in his company had perished in the storm. Someone would come. He just hoped they would find him before something else happened to him.

As the sun climbed higher in the sky, the heat set back in, baking him even more. Faint from hunger, dehydrated, and in pain, he realized no one would come looking for him. Even if someone did, chances were less than decent they would find him before the end. With such thoughts in his head, he reconciled himself to the inevitable.

Just as he'd convinced himself to give up all hope, Walter felt a shadow fall over him. One that wasn't a buzzard or other carrion creature. He could hear the birds fluttering away in anger. But the slight coolness of the shadow jolted him back to a semi state of consciousness. It was enough to encourage him to open his eyes just a crack and look up through sand-gritted lashes. What he saw reminded him of an angel from old legends.

The young man bending over him had light brown hair and astonishingly blue eyes. "What have we here?" he asked in a lyrical voice as he bent over Walter's battered body. "It would appear that fate is on your side this day. I had not intended on coming this way, but something told me it would be beneficial."

Walter was unable to reply. He could only close his eyes and whimper. His tongue felt like a block of sand in his mouth. He opened his eyes again when he felt an unexpected pressure on his body. The stranger had knelt beside him and placed one hand on his chest. A sudden feeling of warmth filled him. The feeling was refreshing in contrast to the sun's scorching rays. He felt as if the almost unbearable pain was melting away.

Tyler closed his eyes as he concentrated on the young soldier's wounds, asking them to heal. The poor man had quite the collection to attend to, but he was more than up for the task. A few minutes passed before he opened his eyes. But when he did, he smiled at the incredulous expression on Walter's face. "They call me Tyler," he introduced as he held out his hand. "Do you think you can stand?"

"I remember looking up into those bottomless eyes," Walter recalled. "It was like looking into the depths of the ocean, only not quite the same. I don't know how, but he'd managed to heal every broken part inside of me, even the ones I didn't know I had. I took his hand, and the rest, as they say, is history."

Courtney smiled as she listened. "That's how he is, isn't it," she mused as she sipped her drink. "He somehow takes every broken part of you and fixes it. He even fixes what you never thought was broken in the first place. But then, now that I think about it, so does Anwen." She tapped the mug with one thoughtful finger.

Walter grunted as he took a sip of his own brew, black and strong. "Something different about that one, too," he agreed. "Course, with Tyler being a dragon and all, what's not to wonder?" He moved to stand, heading towards the far side of the kitchen.

Courtney spewed her mouthful of coffee. "Dragon! You knew Tyler was a dragon?" She stared at him, mouth hanging open.

Walter found some paper towels on the other side of the counter and handed them to her. "You betcha," he answered as he helped her clean up the mess. "Figured something was special about him from moment one. And when he was able to help me find my mates after healing me up--well, I had to ask. Guess he saw no reason not to tell me."

Courtney threw the soiled towels into the trash, reclaiming her stool. "I didn't know until a week or so ago," she confessed. "And Anwen didn't find out until a few days after that. I'm not sure who was more surprised though, me or her."

"Makes sense," Walter commented, "you being a mage and all. He has to be careful 'bout that. Most mages either want him dead or as some kind of slave. That's no way for a dragon to live. He's been waiting a long time for that Porter girl. Wouldn't tell me why though."

Tyler entered the kitchen at that moment, interrupting the conversation. He yawned hugely as he stretched his arms, almost as if intended to pluck the stars from the sky. "Good morning," he greeted with a sleepy wave.

"More like afternoon," Courtney corrected, looking at the clock. The hour hand barely scraped past noon. She accepted a refill of coffee from Walter, adding in more cream and sugar than she had with the previous cup. "About time you woke up," she said, stirring the drink. "You've been out for at least three days straight."

Tyler smiled ruefully as he ran a hand through his unkempt hair. "No wonder I feel so gross," he laughed. "But I do feel infinitely better, which is a huge improvement from before. Though, I wouldn't mind a bite to eat." He turned a half pleading look on Walter who rolled his eyes.

"Figured that would come around eventually." Walter moved out of the dragon lord's way so he could have easy access to the refrigerator. "Help yourself. Just don't eat me out of house and home, okay? I remember that appetite of yours." He gave him an admonishing look.

Tyler opened the fridge and looked around inside. After a moment or two, he took out some fixings. Moving his findings to the kitchen island, he set out to make several sandwiches. "I could probably eat a whole horse," he joked, "but these will have to do."

Watching him prepare and eat his food, Courtney couldn't help but forget what he was. He acted so much like a normal teenage boy that anyone would assume he was nothing more than such. She found herself wondering just how many people knew what he was and how they'd found out.

Halfway through his fourth sandwich, Tyler started to slow down. Even though he was still hungry, he had to remember his mortal form did have limitations. "How's Anwen?" he asked, licking the mustard off his fingers. No matter how many times he'd had it, there was just something about mustard he couldn't resist.

Walter perked at the question as he rolled his coffee mug between his palms. "Vitals are stable," he reported. "No signs of infection. Woke up for a little bit, but passed out soon after."

Tyler nodded at the news. "Did she know who she was?" He dolloped more mustard onto his fifth sandwich. He hoped they'd play the question off as mere curiosity.

Walter set his mug down. "Seemed to," he answered, trying to remember. "Only seemed confused about where she was, but that's not saying much. Didn't have a chance to confirm she knew her name. Didn't think to ask either. She wasn't awake long, really."

Tyler nodded, sighing in relief. If she knew who she was, that was a good sign. It meant Daphne's Ritual hadn't been completed. Though there was still the possibility that it would have some lasting effect. Hopefully he'd know more after tending to her. He could find out for sure when he did.

Having polished off six sandwiches, he excused himself to take a shower. Walter moved to clean up the remaining mess while Courtney sipped her now cold coffee.

SIX

THE WARM WATER OF THE shower felt amazing on Tyler's bare skin. He closed his eyes and let the liquid run over his face and shoulders. He hadn't meant to sleep so long, but he'd needed it. Now, with a week's worth of grime washing away, he felt almost normal.

Despite that, doubts nagged at the back of his mind. Had the Ritual caused any lasting damage to Anwen they had yet to detect? Most individuals subjected to that particular magic had died, erased from history. Those who hadn't, who somehow escaped while the Ritual was in its early stages, tended to live a cursed life. He'd never heard of anyone who'd managed to escape once the Ritual had reached its zenith. Until now.

Tyler's heart pounded in his ribcage. Had he somehow, by giving Anwen part of his soul, negated the effects? Or were they like a cancer, just waiting to rear an ugly head? He didn't have the answers but hoped such was not the case. He didn't know if he could live with that, knowing her life could be snuffed out just like that. Erased from existence.

Finally drying off, Tyler took the liberty of borrowing some of Walter's clothes. They were a bit large but serviceable. He had to roll up both the pant legs and the sleeves. Thankfully, he didn't have to look for a belt. Despite the difference in height, they did have similar builds.

Leaving the bathroom, he could hear Walter and Courtney talking in the kitchen. Chances were good they were still drinking coffee, even though it was mid-afternoon. That was just fine with him. He didn't need them interrupting things. With a full belly and clean skin, it was time to visit Anwen and assess her remaining injuries.

Tyler slipped into Anwen's room and closed the door. Making sure the curtains were closed, he moved the chair to the foot of the bed. It wouldn't do to have outside eyes looking in. Taking a seat, he surveyed the bed in front of him, paying strict attention to its occupant. He leaned elbows against knees, hands pressed together as if in prayer.

Anwen's chest rose and fell rhythmically. Some color had returned to her cheeks, which he took as a good sign. But she was still unnaturally pale. That he did not like at all. He pursed his lips as he took in her appearance, including the brace Walter had found for her broken leg. If everything went well, she wouldn't need it for long.

Taking a deep breath, Tyler conjured six light orbs. He set them floating over Anwen's hands, feet, head, and heart. Satisfied with the arrangement, he moved to one side of the bed. There, he knelt next to where her legs were covered with the quilt. He pushed the quilt aside moments before the orbs shot spears of light down into her body.

Tyler manipulated Anwen's energy to produce a visual representation. The aural projection hovered a foot above her body. It was akin to when he'd purged the poison Daphne had introduced into her body at the Old Mill, but with a few differences. He had to go to a much deeper level; just to be sure the Ritual had dealt no lasting harm.

Carefully, he examined the varying degrees of radiance her energy produced. His lips creased into a frown at a few discolored areas near her upper arms and legs. That explained why he'd been unable to heal the injuries in the corresponding parts of her real body.

He wasn't sure whether these tainted bits of energy were a result of the Ritual. It could have also resulted from Daphne's malice. One thing was certain, though. He had to untangle the dark matter from Anwen's soul before he could heal her.

With the skill of a seasoned surgeon, Tyler carefully manipulated the strands of energy binding Anwen's spirit. He purged each strand of darkness he found, careful to leave no hint of residue behind. It was a long and tricky process and he more than felt the strain as he worked. Most of the dark matter did not want to go quietly. It felt like he waged a battle of wills as he purged each strand.

After close to two hours of intense concentration, Tyler sat back on the chair with relief. He wiped sweat from his brow with the back of one hand. With the other hand, he persuaded Anwen's energy to settle back to its usual home. As her soul reconnected with her body, the orbs began to fade away. As they faded, so too did the spears of light that had connected them with her spirit.

First the orbs over her feet vanished, then the ones over her hands. The orb over her head fizzled like rain before fading out as well. The one over her heart flared with a bright radiance. It threw blue and white light around the room before settling to a faint pulse that also went out. The room looked dark on contrast to the sudden change as his energy disengaged from hers.

As if a string had been cut, Tyler slumped in his chair, almost falling off. Walter startled him when he held out a steadying hand, keeping him from falling to the floor. "Walter," he said, "I didn't hear you come in."

Walter smiled. "You forget I was taught to do that?" he inquired with a laugh. "That was quite the display." He motioned towards the bed where Anwen lay sleeping. "Never seen anything like it before. If every doctor could do that, they'd lose a lot less people. And probably charge an arm and a leg just to do it."

Tyler leaned back in his chair, closing his eyes in exhaustion. "Most mortals lack the discipline or skill for something like that. Let alone the mental capacity. And most dragons wouldn't bother, especially not with an ordinary human. 'Let nature take its course' and all that. I've never met a mage who had enough mastery to separate the soul from the body like I did either."

"Dragon magic, eh?" Walter nodded in appreciation. "Probably best we mortals don't know that stuff. Too many get all high and mighty with what they do know. Can't imagine how they'd behave with more."

"Mortals have their own brand of magic," Tyler countered. "They call it science. As for mages, they use a variation of dragon magic. Even so, it's still not the same."

"Fair enough," Walter nodded. He glanced at his friend critically, evaluating him. He was as fair-skinned as usual. Despite that, there was a decided tired look in his eyes that spoke of more than physical weariness. He was about to comment on that when a sound from the hallway caught both of their attentions.

Looking a bit abashed for being caught, Courtney peered into the room from around the door frame. "How is she?" she inquired, glancing at Anwen's bed.

Standing, Tyler turned towards the mage. "The most difficult part is over," he assured her. "I'm going to let her rest before I finish up. Her soul needs some time to settle before I contemplate repairing her mortal frame. That and I need a break."

Courtney sighed in relief. "Good." She made as if to leave but thought better of it. "Oh. I've tried a few scrying spells to see if I can find out what's going on in the village. I haven't had much success. Everyone might be up on the Mountain, trying to get in. But every time I try to see up there I get something like a busy signal. It's more than a little frustrating."

"Not surprising," Tyler commented as he moved away from the bed. "There are wards and natural means of protection. The stone from the Concentrated Hall, for example, is quite powerful. And similar stone deposits can be found all around the base of the Mountain. You just can't see them unless you go looking for them."

Walter motioned them all out of the room, closing the door behind them. Leading his guests towards the living room, he took a seat on the couch. "I think I've been patient enough so I feel no remorse in saying this. I like being in the dark just as much as the next person. So would you mind telling me what this is all about?"

Tyler plopped down next to his friend while Courtney took a seat on an armchair. He let out a sigh. "Remember back when I told you who and what I am?" Walter nodded. "That girl is the one destined to wake the rest of my kind. With her help, we've already opened the Mountain. But--"

"The mages stand in your way," Walter finished for him. "Makes sense. Been doing a bit of digging in local history. Seems there are plenty of legends to support that. We're going to have to find a way around them."

Courtney sat up in surprise. "We? Surely you don't plan on joining us? I mean, it's going to be dangerous!" It wasn't that she thought him incapable, but against a hoard of mages, she doubted he'd be much help.

Walter shrugged. "Why not? Have you ever planned a mountain campaign? Or any campaign, for that matter?" He smiled as she shook her head. "To be honest, neither have I. But I have a lot more experience in that kind of thing than you do."

Tyler nodded as he leaned back against the couch's frame. "That's true. But I ask you to remember what we're up against. This isn't going to be like some military operation you've done before."

Walter was about to protest but Tyler waves him aside. "Now that the Gates have been opened once, the mages are probably chomping at the bit to get inside. I wouldn't put it past them to camp outside in the City. As things stand, not even my power, combined with Courtney's, will be enough."

"Don't sell yourself short," Courtney protested. "I've seen what you can do. And you're amazing! I'm nowhere near that level."

Tyler waved her comments aside. "Yes, but how much did it take out of me to continue doing all those things for a week? And after bringing Anwen back to the living world, I was left almost incapacitated."

Courtney's mouth fell open as she stared at him, her eyes wide. "You never said anything about that. I just assumed you found her alive. I didn't know you found her--"

"Dead?" Tyler's expression was grim. "Yes. When I finally managed to unearth her from the rubble of that collapsed cavern, she was already dead. I had to make a rather risky decision to bring her back. But, knowing who she is, I feel it was well worth it. After all, there's much more to her than even you realize."

Blinking in confusion, Courtney settled back into her chair. "What do you mean? We already know she's the last Key Keeper. Isn't that enough?"

Tyler passed a hand across his eyes, suppressing a yawn. Even though he'd slept for over seventy-two hours, he was tired after his ministrations. "That was part of it. But remember what Anwen told us about her confrontation with Daphne? Remember what Daphne said to her about a certain name?"

It took a moment but Courtney gasped as realization set in. "Anwen Kaida Porter," she whispered. "It's not just by chance, is it? She really is the Kaida, isn't she?"

Tyler nodded. "I had my suspicions when I first met her on the drive up to the Village of Lindwyrm. She had a journal from one of her grandparents. She didn't know I was looking at the time, but I read the open pages she was studying. That's what first got me to thinking. Then, later that night, I took her to see the dragon boats and discovered she had a dragon gem on her."

Walter watched the exchange as Courtney sat speechless. "You're not talking about just any kind of gem, are you," he asked. "You're talking about those special gems that only come from inside the Mountain, aren't you?"

"That's right," Tyler confirmed. "Back in the day, they were only given to select individuals. But even with that, it's been over a hundred years since one was last seen. Which means the one she has had to be passed down the family line. Of course, we later realized it was actually the Master Key to the Gates of Eternity. Even so, the gem wouldn't have reacted as it did if she had been just a Key Keeper, albeit the Master Key Keeper."

Courtney slipped out her bone knife and began to play with it. She idly ran her fingers down the blade's edge. "So you devised a few tests to make sure, didn't you?"

Tyler couldn't help but smile at that. "Let's just say I used the means at my disposal. Though I did get in a bit of trouble for some of them."

He thought back to when he'd taken Anwen to the Sacred Isle and had her touch the altar inside the sanctuary. That had been the definitive proof, even though the vision dust was also a good indicator. He'd not seen her pictured in the resulting vision show. However, he had seen a dragon form similar to his own. One that was silver with faint cobalt or deep purple shading that he didn't recognize. Perhaps there was something more to that vision than just dragons.

Walter scratched at his stubble. "If Anwen is what you say she is, and yes I've heard of the Kaida, then that will help out a lot. The question is, does she know?"

SEVEN

ANWEN FELT GROGGY AND SLUGGISH, like she'd been submerged in thick tar. Her body was slow to respond to her commands. She vaguely remembered waking up in a strange house, followed by the sensation of falling. Now she felt like she was made from some kind of putty that wouldn't move. She strained to make her muscles work, but to no avail. She was stuck.

The room she was in was dark. It was as if the walls were made of some black pigment. Finally, after a great deal of effort, she managed to reach out her arm. Doing so, she discovered she was touching something smooth and cold that felt a lot like glass. A brief moment of dizziness filled her and she found she was standing with bare feet on the same type of surface.

The room seemed to spin around her, settling after several nauseating moments. Every wall was the same black stone, including the ceiling and floor. It reminded her of the Consecrated Hall. There was no door or window, like she was trapped inside a dark cube.

As if the spinning had somehow freed her ability to move, she found herself running to the nearest wall. Once there, she pounded on the flat surface. It was unyielding. "Let me out!" she yelled as her fists beat against the stone. "Can anyone hear me?"

Laughter filled the air around her as a willowy form emerged from the stone. "No. They can't." Long black hair billowed out like an oil slick. It threatened to engulf everything around its owner.

Anwen let out a gasp as she stepped away from the wall and the encroaching hair. "Daphne. I thought you were dead."

Daphne laughed. "Physically? Sure. Why not? After all, I wasn't expecting you to have that blade. Where did you get it? Did you, by chance, steal it from someone? It's not exactly something you'd find just lying around."

Anwen blinked in confusion as she watched the dark-clad woman move closer. She took a few more steps back. "I've never stolen a thing in my life."

Daphne's smile widened. "Yes you have. You stole Tyler's heart. And now, after reading your memories, I can see everything you've ever thought or done. You have been a naughty girl." She tisked as she shook her head, making her hair rippled with the effort.

Clenching her fists, Anwen stood her ground as Daphne moved right in front of her. "I know you're dead. I know because I saw you die just before I passed out. I saw you get crushed under a ton of stone."

Daphne shrugged. "Does it matter? Before you brought the roof crashing down, I'd started a rather complicated bit of magic. One that invests part of my soul. Ironically, it also invests part of yours. It wouldn't surprise me if the two had a little make-out session in the middle. So, you see, dead or not, you're stuck with me. And I'm going to do everything in my power to make sure you fail in your quest." Her smile turned into a feral glint that sent ice racing through Anwen's veins.

Anwen shook her head. "You're wrong. You're just a figment of my imagination, a post traumatic creation to taunt me."

The mage turned and began to circle the room like a prowling cat. "Does it really matter? Construct or not, you'll still lose. After all, you'll be going up against the full strength of the Mage Circle. It doesn't even matter that your friends think you're something you're not. Remember what I told you? There is only one Kaida, and that's me. An upstart pretender like you can never hope to best that. You see? You're doomed before you even start."

Anwen shook as her knuckles turned white. "Leave me alone."

Daphne moved closer as she circled the room once more. As she did, she let one finger trace across Anwen's cheek. "And why would I do that? I'm afraid you're stuck with me. Well, at least a part of me." Her eyes turned poison-green as she smiled menacingly. "And I'm not going anywhere."

Up on the Mountain, Madame Millard rested in her spacious tent. Several days had passed since the Circle had gathered in the Ruined City. And, despite all their efforts, the Gates remained closed. The master mage pursed her lips as she thought back on all their attempts to break through the solid doors. Looking at those gathered near her, she finally gave in. "We need to find a different approach," she admitted reluctantly.

The other members of the Inner Circle nodded in agreement. Many sported injuries from their efforts, either from carelessness or rebounding spells. The past few days had not been easy, especially with the waning moon. The point of the matter was that as the moon waned, so did their strength. Something had to change.

"But what method have we not used yet?" Maggy Mintaw asked. "We've used every spell at our disposal. We've used physical force as well as magical. What else is there that we haven't yet tried?"

Madame Millard smiled. This was something she'd been mulling over for a while now, ever since the Gates had first been unsealed. "Patience. The Keeper will return. Or do you not remember what our own have foretold?"

Several of the Inner Circle fidgeted in their seats. Almost as one, the group began to chant. *"Open once, a spell undone. Open twice, for the Dragon Born. Open thrice, an era to end. Open all, the Kaida return by the light of the Mage's Moon."*

Madame Millard took up a stick and began scratching the moon phases into the ground. "The Dragon Moon is waning. Soon, The Mage Moon will rise. And when it does, all will be ready." She sketched out a second set of the same cycle, stopping at the second full moon. "We could, of course, send the Fallen in search of her, now that we know who she at least claims to be. And, as luck would have it, some of her belongings remain from my establishment. We can use them for a tracking scent. It pays to be prepared, don't you agree?"

Maggy looked up in surprise at that. "How did you manage that? I thought she took everything when she left the inn?"

In an attempt to smile mysteriously, Madame only managed to look sinister. "Because I took something while she was out with her new little friends." She reached into a chest behind her and pulled out a plain shirt that needed washing. "I took this. The Fallen will have no trouble tracking her with it."

"Whoever controls the Key Keeper controls the Gates," Cadence Carmichael noted. "I say we send the Fallen. Let them track her down and bring her back to the Mountain."

Looking around, Madame nodded in appreciation. "I gather from your expressions that the majority are for this plan." Her expression became grim. "While we seek the Keeper, I urge you to take this into remembrance. It is extremely likely that a lesser member of our own may have sided with her. For that, this mage must be punished. Are we in agreement?"

The others asserted their approval. "Punish the deserter! Death to the betrayer!"

Madame Millard smiled to herself. She'd never much liked Courtney anyway. Even though the girl wasn't officially part of the Circle, she was still a mage. And to turn her back on the other existing mages was something the master mage deemed punishable by death. Even if she wasn't part of the Circle. Part of her hoped it would be by her own hand.

Steam hissed off the last train of the evening as it settled on the tracks. Despite the late hour, Blaucii Station was bustling with activity. Passengers littered the station proper like random flotsam in a stream. Some headed to the long queue of taxis waiting for a fair. Others meandered, waiting for some expected party to pick them out of the crowd. And some waited to board the train, heading to destinations unknown.

Margo Pack stood with a suitcase in hand. She carried a small rucksack slung over one shoulder. Short auburn hair brushed the base of her neck as she turned to look around. It had been a long time since she'd last visited Blaucii City, let alone the Drakonii Mountain Range. It had to be twenty years at least, long before she'd married. Not much had changed, except for a little upgrading of equipment and structures.

Looking around the platform, one unclaimed taxi caught her eye. She strode towards the waiting vehicle, ignoring the press of people around her. The way seemed to open up before her, almost as if an invisible force kept the masses at bay. Reaching the cab, Margo helped the driver with her luggage. "5792 Driscoll Lane," she instructed him as she settled into the back seat. Part of her wondered how those residing there would react to her sudden and therefore unexpected arrival.

EIGHT

TYLER NODDED IN SATISFACTION. He could feel the last few filaments of bone weave back together under his mental urging. He'd waited a full day before attempting to heal the rest of Anwen's injuries. After one last inspection, he felt confident he'd repaired all of the damage inflicted on her body. "That should just about do it," he commented as he opened his eyes and removed his hand from Anwen's left knee. "Good as new."

Anwen smiled as she sat up. She'd only been up for a few hours, but what a few hours those had been. Watching Tyler coax her body back into normalcy had given her a new perspective. That and his ministrations left her skin tingling. The sensation wasn't unpleasant. "Thanks," she said, rubbing where the brace had supported her no longer broken leg.

Walter got up and gave Tyler a pat on the back. "Good work, as usual," he said in appreciation. With permission, he moved to run one hand down the length of Anwen's leg. "Not so much as a spur out of place."

Tyler smiled at that. "Just because the flesh has mended doesn't mean you shouldn't take things easy," he warned her. "You're bound to be a bit weak at first. But, given time, you'll get stronger."

Anwen nodded as she pulled the covers back over her legs. "And you're sure whatever Daphne did to me won't have any lasting effects?"

Standing, Tyler pushed his chair back to the wall. "As far as I can tell," he assured. "I purged all the taint I could find, down to the smallest particle. Why?"

Anwen turned away as she pulled the quilt further up her body. "No reason." Tyler was right about her feeling weak.

A sudden commotion could be heard from down the hallway. Footsteps scuffed on the floor and Courtney's voice could be heard, protesting. "I told you, you can't come in here! You weren't invited and need to leave! Hey! Listen!"

Both Tyler and Walter started for the door but stopped in surprise before they could reach it. An older version of Anwen filled the open frame. A sense of power seemed to fill the room, giving the dragon pause. He almost looked like someone had slapped him.

Realizing something was going on, Anwen looked up and gasped. "Mom! What are you doing here?"

Margo Pack raised her eyebrows, hands on her hips as she stared into the room. "I might ask you the same question," she retorted. Her voice rang a bit lower than Anwen's in tone, but with far more authority. Every inch of her spoke of a maturity beyond her visible years.

Tyler was the first to recover from the shock. He swept a slight bow. "Mrs. Porter, it's a pleasure to make your acquaintance."

Margo strode into the room, eyeing both Walter and Tyler. "That's Ms. Pack to you," she announced. "Got it?" Hands still on her hips, she glared at the young-looking man.

Tyler acknowledged the correction with a bob of his head. "Of course, Ms. Pack. I can only presume that my 'brother' sent you word on where to find your daughter?"

Anwen stared in horrified silence as her mother gave Tyler a dressing down about her name. According to the courts, Margo was still a Porter. Despite that detail, she'd opted to use her maiden name after her husband's murder. "Mom! Do you have any idea who this is?" She began to fumble with the covers but stopped at a look from Tyler.

The dragon lord turned and gave Anwen a reassuring smile. "It's alright. I don't mind." He turned to look back at the woman who looked so much like but not like her daughter.

Margo paused for thought at the mention of Tyler's 'brother'. In truth, she had gotten word from a most unusual source. At least, it was unusual by most standards. Few people could claim having a close relationship with the soul of a dragon. "Are you, by chance, a Durand?"

Tyler moved closer to her. "Yes, ma'am. Tyler Durand at your service." He gave a more formal bow, one hand in front, the other behind his waist.

Margo blinked a few times in quick succession. Kern Nurrim was the father of all Mage lines, her direct ancestor. He had once told her one of his kin lived outside the Mountain. As a child, she'd often dreamed of finding him and befriending him. But now, to have actually found him, and in such a young form! She wasn't sure what to think.

Seeing her discomfort, Tyler took one of Margo's hands in his and kissed it before bowing once more. "Well met, Margo Kaida Pack. As you have correctly discerned, I am one of the Immortal, a living remnant of a once grand line. At the request of my brethren, I alone remained to guard the Gates of Eternity at the conclusion of the Great War. I have long waited for the return of the last Keeper of the Keys. Disguised as one living among the mortals, I have long accepted this burden. Until this past fortnight, when I met your daughter and discovered her lineage."

A faint hint of red crept up Margo's hairline when Tyler's lips gently pressed against the back of her hand. It was hard to not feel as giddy as a schoolgirl over her first crush. Tyler was certainly a most attractive young man. Having Tyler confirm he was the last of dragon kind outside the Mountain was incredible. It left Margo feeling almost as though she'd regained her long forgotten childhood.

"With the advent of the Dragon Moon, I was blessed with the companionship of your daughter." Tyler continued to look her in the eye as he spoke. "And in such position, I was able to befriend her as a champion and guide." He nodded towards Courtney who had remained in shocked silence. "With the aid of those before me, and a mage from the village, we journeyed to reach the Gates. After much travail, we were able to overcome the obstacles in our path and unbar them."

Margo couldn't take it anymore and slipped her hand from Tyler's. She pressed her other hand to one temple. "Please stop. This is all giving me a headache. Kern warned me this might happen, but to hear you talk like that…" she trailed off.

Anwen rolled her eyes. "If it makes you feel any better, mom, he never once talked to me like that. It was more along the lines of, 'Hey, I'm Tyler. I think you're here for weird reasons and I'm going to try and get you killed so we can open up a mountain pass'. Or something like that." She made a face at Tyler when he glanced her way with a raised eyebrow.

Courtney switched her gaze between Tyler, Margo, and Anwen. As the conversation continued, she felt something bubbling up inside her belly. It took her a moment to realize what it was. She covered her mouth just in time to almost catch an odd sort of squeak. She tried to contain what wanted to naturally follow but couldn't keep it from leaking out. Laughter simply burst out, followed by tears of mirth. "Oh my lord!" she gasped. "Are you guys for real?"

Tyler looked from Anwen to the older mage. He then looked at Courtney, who had turned red from the amount of laughter she'd tried to keep bottled up. The corners of his lips turned up and, before he could suppress it, he'd joined in the laughter. "You're right," he agreed between bursts. "It did sound pretty ridiculous."

Walter coughed politely to remind them of the current state of affairs. But he smiled as Courtney flopped onto the bedroom floor, near to hysterics in her mirth. He wiped away a few laughter tears of his own as he looked towards Tyler. "After having heard the whole story myself, I think I can say with confidence you deserved that one." He stared pointedly at his dragon friend, a hint of amusement in his eyes.

Anwen snorted, soon joining in with the chortle fest. "Oh my gosh! Your face!" She pointed at Tyler. "When I said that! Your face!" She dissolved into a puddle of giggles.

Margo shook her head at the nonsense. Inside, she was pleased to see her daughter letting some of the stress out. Kern had warned her she was neigh unto the breaking point. Though she knew the giggle fest might go too far. Tyler's speech had amused her as well. From what Kern had told her, she admitted Anwen's truncated view was probably accurate.

"If you've all had your fill," Margo admonished, "perhaps it's time to get down to business?" She gave them all a disapproving look, the kind only a mother could give.

With some difficulty, Courtney managed to calm herself. Unfortunately, Anwen was laughing so hard tears trickled down her cheeks. She couldn't catch her breath from the intense spasms caused by her laughter. Nor did she have the control necessary to make herself calm down, even if she had the mind to do it.

Tyler shook his head at the sad lot, giving Walter a sideways glance. "If this keeps up," he noted, "she'll never be able to stop."

Margo rolled her eyes and moved towards the bed. Before anyone could even think about reacting, she smacked her daughter across the face. It wasn't overly hard, but enough to jolt the adolescent girl back to some semblance of sense.

Anwen fell back against the pillows, completely out of breath. Her eyes were wide in shock. She let out one last hiccup before that was the end of it.

Margo rearranged her blouse with a look of satisfaction. Walter and Courtney stood in shocked silence. Neither seemed willing to move, let alone reprimand her for hitting an injured girl.

Tyler moved to insert himself between Anwen and her mother. He turned to glare at the older woman. "That was uncalled for," he reprimanded. "Surely there was another way."

Margo let out an exasperated sigh. "Let me share something with you, Tyler Durand. When Anwen was just a child, her father would tickle her to the same point of near hysteria. There was only one way to pull her out of it. Oh both James and I tried various means, but this was the only sure way to make her stop so she wouldn't hurt herself."

But Tyler wasn't about to back down. "That doesn't mean you had to slap her so hard!" he protested.

The fires of indignation began to burn inside him. He felt a sudden desire to transform. Instead, he curled himself around Anwen like someone protecting their beloved treasure. If he had transformed, however, it was more likely he'd first try to bite Margo's head off. Literally. If he didn't break the bounds of the entire house first due to the sheer size of his draconic form.

Having recovered herself, Anwen slid towards the edge of the bed. Once there, she grabbed Tyler's arm, making him turn. "That's enough. I'm fine," she admonished. "You both sound like a bunch of sulky kids. It almost makes me ashamed to be seen with you guys."

Tyler placed his hands on Anwen's shoulders, turning her to face him full on. He then carefully inspected her face. Although there was a faint red mark from her mother's aggressive action, no welt had been raised. He sighed as he pulled her towards his chest and hugged her. "That's a relief."

Watching them, Margo raised her eyebrows once more. Kern had mentioned nothing of this development. And she meant to have words with him the next time he made contact. "Now are we ready to discuss things?" She resisted the urge to massage her temples again.

Reluctantly, Tyler released Anwen from his arms as Walter moved towards them. "Not to butt in, but," Walter hesitated, "Maybe we should go to the kitchen for some food or something. I'm sure Anwen wants to," he cleared his throat, "clean up. She *has* been cooped up for several days now. At the very least, she might like a change of clothes?"

Anwen felt like everyone was suddenly staring at her. It was true that she was wearing clothes more appropriate for sleeping. Not to mention she felt the need for a good scrubbing. But did they all have to stare at her like that?

Margo nodded, taking charge. "That's fine." She ushered everyone towards the door, turning to look at her daughter. "Just don't take too long, Anwen. I have a lot to tell you and there isn't all that much time."

Remembering her dream from before, Anwen groaned. No rest for the weary. "I'll hurry," she appeased and went in search of her clothes.

NINE

TWENTY MINUTES AFTER LEAVING ANWEN'S room, Margo was complimenting Walter on his cooking. The tantalizing smell of grilled chops with mushrooms and onions wafted through the air. The scent caused more than one stomach to rumble. "I think your cooking would put my husband's to shame." She sampled the slaw Walter had finished before moving on to the meat.

"Cooking's a passion of mine," he smiled as he checked the food on the stove. With perhaps a bit more flair than necessary, he flipped several of the chops. He then seasoned the now exposed sides.

Margo leaned against the counter as she sat in one of the bar stools. "James was the same way," she sighed. "He usually let me do the cooking though. Such a stubborn insistent man. It was infuriating. But I loved him with everything I had." She got a bit of a faraway look in her eye as she thought about her departed husband.

Tyler tried to at least pretend to ignore the two mortals as he sliced up vegetables for steaming. The smell of the meat was making him feel hungrier than he really was. The conversation, however, was interesting. And he was gaining some new insights into Anwen's mother while listening. And, by extension, Anwen.

Courtney played with a pencil as she sat at the table. It had taken some doing to clear off the surface so they could all comfortably sit once the meal was ready. She'd somehow managed to displace most of the junk littering the surface. As a reward, she was taking a break and just enjoying being idle.

Walter threw some more onions into the pan and stirred them around. "Not much into cooking?" he inquired as he looked over his shoulder at Anwen's mother.

Margo shook her head. "I like to cook, but he had a true gift for it. Among other things. I just let him do those other things so he decided to be stubborn and refused to cook when I offered to let him. I think he was more disappointed Anwen didn't share the cooking gene."

Courtney perked up at that. "Anwen can't cook?" Now that she thought about it, she hadn't seen her help with the meals while they'd been out and about. Of course, she'd assumed it was because Tyler insisted on doing all the cooking himself. That was something he had in common with Walter, she guessed.

Turning to face the young woman, Margo smiled. "Not really. She can follow a recipe. But ask her to cook from scratch and she couldn't make anything more than a gluey mass of flour and water in a bowl. Believe me when I say she's tried but it never turned out well. No, her strengths lie elsewhere."

Margo toyed with a ring on a chain around her neck. There was a green stone set among the twining filaments of silver metal. It looked almost like a signet ring, with something carved into the green stone. It was flat across the top but cut in an almost oval shape.

Tyler caught sight of the green gem as light flash off it. He blinked, wondering about the trinket. But his attention was averted as Walter called for the vegetables. "Coming," he responded as he brought the sliced plants over. His curiosity could wait.

Sensing she'd drawn some unwanted attention, Margo slipped the ring back under her shirt. "For example," she continued, "Anwen has always been curious. She also has a strong sense of justice and family, thanks to her father. And, despite her fears, she's willing to give most things a try. She'll seldom complain about her own problems."

Tyler smiled at her last comment. He'd experienced that first hand time and again since he'd met her. Anwen was indeed selfless. She'd give the clothes off her back if someone else needed them, he was sure. That was part of why he liked her. She was far from anything close to the girls he'd watched grow up in the village, Courtney included. If the blond had behaved more like she did now, he might have been in some danger.

Courtney nodded in understanding. "Yes, she is like that, isn't she," she said thoughtfully. "And she has a way of bringing out the best in you. Kind of like a certain dragon I know." She gave Tyler a wry glance.

Before Margo had a chance to reply to that, however, Anwen entered the room. She wore clean clothes. Her hair was still damp from the shower. "That smells good," she commented as she headed towards the kitchen island and took a stool near her mother.

Walter turned from the stove and gave a heartfelt smile. "Sounds like you've got a good appetite, which is decidedly a good sign. Don't worry. It's almost done." He turned back to the stove to make sure the vegetables were steaming as they should. He'd placed them in a finely woven steaming basket over a pot of boiling water.

At Walter's request, Courtney began to set the table. She glanced out the window overlooking the dining area as she did. Overhead, something momentarily blotted out the sun. It looked like some kind of bird, though none she could identify. She moved closer to the window, trying to decide if she'd really seen something or not. "Hey, Tyler, have you heard of there being any kind of large bird in the area?"

Tyler looked up from cleaning the counter with a dishtowel. "Large birds?" He abandoned his cloth and walked over to the window. The hair on the back of his neck began to prickle as he saw another shadow cross over the sun. It didn't look like the typical fowl.

The silhouette looked like some kind of flying creature. It resembled something he'd seen several years ago, but not like any bird he knew. He could clearly see two creatures, even though they were both relatively far away. "That's not a bird," he warned. He reached for the nearest weapon, which happened to be a wooden walking stick from against the wall.

Seeing Tyler's unusual reaction, Anwen felt her chest tighten. "How did they find us?" she asked as she slipped off her stool. The only weapon immediately at hand was the key around her neck. Unfortunately, she had no idea how to make it become a sword again, like she had back in the Mountain. Instead of pulling it out, she reached for the next best thing, a butcher's knife from a block on the far side of the island counter.

Margo's head jerked up as something slammed into the side of the house. "Fallen? Here?" She dove for a knife matching Anwen's, only longer. And with the right application, the knife extended into a thin sword.

Walter abandoned the stove and ran for a stash of automatic weaponry he kept hidden in a low cupboard. He reappeared with a loaded weapon and a belt full of extra clips slung over one shoulder. "Please tell me bullets can kill those things!"

Courtney ducked away from the window as she pulled out her bone knife. Whispering the proper incantation, the blade shot out like a spear. "We should have set wards," she said, mentally kicking herself for the lack of foresight.

"No time to worry about that now," Tyler exclaimed. Loud scratching sounds came from outside. The noise might have come from the roof. More noise came from one of the back rooms as a window shattered into the building, causing Anwen to jump. "Here they come," Tyler said in an all too calm manner.

Something swept past the window in the dining room, blocking out the light from outside. It rammed the glass, making shards fly inward. At that exact moment, another creature bounded down the hallway. It all but flew into the room. They were both hideous. One looked like a demented bird mixed with a panther. The other looked like a rabid wolf with great tufts of hair yanked out at random.

Anwen cried out as the wolf Fallen slammed into one of the bar stools, knocking it over. She somehow avoided getting hit because Margo pulled her to one side. Her mother stabbed the beast with her borrowed knife. The creature cried out, whipping its ugly head around. Black blood mixed with saliva flew from the creature's mouth. Some of it landed on Anwen's arm, burning her like acid.

The panther bird kept Tyler occupied as it attacked from the window. With Courtney's help, they managed to push it back outside. But, before they could destroy it, another similar beast flew down to help its mate. It called out in defiance.

"Not good," Tyler sweated as he jabbed the second bird with his stick. He'd also transformed the wooden tool into a form resembling a spear.

Walter sprayed the back entryway with bullets as another creature burst through the door. He riddled it with holes that steamed with a sickly scent. After almost a dozen rounds, the creature fell to the earth before turning to ash. Unfortunately, several other Fallen jumped forward to take its place. "Just how many of these things are there!" he yelled before ducking for cover.

Anwen wasn't sure which direction to look. Too many things were going on all at once. Her mother battled the wolf demon and her friends battled the others. Her heart beat like a fast-paced drum. Around her neck, the key seemed to heat up like something left on the stove. It grew hotter and hotter as blue light filled the room. One of the Fallen broke free from the pack attacking Walter's position. It jumped straight at her.

Letting out a scream, Anwen thrust her hands up in an attempt to ward off pawing claws. The knife she held bit into the creature, which let out a scream of its own. Almost as if swatting at some insect, Anwen moved her arms like a mad man. The knife blade flashed again and again as the Fallen tried to break free and pin her to the ground.

Seeing Anwen in peril, Tyler became distracted from the panther-bird demons. "Anwen!" He was about to turn and help her when one of the beasts gouged his cheek with a talon, drawing blood. He grunted as he turned to reengage the monster. Something inside him began to burn as his anger mounted. How dare they come to his friend's home and attack? And how dare they come after Anwen yet again? It would not be allowed to continue.

Anwen was too busy to notice that Tyler had begun to glow with a white light. It contrasted with the blue thrown off by the Master Key. With her own eyes closed, she could feel the heat rising in the room, but attributed it to her own panic. Continuing to swipe at the creature in front of her, she somehow managed to trip over one of the stools and slammed into the floor as a result.

Seeing a moment of weakness, the Fallen sprang forward, paws extended to dig into her chest. But it never got the chance as Anwen held her blade pointing outward. The creature flew into the knife, sinking it deep into its underbelly. The creature fell on top of her, lifeless, and then turned to ash.

Tyler's eyes turned liquid amber as his anger mounted. It wasn't enough that they'd hunted Anwen on the Mountain. Nor that they'd attacked them while in the Ruined City. Now they had attacked them in the one place of refuge he had left and he wasn't going to stand for it.

Having killed her own attacker, Margo turned to see

Tyler's expression with a sense of alarm. "Look out!" She dived for cover as Tyler opened his mouth and white-hot flame spewed from his throat.

Courtney reacted to the cry with a backhanded swipe of her blade. The movement cut into the panther-bird nearest her. She pivoted on the balls of her feet and dropped to the ground as the flames flew over her head.

Walter was less lucky as the edge of the flames passed over his arm before he could hit the deck. They set his sleeve on fire, though that seemed of little consequence. All around him, fire burned, raw and angry. It was only encouraged by the gas stove that had yet to be turned off.

Anwen lay on the ground, completely stunned. She stared upwards at the swirl of almost silver flames above her. The fire licked around her, scorching the furnishing of the room. Despite the intensity of the heat, she only felt numb. Black liquid dripped from her knife and onto her clothes. Steam seemed to rise into the air, only to be completely destroyed by the intense heat.

All around, Fallen cried out in fear and pain before being vaporized by the intense dragon flames. Their cries filled the air with a sound worse than anything Courtney had ever heard. She covered her ears with her hands and prayed for it to be over.

Tyler, having swept the entire area with his flame, turned back towards the window. He glared out into the afternoon sky with his amber eyes, expression almost feral. No more Fallen came to challenge him. They had either been cowed or defeated. With one more look around, Tyler swallowed his flame. His eyes returned to a more normal slate blue, then settled on their usual color.

Margo cautiously moved from her position behind the kitchen island. Looking around, she felt a sense of awed fear. The stream of dragon breath had blackened most of the room. Parts of the counter were still on fire, but with the usual flames instead of the white that had started them. She quickly willed the flames out, and then moved to turn off the stove.

Tyler pushed through the debris, which included part of the ceiling, as he made his way to Anwen's side. He knelt next to her, full of concern as he saw her staring unblinkingly upward. "Anwen? Can you hear me?" He brushed a gentle finger down her face.

Anwen shuddered as her fingers relaxed on the knife, which clattered to the floor. "I... I killed it," she said, her voice far from steady. "I actually...." Tears leaked from her eyes. "I didn't mean to kill it. It just..." She turned towards Tyler, her body curling around him as she shook with tears.

Tyler caressed her hair, pulling her closer. "Shh. It's okay. It's going to be okay." He couldn't help but notice how silky her hair felt under his fingers. He wanted to stay like this forever, immortalized in this moment, ash and all.

Anwen continued to sob as he stroked her hair, but her heart beat less quickly. Inside her chest something radiated a comforting warmth unlike any she'd felt before. Over and over again, she heard his words in her mind. *It's okay. It's going to be okay.*

Courtney moved from her spot near the window, her bone knife back in its original form. She walked a bit unsteadily towards the kitchen bar. Looking around, she noticed Walter nursing his burns. She quickly moved over to him. "Let me help," she offered. She used a minor spell to capture water from the faucet and cocoon the fluid around the worst of his injuries.

Margo watched Tyler as he scooped Anwen up into his arms. The girl had fallen asleep against him, her body still shuddering from the unconscious sobs. "The first one is always the hardest," she commented. Wisps of hair had matted against her face and she moved to brush them back.

Tyler gave a grim smile. "I never thought they'd attack here," he admitted. "Unfortunately, now that they know where we are, we have no choice but to leave. I'm not sure if they were trying to kill Anwen or capture her. Either way, we can't stay here. They will be back."

His announcement brought a slight gasp from Courtney. As a result, she almost lost concentration on her task, the water threatening to fall to the floor. "But I thought you said we'd be safe here."

"Margo," Tyler looked directly at the older woman as he ignored Courtney's comment. "Something tells me there is more to you than meets the eye."

Margo returned his gaze with a worn smile. "I am a daughter of the line of Kaida, as I'm sure you already know. And even though I never told Anwen about it, I am a practicing dragon mage. My grandmother didn't agree with those in the Circle and left the village. She wanted to break all ties, along with several others. But she also knew that someday someone would have to return to bring order. We mages have our own prophecies. And, knowing that one of the Kaida line would return to the Mountain, she made sure we knew how to use our abilities."

Nodding, Tyler moved towards the living room. He hoped the others were following him. It would be best, after all, to leave the battle zone. He doubted there would be any more attacks that day, but safety in numbers was better than being alone. And he didn't want to risk Anwen getting hurt again. She'd only just healed.

Thankfully, the others followed him into the adjoining room. Courtney ran to grab the medical kit Walter kept in the back. Margo helped the veteran find a comfortable chair while they waited for the young mage to return. Tyler set Anwen on the couch.

Margo examined the burned tissue on Walter's arms and chest. "If you would allow it, I can heal most of this," she offered. "It won't be the same as what Tyler can do, I'm sure, but I have a knack for coaxing flesh back together."

Tyler looked over at her comment but didn't say anything. He turned his attention back to Anwen and examined the burn marks she'd received from the Fallen's bodily fluids. He was pleased to note none were bad. It took little effort to heal the damaged skin.

He just wasn't sure about the psychological damage from the unexpected fight. This was technically her first real battle. He didn't count the one where they were attacked near the Lake. She hadn't fought there, though he doubted it was any less traumatic, just in a different way.

Walter glanced down at the blackened skin on his arms and tried not to wince. "Might as well give it a go," he said. "Looks like Tyler's busy and all that anyway." He shuddered when Margo placed a cool hand on his shoulder.

Margo took a deep breath as she mentally coaxed the damaged tissue back to a more healthy state. When that didn't work, she tried to persuade the healthy flesh to regenerate. At her prodding, it created a new layer of skin. Flakes of blackened dermis fell to the ground as Walter's body responded to the silent pressing.

Courtney came back into the room as Margo moved her hand from Walter's shoulder. She blinked in surprise to see the pink of healing flesh where charred skin had been only minutes before. "How did you do that?" she asked in awe as she set the medical kit down.

Margo sat back in the closest chair. "Being a mage isn't all about destruction, illusion, or wards," she replied. "Unfortunately, the Circle has lost sight of that. Along with some of the more useful and original spells. I just asked Walter's body to generate several new layers of skin to replace the damaged ones."

Tyler glanced over at the comment. It was definitely true, though. Over time, the mages had lost a lot of the more essential knowledge given them. He supposed it was a result of wanting to distance themselves from dragon-kind. Instead of interacting, they wanted control.

"Sadly," Margo continued, "it's not a full healing. You're skin will likely be sensitive for a day or two. I can't do anything to lessen the pain. I'm not that good."

Courtney was about to ask for a lesson when Anwen opened her eyes. Seeing only shadows, the Key Keeper flinched away from Tyler. After a brief moment, she was scrambling to apologize. "I'm sorry! For a moment, I thought... I thought..." she trailed off in embarrassment.

"You thought I was a Fallen One?" Tyler finished for her. It was understandable. "I'm pretty sure you were their target, so it's not surprising. But I don't think they were out to kill you. I believe the Mage Circle is now intent on getting inside the Mountain before the dragons wake. If they can do that, there's a chance they can either destroy them or control them. And to do that, they need you."

"Makes sense," Margo mused. "And if that's the case, they'll definitely try again. Good thing we have the advantage."

Walter looked up from admiring his new skin. "Advantage? How's that? They've a whole mountain's worth of magicians or whatever they are. What do we have that can at least match that?"

Courtney looked back and forth between the three adults. She had to consider Tyler an adult, even though he looked her age. "Walter's right. Even with a dragon, two mages, and a well trained veteran, how can we compete? Remember what you told us earlier, Tyler? You may be a dragon, but you don't have an endless supply of energy. This past few weeks showed us that."

Tyler smiled as he leaned against the couch. "We have three trained mages. Or we will. And one of those isn't just an ordinary mage. We have the Kaida, remember?"

Anwen almost bolted upright as Tyler, Walter, and Courtney turned to look at her. "But I'm not the Kaida!" she protested. "Daphne said so herself! I can't be the one!"

Margo leaned forward in her chair. "You're great grandmother, Emma Kaida Garret, left the village when she was almost eight. She only had one daughter, who was your grandmother. And, as you know, I was her only child, just like you. That makes you the next in line."

"Emma Garret," Tyler broke in, "was a direct descendent of the first Kaida. Each in that line was the first female child. Which, as your mother said, makes you the heir to that title."

"But what about Daphne?" Anwen protested. "She claimed to be the Kaida. She even said it was part of her name. Doesn't that mean something?"

Tyler frowned as he thought back. "Daphne is a great granddaughter of Anna Kaida Magus. A second daughter, I believe. After it skipped a generation. If I remember correctly, her great grandmother's sister, Samantha, was not the favored child. Even though she was the first born."

Anwen's eyes almost bugged out. "You mean Daphne and I are somehow related?"

Margo nodded with Tyler. "Distantly, but yes. That doesn't change the fact that you are the last in a direct line of firstborn. For now, Kaida is a title I hold as a sort of honoree. It's a title I will pass on to you once you have completed your training. Every daughter destined to inherit that title is given the same middle name. It looks like the parents of this Daphne girl you mentioned were being rather presumptuous."

Anwen rubbed at her temples. "I'm getting confused. Why didn't you tell me about all this before?"

"Kern," Margo sighed. "In return for his protection, I promised not to tell you. Not until you were ready."

Courtney's mouth fell open in surprise. "Kern? As in the first of the Dragons? The Oldest of Old? *That* Kern?"

Margo smiled with great patience. "Yes. He has spoken to me since I was a little girl. It was with his encouragement that I found my husband James. He seemed to think it important we meet. And when we fell in love, it was as if he'd blessed our union. He was the one who named Anwen." She turned towards her daughter.

"What?" Anwen fell back against the couch cushions. "But how? Why?" She looked at her mother with complete bewilderment.

Walter looked at the clock on the wall and cleared his throat. "Not to be rude, but didn't someone say it wasn't safe here anymore? Shouldn't we get a move on? Find a new base of operations or something?"

Tyler nodded. "Yes, we should. But first, we need pack a few things. I've no idea how long we'll be gone so it's best to plan for the long term. Wherever we go, we need an area with plenty of space and materials to train Anwen. She's our ace up the sleeve." He gave her an apologetic shrug when she gave him an incredulous look.

Margo pursed her lips. "Since the Fallen have attacked here, it would be safe to assume they don't mind crowds. Our best bet is somewhere more remote. That way no innocent bystanders will get caught up in all of this. I wouldn't put it past them to kill whoever gets in their way, regardless of their innocence."

Courtney agreed. She tried to think of any places she knew. The outpost near the waterfall didn't have enough room, even if it had the wards. And although the Old Mill did have the space, it probably wouldn't work either. They'd found them there already. That and it would likely bring up bad memories for Anwen.

Tyler closed his eyes as he thought about the possibilities. Any previous locations would not do, he decided. "Somewhere remote," he mused. "Close to plenty of water and a food supply. Somewhere where the Fallen can't come." He stood up abruptly. "I need to meditate." Courtney and Anwen watched him leave the room, not really sure how to interpret this behavior.

Margo clapped her hands together for attention as she stood from her chair. "While he's off doing his thing, we should gather together any supplies we'll need. I have a feeling it will be some time before we come back, so we should try and repair what outward damage we can. We don't want to tempt any looters or thieves while we're away. Courtney, this task is up to the two of us. Anwen, you help Walter get the supplies."

Courtney followed Margo towards the kitchen. It was true she and Margo were the only ones who could accomplish the repairs the older woman had in mind. With Tyler off meditating, he was off the hook. She just hoped it wouldn't be a massive repair job and that they'd be fine with just surface repairs. Anything more would be exhausting and take too long.

Anwen followed Walter to the back room where he pulled out several large hiking packs. "Never know when you'll need these." He began to fill the bags with various camping and food supplies. Anwen silently agreed. Part of her wondered if she would ever get away from the more rough aspects of this venture.

TEN

ONE HOUR LATER, EVERYONE MET back in the living room. Walter and Anwen had prepared four mountain packs. Courtney and Margo had repaired the surface damage to the outside of the house. Any further repairs would have to wait. At least the repairs they had managed wouldn't invite any unwanted guests.

When Tyler emerged from the spare bedroom, he looked almost resigned. "I've decided where we're going," he announced. "It took some convincing of my closest kin, but they all agree it's the best place. And all are welcome." He didn't mention how his brother had almost opposed the idea. Letting three more mortals set foot on sacred soil was not high on his priority list.

"So where *are* we going?" Courtney asked.

Tyler smiled with weariness. It had been a trying negotiation. "Back up in the mountains. We make for Lake Wyvern and the Sacred Isle."

Anwen's eyes went almost as wide as the others' did. "To the Sacred Grove? Are you kidding?"

Thoughts of a circular alter inside the shrine filled Anwen's thoughts. Along with the memory of sustaining a concussion there. It was something she definitely didn't want to repeat.

Shaking his head, Tyler moved to pick up one of the packs. "No. Not that far in. As part of the conditions of using the island, no one is allowed to pass the Bounding Circle. To do so, without permission, means immediate death. And we really can't afford that to happen."

Walter looked after Tyler with misgivings. "Sounds… daunting." He doubted the dragon was joking. It wasn't in his nature to joke about such things.

"But that's right under the Mountain!" Courtney protested. "That's where the Circle is gathered! Doesn't that make it even more dangerous?"

"The Fallen cannot go there," Tyler stated. "It has long been said that the lake water has special properties. It destroys any unclean thing that touches it. Remember what happened when one fell into the water? And should they try to fly over it, well… let's just say they would not get far."

Margo pursed her lips. "Then let's hope everyone in our group is 'clean', with pure intentions."

Courtney glanced over at Anwen. Out of the entire party, she and Tyler were the only ones to taste the waters of that lake. And yet, Anwen was still living. Was it because she carried no ill intent? Or was it because Tyler refused to let her die? Or because they had not been tainted by evil?

Walter picked up his pack, following Tyler out the door. "Time's wasting. Best be off before anything else happens."

Margo and Anwen grabbed a pack and followed him outside. Courtney wasn't too far behind. Tyler had already put his pack in the back of Walter's truck and was waiting to help the others do the same.

Holding his hands out for the keys, Tyler resisted the urge ask Walter to stay. Kern had only allowed this man's inclusion because of his history with Tyler. "I think I should drive," he said instead. "No one knows the area like I do."

Walter raised a brow as he took the keys out of his pocket. "Sure about that? I know how you drive." He gave him a knowing look, laced with a hint of humor.

Tyler rolled his eyes. "The last time you were in a vehicle I drove was back in the desert. And we were threatened by another sandstorm at the time, as I recall. You were still recovering from exposure. I had to use whatever means available to make sure you stayed alive. Sorry if that makes me a bad driver in your eyes. Just remember I've been doing this much longer than you have."

Smiling in amusement, Walter tossed the keys to Tyler. "Just make sure you all buckle up," he advised the ladies. "Tyler loves offroading."

Taking Walter's joke aside, everyone made sure seat belts were fastened before starting out. It never hurt to be cautious.

Streaks of color began to fill the sky as the sun began its long journey back to the other side of the world. Their party was a good ways away from the city limits by the time it had dropped behind the higher peaks. Tyler followed the same route the bus had used back when Anwen first set foot in the Drakonii Mountains. They climbed steadily for hours. Both Courtney and Anwen dozed in the back, even though it was cramped with their gear.

About fifteen miles outside the Village of Lindwyrm, Tyler pulled off the main road. There was a small track off to one side that was hard to see from the main highway. It had once been used as a fire road, in case of natural disasters. Due to the lack of such disasters, it had fallen into disuse. Ultimately, it had been left to the mountains to reclaim.

Anwen woke with a jolt as the vehicle bounced over a fallen branch. She tried to peer out the windows but only saw a mass of black flashing by. Dark trees lined the little-used path. And, with the moon not yet rising, everything was dark except where the headlights shown.

Yawning, Anwen tried to guess at the time. She supposed

it was still before midnight but wasn't sure. She'd been rather tired, even with the recent rest she'd received. Though she supposed she shouldn't have be surprised. The adrenaline rush from the Fallen attack had given her more than ample reason to crash.

"The path's a little more rugged then I remember," Tyler confessed as they hit another bump. "But we should almost be to an old ranger station where we'll leave the truck. From there, we'll hike the rest of the way to the Lake."

Margo tried to calculate where they were based off of her own memories and the maps she'd studied. She figured they were off to the right of the highway, though she wasn't exactly sure where. "How long of a jaunt are we talking about?" she asked. She glanced back at her daughter, realizing she was awake.

Tyler didn't so much as look away from the road as he thought about it. He kept the vehicle going at a steady rate. Despite the conditions, the trees went by at a rapid speed. "I'd have to estimate an hour or two," he finally replied. "After that, it will take some time to cross the Lake. Regardless of the actual time involved, we must reach the Island before daybreak. We can't let the Mage Circle know we're here. And until we're on the Island, we won't be safe."

"I knew I should have taken that nap," Walter groaned. Having been up since the small hours of the morning, he was starting to feel the weariness set in.

Realizing this, Tyler smiled in compassion. Even though he knew his friend couldn't see it. "Once we arrive on the Island, we can rest as much as needed. We should be free from prying eyes so long as we're under the cover of the trees."

Half an hour later, Tyler stopped the truck, parking in a small clearing. Half a dozen logs formed a semi-circle where someone had packed the earth solid. A dilapidated wooden building stood off to one side. The door had fallen in and vines reached out from the windows. Overhead, stars filled the sky as Tyler killed the engine. The sound of insects and nocturnal creatures rushed in to fill the silence.

Anwen nudged Courtney, trying to wake her. "Hey, we're here," she whispered. She knew they were miles away from the village, or the Mountain. Despite that, she somehow felt if she talked any louder the Mage Circle would hear her.

Courtney groaned but opened her eyes. She had to blink a few times to adjust to the near black darkness surrounding them. After a minute or so, her eyes had adjusted to the starlight. "Doesn't look like the lake to me," she complained.

Tyler left the truck's cabin and walked around to the back, retrieving his pack. "We have a long hike ahead of us," he said in reply to Courtney's sleepy observations. "And then a bit of a ride over water. Nothing to it."

Courtney rolled her eyes as she stiffly got out of the truck. "Easy for you to say. You have the stamina of the undead."

Anwen felt tempted to laugh but didn't as she accepted her pack. It suddenly seemed so much heavier now that she had to carry it for several long miles. "I wish we could just fly there," she sighed.

"And alert the entire Mountain to our presence?" Margo asked. "I wouldn't even harbor the possibility. Even if Tyler offered it."

"I know." Anwen stared at the ground. She thought she heard the distant sound of laughter. It sounded like Daphne. "Leave me alone," she hissed at the sound.

Courtney gave her friend a rather odd look, not sure why she'd earned that comment. She was about to say something when the other girl spoke up again.

"Not you," Anwen amended, hoping Courtney wasn't offended. "Just a little insect trying to make me mad."

With everyone ready to go, Tyler led the way. He summoned a small light orb. He then masked it enough so the light wouldn't alert anyone to their presence. He nodded in satisfaction at the wards Courtney and Margo had created before heading out. They should keep them from being detected. He added an extra layer from his added wards. Even the most skilled member of the Circle would have a hard time discerning their presence.

Unfortunately, the path was not as direct a route as some of the party had hoped. To be extra sure they were not discovered, Tyler took them on a more round about direction. That meant he sometimes backtracked. After several hours of this, he finally let them rest for more than a few minutes. During this time, they broke out small rations.

"Aren't we there yet," Courtney complained. She inspected a long scratch that ran down her exposed arm. She wished they'd had time to at least go to a store and get more clothing. The branches were murder on her skin. As things were, she only had the sets they'd brought from the village. And those were starting to get ragged, even with some minor repairs.

Anwen looked around, noticing a slight change in the lightness of the sky. The air was also cooler. "Looks like the sun might be rising soon," she said. Inside her head, Daphne laughed.

Tyler looked towards the sky. What Anwen had said was true. It was still in the early hours of the morning. But the sun would start to ascend the mountainside before long. Time was indeed running out. "We're almost there," he assured as he recapped his canteen. "Let's go."

Picking their way through fallen foliage, Tyler led them once more. The air began to grow more damp the closer they came to the Lake. Within another half hour, they had reached the shore. But there was no visible way of crossing the large span between the bank and the island. Unless they swam.

Walter shaded his eyes with one hand as he looked out towards the far shore. It wasn't to keep off any light, but as a sort of makeshift binoculars. "I knew I should have packed that inflatable raft," he joked with a low whistle. "That's a bit away isn't it?"

Margo stared impassably towards the east. The faintest

hints of color were beginning to show between the mountain peaks. "I hope you have something in mind for this situation," she commented as she turned to Tyler. "Otherwise, we won't make it there in time. Unless you want to transform into your true form and fly us over. Not that I'm recommending it."

The dragon ignored her dry words. Instead, he continued the work he'd started upon reaching the shore. While the others had admired the view, he'd been busy hauling over several fallen logs. Seeing his efforts, Walter joined him. Soon, they both had gathered a good collection of odd sized branches and drift.

Finding some vines, Tyler quickly laced them over the wooden limbs. With that finished, he placed one hand on the rickety raft they'd created. Closing his eyes, he concentrated on the form.

"Hate to break it to you, mate," Walter interposed, "but that won't hold us all, even if it will float."

Tyler either ignored him or didn't hear. For a moment, it seemed as though light had flown from him into the dead wood as he closed his eyes. The gnarled branches began to change, smoothing out. With a few more minutes' worth of coaxing, the wood flattened out. The ends bowed together to create a stern and prow. The widened surface curled up to make a water-tight vessel

Finished, Tyler opened his eyes, pleased with his efforts. A thin but durable boat bobbed lightly on the lake's edge. It was more than large enough to accommodate the five travelers and their gear. "You were saying?" He turned to look questioningly at Walter.

Courtney clapped her hands in anticipation. "Now all we need is a pair or two of oars." She looked around for several sturdy branches of a smaller size. She found two. Using a similar spell to Tyler's, she coaxed the wood to change according to their needs. When she was done, she noticed Margo had done the same.

Under Tyler's direction, Walter and Anwen stored the

packs in the middle of the boat. They used one of the ropes Walter had packed to secure them in place. By the time they'd finished, both Margo and Courtney had completed their tasks.

After everyone had climbed aboard and situated themselves, Tyler pushed off from the shore. Margo sat with Courtney in the front. Tyler paired with Walter in the back, each with a paddle. Anwen sat in the middle, as far from the sides as possible. Tyler didn't want to risk retesting her lack of swimming skills.

Even with Tyler's reassurances, Anwen felt ill at ease. The last time she'd been on the Lake's waters had not been a good experience. She still remembered the feel of the water pushing her down. It was not something she wanted to repeat. Even if she'd had visions of dragons while under the surface.

Paddles dipped quietly but strongly in the water. With two sets of rowers, their makeshift boat seemed to move more like a swift current carried it.

By the time the morning light began to climb down the Mountain's side, they were halfway to the Island. Maybe it had something to do with Tyler's mental request to the Lake waters for swift passage. Maybe it was because they had more help than the last time he and Anwen had been on the Lake. Either way, Anwen was glad.

Tyler directed the boat towards the far side of the Island, away from the prying eyes on the Mountain. A second, smaller jetty sat near where the tail would have jutted out from the rear of the Island's main body.

Several smaller islands moved away, as though the tail was only partially submerged. If the water's level had been lower, they'd have all connected. Instead, a small beach waited where the spur flowed downward.

Both Tyler and Walter jumped out to guide the boat up onto the shore, landing them several dozen yards away from the jetty they'd seen earlier. Safely secured, they helped the others out as the sun's light hit the Lake. "Just in time,"

Tyler noted as he looked out over the water. "Up and in now."

Trees lined the shore, making it easy to conceal the boat. Keeping to Tyler's words, they moved further in. Maybe half a mile up the slope, Tyler called a halt. "We'll make camp here," he announced.

Walter looked around the green foliage. "Not bad," he said in approval.

They stood in a small clearing. A stream ran nearby, providing ample water. And with plenty of dead wood to make a fire, it made an ideal camping site.

After another hour, the small group had two tents set up. Walter collected stones to create a decent-sized fire pit. Courtney went to collect the first batch of firewood.

Anwen found a stone to use as a seat near the tent she was to share with Courtney and her mother. She felt strange setting foot back on the Sacred Island. It was as though static electricity lined her body. She almost felt afraid to touch anything because of the possibility of static shock.

Having finished unpacking her gear, Margo walked over to her daughter. "Anwen, due to the serious nature of our quest, time is not granted you to be idle. Training begins now. You will do exactly as I say, when I say it. Is that clear?"

Anwen looked up at her mother's serious tone. She was still tired from the ordeal the day before. Not to mention their most recent hike. All she wanted to do was crawl inside the tent and sleep. That or to find some food. She hadn't eaten in days. No one had thought to offer a snack on the way over and she'd not felt hungry enough to ask for one. But she knew her mother all too well. "Now?" She looked up with wistful eyes, already knowing the answer.

Margo raised her eyebrows a bit, hands on her hips as she gave her that no-nonsense look. "Now."

With a sigh, Anwen stood and followed her mother. "What kind of training?" she wondered out loud, hoping she'd at least get the chance to eat something first.

Margo picked up a canteen on the way out of camp. "You'll see," she promised.

Not wanting to go too far, Margo kept careful watch on her directions. After half an hour of easy walking, they came across a little glen with another small stream. "This will do," she commented to herself. She thrust the canteen at her daughter. "You'll need this," she explained. "Your first task is to sit and listen."

Anwen looked at her in disbelief. "You want me to just sit here and listen? For how long? And what am I listening for?"

Margo's eyes looked like a stormy sky. "Until you can hear everything. A mage understands her surroundings and heeds them. Being in tune with nature is the first step. No nodding off." With that, she turned and walked away.

Anwen stared after her, the canteen dangling from her fingers. "You're serious? I have to sit here and just listen?"

"Until you can hear everything," her mother reminded as she disappeared into the foliage.

Anwen wasn't sure what she meant by that but decided it was best to do as her mother ordered. So she found a relatively comfortable spot and sat down to meditate. It was hard, especially since all she really wanted to do was go to sleep.

ELEVEN

MARGO WALKED SLOWLY BACK TO camp. She exhaled, stopping to lean against a tree. "Oh, Anwen," she sighed. She wished there was another way but knew there wasn't. Not if they were to make sure Anwen was ready in time. And even with her method of choice, there were no guarantees it would work.

Tyler watched her from a small ways away. He cleared his throat to announce himself before coming any closer. "It's never easy," he commented as he caught up to her. "Being the responsible one that is."

Margo turned at the sound of his voice. "No," she agreed, identifying his face. "I felt the same way when I allowed her to come here. It was like I was abandoning her. In a way, it was the same when she went off with her father that one night." She pushed away from the tree and brushed the dirt from her hands.

Tyler closed the gap between them. He then offered his canteen as he ignored the minute amounts of moisture in her eyes. Even though he was aware of those events, he didn't feel he should comment on them. It was a private memory and she didn't seem inclined to share. "I knew the moment I met her she wasn't destined to be a warrior," he admitted. "I wasn't sure what she was meant to be, but I was sure of that. With that in mind, I think you've chosen the right path."

Margo accepted the canteen and took a sip. "I hope you're right. Anwen has always been a quiet child. She's already been through so much. But if she can't master this lesson, we can't move on. And you and I both know what that means."

Tyler nodded. "She will understand. It's her destiny." He didn't want to add the few other things he knew. Not yet. Things like how Anwen was no longer quite mortal. Or how she'd already begun to change the fabric of reality. "Just look at how far she's come."

They fell into step, heading back to camp. Margo returned the canteen. "Yes," she agreed. "She is different. And I don't think it's just because she almost died. There's something more. I just can't put it into words."

Tyler resisted the urge to correct her on that one point. Anwen hadn't almost died. She had. But Margo didn't need to know that. At least not yet.

Anwen sat cross-legged on some moss she'd discovered. When her first position hadn't afforded comfort, she'd opted to look for something better. Part of her wondered if it might have been better to be uncomfortable. It kept her from wanting to doze off, or at least made it less likely that she would.

Her hands rested lightly on her knees as she closed her eyes. About an hour had passed since her mother had left her there. She still wasn't sure what she was supposed to do. She'd tried listening for the sounds of insects and animals. Somehow, she was sure that wasn't quite what her mother had in mind.

A slight breeze made the tree branches rustle. The wind raised goose bumps along Anwen's skin and she shivered. It wasn't cold out, but it somehow felt as though the temperature had dropped.

"You're pathetic," Daphne said in her mind, slowly taking shape. "You'll never be as great as I am by just sitting here. Don't you even know what it means to be a mage?" She snorted in disdain as her body took on more definition in Anwen's thoughts. "I somehow doubt you do. This exercise is pointless."

Anwen tried her best to ignore the mental taunts. But part of her feared Daphne was right. What was the point of sitting in the middle of nowhere? She was no closer to hearing everything, as her mother put it, than she had been back before she'd met Tyler. "No," she shook her head. "There has to be a reason."

"So sure, are you?" Daphne asked. "But what if you're wrong? What if you're both wrong? What then? Will you whine and complain that life isn't fair? Because it's not."

A sigh escaped Anwen's lips, more out of irritation than anything. "I'd be able to hear things better if you'd just shut up," she admonished. "Can't you go haunt someone else?"

Daphne snorted. "Fat chance there," she retorted. "You're mine to torment for forever. Even if my spell didn't destroy your soul, you're now stuck with me. You know that. I'm not going anywhere."

Anwen tried to mentally push the other girl away. After all, Daphne was far from helpful. She resettled herself and continued to try and meditate.

Madame Millard stroked the coat of a particularly ugly Fallen. This one looked like a cross between a bear cub and a hairless dog. "It's alright," she crooned. Things had not quite gone as planned. The Key Keeper was still outside her reach. But time would change that. "It's alright. Soon you will feast on dragon flesh."

Outside her tent, someone argued with her second in command. After more rustling, the flap lifted and Josef entered. "Madame Millard, we need to talk." He paused at the sight of the Fallen, cringing away. No matter how many he'd seen over the last few days, he still could not get used to their ugly appearance.

Madame Millard noticed his disconcerted staring. But she only smiled as she continued to stroke the hairless head. "I thought you were assigned to guard duty," she commented. "Why did you abandon your post?" She continued to croon, her voice level and calm.

Josef steeled himself, keeping a wary eye on the creature. Madame Millard was known for having a honey tongue when she wanted to use it. "You still haven't found Daphne," he answered. "It's been almost a week and no one has so much as looked for her. Why?"

Standing, Madame Millard sent her Fallen outside. "My niece is perfectly capable of taking care of herself," she responded. "I'm sure she's off on some errand of her own." She moved over to the low table where a map of the mountain range sat. "Now, if you don't mind, I have some business to attend to."

Josef puffed up his chest, looking as though he was preparing to give battle. He backed down when the mage continued to ignore him. With a bit of a huff, he left the tent. Striding away, he headed, not back to his post, but towards the destroyed amphitheater. He felt sure Daphne had been there. If no one else was going to look for her, he would. And he'd find her, one way or another.

Courtney had gathered a sizable amount of dead wood by the time Margo and Tyler returned to camp. She'd not even realized the dragon had gone off until she saw him walking back with Anwen's mother. Dropping her last armful into the growing pile, she looked for Anwen. She felt sure her friend would not be too far behind. When she didn't see her, she went to meet them.

Easily interpreting the girl's thoughts, Margo sighed as she entered camp. "Anwen will be doing some special training on her own," she announced.

Courtney blinked in confusion. "But I thought…?" She turned to follow the other two back towards the main clearing.

Tyler moved around the makeshift fire pit and found a seat on an old stump. "Anwen's not a fighter like we are," he reminded. "It would go against her nature to force her to become one. I'm sure Margo means the best by giving her a different kind of lesson."

Courtney's mouth fell open. She couldn't believe what she was hearing. "But doesn't she need to know how to defend herself? I mean, what if something happens? The Fallen could come again, just like they did back at Walter's house. How is she supposed to defend herself if you've left her out there on her own?" She indicated the forest with a shrug of her shoulder.

Margo found another stump to sit on. It sat close to the other two. But it was still far enough away that she couldn't just reach out and touch either of them. "I have always known Anwen's nature is not a typical one," she said. "It's not her job to fight, but to unite two halves of the same whole. Forcing her to go against that nature will only break her."

Courtney shook her head as she moved to place several small logs into the fire pit. "I don't understand."

Tyler exchanged looks with Margo as Walter came back to camp with his own armful of wood. "It's our job to protect her," he informed. "And remember, no Fallen can come here. She'll be fine."

Walter dropped his load of wood into the pile. He brushed off the resulting bark and dirt on his clothes as he walked over to the group. "To protect who?"

"Anwen," Margo answered. "I've known for a long time that her destiny is a special one. Kern wouldn't have taken such an interest in her if it wasn't."

Courtney dropped down in defeat, declining the stump Tyler offered her. "But you can't seriously mean to just leave her out there, on her own. You'll at least bring her some food, right? And what about wild animals? She'll have to defend herself against those, won't she?"

Margo shook her head. "She has everything she needs. And Tyler assures me there are no creatures on this island that will disturb her. When she is ready, I will bring her back. End of discussion. Until then, we must do what we can to prepare for what is coming. I suggest weapons practice, especially for you," she pointed at Courtney. "And spell work."

Tyler tried to repress a smile as he watched Margo take charge. She would have made a wonderful matriarch, or a general, he mused. He didn't mind so long as she didn't overstep her bounds. She may have the skills and authority of a leader, but she wasn't technically the one in charge.

Courtney sat back on her heels. "Me? Why me? My skills are fine. You saw them back at Walter's house. Tyler, you tell her." She gave the dragon a half-pleading look.

Margo shook her head. "What I've seen of your skills has led me to believe them lacking. That has to change if you want to stand a chance against the Mage Circle. We should work on your speed of execution as well."

Courtney groaned. "Sounds like boot camp to me."

Walter sympathized with the girl. Margo reminded him of one of his old drill sergeants, firm and unrelenting. "I've been thinking, since I don't have any of that dragon mojo ability, I'd sneak back to the mainland tonight. You know, to get a few special supplies. I could be back before dawn. What do you think?"

Margo glanced at the former soldier, deciding what to say when Tyler smoothly interceded. "It would be better if I go with you," he pointed out. "Navigating the Lake is hard enough for non-dragon folk during the day. That's part of the ward on the waters. But at night, unless you have a mage or a dragon with you, it's ten times more dangerous."

Strictly speaking, that wasn't entirely true. But he didn't think they needed to know that. Of course, once the Mountain was reopened, and the dragons awakened, it might as well be. With the return of the dragons, the Isle would be more carefully guarded from outsiders. As things stood, it was only a half-truth.

"Not to mention," Tyler continued, "If I go, we can bring back twice as much. And maybe find a more secure boat for our troubles. Who knows? I might even be tempted to do a bit of reconnoitering."

Margo looked like she wanted to protest but didn't. Instead, she simply nodded. It would be easier to let Tyler worry about the non-mage. That way she could focus on the two girls. "That's fine by me. Just don't get caught."

Tyler smiled; sure she'd tacked the last bit on to feel as though she had some control over the decision. "Wouldn't dream of it," he replied. "Since that's been settled, I suggest Walter and I catch a few hours of sleep." With that, he moved to the smaller of the two tents and crawled inside. Walter was not far behind him.

Margo pursed her lips, staring at the tent flap. Turning, she focused on Courtney. "If you're not too tired, I suggest we start working on your sword and spear techniques."

TWELVE

ANWEN THUMPED THE CIRCULATION BACK into her legs. Sitting in the quiet glen didn't seem to do much. She was no closer to understanding what her mother meant than she had been hours before. She wasn't even sure how to go about figuring things out. Listening for all she was worth was not working. It was possible she was trying too hard, she reasoned.

"Maybe you should just try standing on your head," Daphne snickered in her mind. "At least you'd be doing something productive. Of course, I really don't mind if you don't succeed. It's no skin off my back I mean, you are just going to lose anyway."

Anwen rolled her eyes. "I thought I told you to be quiet," she retorted. "How can I hear anything if you're always buzzing around in my head?" Her stomach rumbled, reminding her she hadn't eaten anything in quite some time. With a sigh, she opened her canteen and took a sip. The way things were looking, she wouldn't get the chance to have a decent meal any time soon either.

"You'd do better to focus on your own needs," Daphne pointed out. "I'm sure you could find an edible plant or two. That way your infernal stomach would finally shut up. It's annoying."

Anwen clenched her fists. "No. Mom told me to stay here. I'm not going to disobey her. I already told you that."

Daphne just laughed. "And what will you do when you are so faint with hunger you can't even move? Or when there's no water left in your precious canteen? You know it will happen sooner than later. You're already more than halfway there. Will you continue to be stubborn and starve yourself to complete this impossible task? If you're that determined, I can just show you what you need to know."

Anwen resettled herself, canteen between her legs. She'd tried to be careful about how much she drank, but knew Daphne was right. She would run out of water before too long. Combine that with her not having eaten anything in who knew how many days, things did not look good. "No thanks," she told the ghost in her mind.

Daphne shrugged shadowy shoulders. "We'll see. Just wait until the hunger and thirst really register in your pathetic little brain. Then you'll change your mind."

Josef stumbled over rubble in the small alley leading back to the main courtyard of the Ruined City. "Stupid mages," he cursed. "You'd think they'd be more interested in finding one of their own. Instead, they waste their time trying to break into some forsaken fortress!" He kicked at a lose stone for good measure.

The ruined amphitheater left much to be desired. There were just too many broken stones and pillars to do an effective search without any help. He did is best though, despite his limitations. In the end, he had little to show for his efforts.

Finding nothing there, he'd gone back to the buildings in the secondary courtyard. He took his time looking into every last one of them. He even went so far as to look in the little out of the way corner where he and Daphne had made out only a few weeks before. Nothing. But she couldn't have just vanished into thin air, he reasoned. Unless those people the mages wanted had killed her. If that was the case, he'd have his revenge.

Finding nothing but more mages in the central courtyard, he abandoned his search of the City. He decided to head back down the trail instead. Maybe there would be some clues there.

Courtney wiped sweat from her face as she leaned against a convenient tree. Margo's training was hard, a lot harder than she'd anticipated. She found herself wondering just how the woman had so much stamina. She looked like a weakling some punk could take out in a heartbeat. And yet, she seemed able to bulldoze down any obstacle in her way.

"Not bad," Margo commented. "You're strokes are becoming more sure, but you keep dropping your guard. That's a luxury you can't afford in battle. The others will take advantage of that and cut you into bits."

The older woman stood at ease, an elongated branch in her hands. It wasn't as deadly as a bone knife, but was a useful training tool. She took a moment to examine the smooth bark. She even checked it for any notches the girl might have inflicted in their mock battle. Courtney had managed to get in a few good hits with her own wooden weapon. She'd received much more in return, and Margo felt sure the girl was feeling it.

"We'll take a five minute break, and then get back to work," Margo announced.

Courtney was too tired to argue. She'd never had such a workout in her life, unless she counted her fight with Daphne's manticore. That, of course, had been more of a life or death situation, with her adrenaline pumping. Now, the work felt more grueling and twice as exhausting. She reached for her canteen and took a quick swig. It was good to stay hydrated but she didn't want to overdo it.

Margo pulled out her own canteen. "I suppose now is as good a time as any to give you may thanks," she commented.

Courtney looked up in surprise. "For what?" She cradled her water container between her knees as she slid down to the ground in relief.

Taking a sip from her water, Margo looked around the clearing they were using as a practice ring. "For protecting my daughter. I didn't thank you before."

Courtney brushed that aside. "I should be thanking you for how she was brought up. She saved me from my own vanity. If it weren't for her, I'd still be trying to catch every boy I met, and in the most pitiful manner. She showed me how shallow I was. And, because of that, I decided I wanted to become something more. To do something meaningful with my life."

Margo smiled. "One of her many gifts," she commented. "Perhaps that's part of why Kern thinks her special. She's not a fighter. Despite, that, she has the ability to inspire and put into effect change in a non-threatening way. A natural leader, if you like."

Courtney nodded, though she wasn't sure about the leader part. Tyler had done more leading than either combined. But then again, Tyler was a dragon. And apparently an important one at that. Leading was as natural to him as breathing.

"But back to work," Margo interrupted her thoughts. "We still have a few hours left before nightfall and I want to engrain those lessons into your muscles. You can't afford to forget them in battle."

With a groan, Courtney moved back into the meadow, wondering what the master mage had in mind for the rest of the afternoon.

Tyler emerged from his tent just after dark, followed closely by Walter. Firelight flickered off the tent wall from the fire pit. "Looks like they've turned in early," he commented, noting the empty area. He could hear the sounds of two people breathing from the girls' tent. And, if he really focused, he could faintly hear Anwen's breathing as well. Even though she was some ways away.

Walter nodded. Though they'd already agreed to go after more supplies, he felt like sneaking around. Maybe it was the need for practice in stealth. He wasn't sure. Or maybe it was because he felt like he was in a place he didn't really belong. Either way, he moved with discretion as he followed Tyler down to the lake's shore.

Tyler pulled the thin frame of the boat towards the water. Deciding the large boat would be too much for just the two of them to handle, Tyler coaxed the wood to a more compact size. "We're good to go," he announced as he slid the small canoe-like craft into the water.

Walter grabbed two of the oars and stepped into the boat. He then distributed his weight to make sure it didn't capsize. "We're going to need a bigger boat for the return trip," he observed. "One that's a lot sturdier than this one. One canister of ammunition could sink it faster than a torpedoed pleasure boat."

Tyler nodded as he situated himself behind Walter. "We can worry about that once we get back to the mainland." Taking up a paddle, he pushed the boat away from the bank, sending them smoothly across the water.

THIRTEEN

ANWEN HADN'T MEANT TO FALL asleep. But having stayed awake for longer than she was used to, she couldn't resist the pull of tired eyelids. Slumped over, with one arm twisted underneath her, she slept the sleep of the exhausted.

She found herself inside an immense chamber of stone. The vast cavern was carved in an ornate fashion, with pillars helping to support the high ceiling. The whole expanse appeared to be some kind of gallery. Marble and quartz shone in the chamber. A giant pulsating crystal sat in the middle of the room, casting the half-light.

The crystal was multi-faceted and radiated several different colors. It felt as though the stone was alive, with each color branching out in a different direction. The formation reminded her of the sugar rock candy she'd once had as a child. Only instead of being in one upward direction, it reached out all around.

And deep within the center of that glowing mass, an even brighter point signified the heart. It was a rich ruby-red in color, and seemed liquid behind the many facets of the outer crystals around it. The rest of the rock seemed dim and transparent in comparison.

Anwen walked around the giant collection of crystal spikes. She couldn't help but take in the absolute size of the living rock. One section in particular caught her eye. It was deep blue, graduating to varying shades of the same hue. Beneath her shirt, the key glowed, pulsing in time with the Heart of the stone.

"That which the Mountain giveth," she heard in her mind. It sounded like a chorus of ancient voices. *"Let us give in return."*

Dragons of all kinds filled the empty spaces of the gallery. Their silent forms surrounded the glowing mass. They seemed to hum deep from within their bellies as three dragons moved closer to the crystal. One was white. The other two were silver, one with blue undertones, and the other with green. She instantly recognized the three dragons. The green and silver dragon had flown her to the peak of the Mountain where she'd met the white one, the Nurrim. The silver with blue dragon had saved her life when she'd fallen off the Mountain. She somehow knew that one was Tyler.

Nearby, a bronze dragon heated metal in a large stone basin. Two men beat at the cooling metal with hammer and mallets. They didn't so much as flinch at the intense heat of the dragon flames next to them. Their actions led Anwen to believe they were dragons in human guise.

As she watched the events unfold, Tyler transformed into the form she knew so well. Light complexion. Light hair. Blue eyes that were bluer than the waters of Lake Wyvern. He stepped past her as if she didn't exist. And then he reached up to grasp a segment of crystal that was deep blue throughout. With extreme care, he broke the fragment free from the main cluster. Almost reverently, he carried it over to the two blacksmiths.

A shower of sparks filled the air as they took the shard and hammered away. The other dragon breathed out white flame, engulfing them so they were lost from view. But the flames finally stopped and Anwen could see again. She saw

Tyler wielding a familiar crystal sword. As he carried it towards Kern, the blade shrank until all that remained was the key. It was an exact replica of the one around her neck.

Anwen turned and the image faded. It was replaced with one of a smaller chamber where twelve were seated, two mortals and ten dragons. They were sitting around a circular table similar to the shrine in the Sacred Grove. Of the two mortals, one was a woman. She recognized Matthias, even though he was much younger than in her previous dreams. She did not recognize the woman.

Once more, Kern and Tyler, with the other silver dragon, presided over the meeting. Kern sat with one silver dragon on either side of his massive body. Among the other dragons sat an aged yellow, a light brown, a bronze, and a blue. The others were harder to discern in the low light.

Kern thumped his tail for order as the brown, bronze and blue dragons squabbled. "Let the Kaida speak." The Nurrim's voice filled the chamber, silencing the cries of the other dragons.

The woman Anwen had noticed stood from her cushioned seat. She appeared to be younger than Margo. Anwen guessed her to be in her twenties or thirties but wasn't sure. All she knew was that this woman they'd named Kaida was older than her.

The Kaida looked around the room with grave eyes. "My Kinsmen, I bring unsettling news. It would seem there are among those of the mage line who wish to challenge dragon kind. They are still small and few in number, but growing."

A murmur rolled through the chamber as those assembled contemplated the news. Kern looked troubled, as did Tyler. They exchanged words that Anwen couldn't hear.

Aria Kaida waited for the dragons to settle once more. She knew what she had to say next would be even more upsetting.

"It has also come to my attention that some have even attempted to summon Revenants. I have learned this move is an attempt to form an alliance with them. They mean to overthrow those dragons who refuse to become subservient to their whims."

The chamber filled with cries of outrage. Deep growls and roars rumbled through the air to such a point that Anwen had to cover her ears. She went to her knees and closed her eyes, willing the madness to stop. And, after a few more moments, it did.

When Anwen opened her eyes once more, she found herself back in the forest on the Sacred Island. Her arm had fallen asleep from being twisted underneath her and she moved it with some difficulty. Painful tingling coursed up the starved appendage once the blood flow was restored, though the sensation wasn't unpleasant.

Anwen bit back a scream as the pain changed to a piercing one that threatened to overwhelm her. It almost felt like Daphne had thrust a spear into her arm all over again. Sweat trickled down her forehead as the other areas the spear had touched began to burn. She fell against the ground, her entire body shaking. But she refused to scream.

In her mind, Daphne laughed. The wounds she'd inflicted on the girl while yet alive were apparently still present. "You'll never be free of those scars," she cried out with glee. "My blade was blessed by the blood of a Revenant. You will suffer from them for the rest of your miserable little life!"

Almost vaguely, Anwen recalled sitting on the Mountain, just past the Endless Chasm. Tyler had reached out to examine the throwing knife Courtney had retrieved from the path. Upon touching it, Tyler recoiled as if burned.

"This is a Mage Blade," he'd said. *"It has been infused with the blood of a Revenant."*

"I admit," Daphne continued, "I was wondering when the pain would return. I was tempted to provoke it myself. Who knew your dreams would do the job for me?"

If it hadn't been for the fire coursing through her veins, Anwen would have made some kind of retort. But as things were, she didn't have the strength. It took all she had to not cry out, knowing it would bring the others running. She knew Tyler would be able to hear, even if no one else could. She wasn't sure why, but knew she didn't want that to happen. Maybe it was kin to admitting defeat, that she couldn't handle it. She wasn't about to prove she was weak.

Daphne conjured a spectral stool and sat down. "Oh, go ahead and call them. There's nothing they can do to stop it. After all, the poison's already a part of you. It's just unfortunate the process was stopped before it could obliterate you." Her phantom eyes blazed with malice.

"I remember hearing something about that," Anwen managed to say through her clenched teeth. The others seemed to have whispered it around her. Something about a Ritual of Obliteration. She tried to remember what she'd half heard while dreaming but couldn't.

Daphne smirked. "Ah yes," she said. "So you did hear a bit about that. Then you know the absolute basics. But Tyler did get a few things wrong. Easy to do when no one survives the whole thing. It doesn't help that only those of the Inner Circle know how to perform it, and they're not telling anyone."

Anwen froze in shock, the pain momentarily suspended with her surprise. "What? You don't mean--"

The phantom mage only smiled, teeth gleaming in the light like a predator stalking its prey.

FOURTEEN

THE TRIP BACK TO THE mainland was uneventful. With just the two of them in the boat, Tyler and Walter made good time. And, after retracing their steps, they found the truck. It was still hidden at the abandoned ranger station. Despite a few technical difficulties, Tyler got the vehicle back on the road.

"So where is this stash of yours?" Tyler asked as he navigated back up to the main highway. He didn't so much as deviate from the overgrown path. Instead, he followed in the exact tracks they'd made only a day before.

Walter held the handle above the door as if his life depended on it. Tyler was driving a lot faster than he'd ever dare on such terrain. He was going even faster than he had the night before. "Just outside Blaucii," he directed. "There's a little suburb to the south."

Tyler nodded. "I think I know the place."

Two hours passed in silence as they traveled back down to the low lands. Their only deviation was to get more gas. With the late hour, there wasn't much traffic, not even when they breached the city limits. Thankful for the small respite, Tyler followed his companion's directions. This part of the city had changed a bit since he'd last come down. Either that or he was just tired.

"Over there," Walter called out as he pointed to a sagging sign. The board advertised a rather rundown looking storage facility. It boasted low rent and great security. Weeds filled the spaces between concrete driveway and chain link fencing. It gave it an almost abandoned feel. But there was a coded gate in fairly new condition at the entrance.

Once inside the complex, Walter directed Tyler down several rows of units. Each aisle looked more derelict than the one before. "You sure this is the right place?" the dragon asked. Despite the new gate, the rest of the area looked rundown. It looked like a jungle trying to reclaim its surroundings.

The smile the veteran gave him was a little disconcerting. But it more than conveyed the affirmative answer he gave in response to the question. "Despite its outward condition, this place is actually pretty secure. Besides, there's a rumor the place is haunted. Most people stay away. And those dumb enough to try and trespass pay the consequences. It's part of the charm."

With a few more directions, Tyler pulled the truck to a stop outside a long line of units. Each stall had an upward sliding metal door with a slide bolt and lock. But, upon further inspection, it became obvious that this was, for the most part, just for show. Off to one side of each unit was a small box that blended in with the stucco siding. Each box contained a key-coded entry pad.

Making a bit of a show of it, Walter opened the box and entered his code. A few clicks announced the system's deactivation. Sure the process was complete; he pulled out a normal key and undid the lock before sliding the bolt.

Tyler let out a low whistle as Walter opened the sliding door. "That's quite the collection," he said in admiration. "Saving up for a special occasion?"

Walter walked into the storage space. Once inside, he began moving around various boxes of explosives and ammunition. "Nah," he replied. "You know me. Just like to be prepared. That, and if a zombie apocalypse happens, I want to be ready. I've got another unit a door or two down packed with survival rations."

Shaking his head, Tyler went to help his friend. "You wouldn't happen to have a boat in here, would you?" Shelves lined the walls. Some created a sort of labyrinth in the space that was large enough to house a mid-sized motor boat, or maybe a small dragon.

Walter laughed as he moved a canister of grenades to the front. "Nah. That's in my other locker." His grin widened with Tyler's expression. "Kidding! Kidding! I do have an inflatable raft though."

Tyler shook his head. "We'd better get this stuff in the truck. Anything else you want to bring back? Keep in mind we can't take everything with us. No kitchen sinks this go around."

Looking around, Walter spotted a box of small grey cans. Grabbing it, he navigated back to the front of the locker. After pulling out a folded mass of rubber, he locked the storage space. "That should do it," he confirmed as he carried his load to the truck. "All those boxes and cans right there."

Tyler sighed at the amount of equipment but helped move it into the back of the truck. He just hoped Walter's raft was up to the challenge of shuttling it all across the water in one trip. Picking up the last box, he pushed it over the hanging tailgate. A sudden wave of dizziness washed over him and he swayed ever so slightly.

Walter pushed the box further in and closed the tailgate. He wiped sweat from his brow. "Good thing that raft's military grade, ain't it? Now we just have to figure a way to drag all this stuff to the shore."

Tyler closed his eyes as he leaned against the auto's metal body. Something was definitely not right. He never felt this way. Not unless he was at his strength's end. And he knew that wasn't possible. He'd had more than ample time to recover while back at Walter's house.

"Hey," Walter said, clapping him on the back. "You not falling asleep on me, are you? Ready to go?" He paused, noting his friend's unusual behavior. "You okay? Want me to drive?"

Tyler shook his head again. "It's nothing. Chances are good it's just a side effect from wearing myself out." He shrugged away the man's hand and took his place behind the steering wheel.

Walter followed him around the vehicle, and then continued to the passenger side. It was possible Tyler was only suffering a bit of relapse, or a "side effect", as he put it. He'd never seen the dragon so worn down before. But he doubted that was the problem. With that in mind, he decided to keep a closer eye on his friend.

Starting the engine, Tyler put the vehicle into gear and headed down the road. He mentally pushed past the dizziness to focus on driving. But, keeping his current condition in mind, he decided to take a different, much closer route to the Lake. Without Anwen with them, it was less likely the Mage Circle would notice two men in a boat.

Daphne all but laughed at the look on Anwen's face. It was such a nice expression, a mix of physical anguish and absolute shock. It made her announcement more than worth it. "You didn't know? Oh, that's right. You're just a wannabe mage." She flicked at imaginary nail polish on her nails. "And what does a wannabe know? Nothing. So how could you know about my position in the Mage Circle? Not even Courtney knows," she scoffed.

Anwen could only stare with unseeing eyes. Her face felt frozen with the realization of what Daphne had just told her. She couldn't be that powerful. It couldn't be true. Her soul cried out from the frozen flesh. She silently screamed as the scars flared like burning brands.

What Daphne was suggesting wasn't possible. She was just teenager, albeit a rather ambitious and malicious one. But there was no way she could be that high up in the Circle. Then again, what did Anwen know about it? She barely had any knowledge of dragon mages, let alone the different factions. Everything she knew about them she'd learned from Courtney and Tyler.

Daphne flounced off her imaginary stool. "It's true, though. I was part of the Inner Circle. The higher ups, if you will, right up there with Madame Millard. We were probably on equal footing, honestly, until you killed me. But it doesn't really matter. It is what it is."

An image of the overweight innkeeper flashed in Anwen's mind. There had always been something creepy about that woman. Now she knew why.

Tyler parked the truck at different ranger station. This one looked even more run down than the other. But, more importantly, it was further ahead than the previous one, and closer to the water's edge. It meant less of a walk to the shore, something he felt would be better for the both of them.

Walter began unloading the boxes from the truck's bed, carrying them the fifty or so yards to the lake. After a few boxes, they worked out a system. One man brought a container half the distance while the other took it the rest of the way. Tyler stayed at the top while Walter took the bottom half of the trail.

Between loads, Tyler leaned against the truck. With his eyes closed, he tried to regain some semblance of normalcy. Despite his best attempts to shunt it aside, the dizziness had not left him. And now it was getting worse. It became so bad that he stumbled with the last load, his vision blurring enough to make him see double.

Walter came back in time to relieve him of the bundle of rubber he'd been carrying. Seeing the strain on his face, he made Tyler sit down with his head between his knees.

"You're no good if you can't see straight," he warned as he looked his friend in the eyes.

With a sigh, Tyler nodded. He watched the veteran carry the rubber raft down to the water's edge from his log perch. The process was quickly carried out and Tyler moved to go help the man inflate the raft. Halfway there, pain shot through his arms and legs as though they'd been pierced with a searing flame. He let out a strangled cry as he crumpled to the ground, his breath coming in short spurts. As he lay there, the searing sensation spread throughout his extremities. The experience made him unable to move. It was worse than anything he'd ever felt. Before any further sounds of anguish could escape his lips, he clamped his mouth shut. He knew any further sounds he made would be anything but quiet.

Hearing the initial outcry, Walter turned to check on his friend. He half expected to see the dragon sitting where he'd left him, maybe throwing up. But he was surprised to see him on the ground. Quickly making sure the raft was secure, he ran to his Tyler's side.

Tyler had closed his eyes. The sight of the tree branches waving overhead made him nauseous. He continued to clench his teeth to keep from screaming. The sound would carry to at least the far side of the Lake if he didn't. Sweat beaded up on his skin with the effort to remain silent.

"Not good," Walter groaned as he knelt by the dragon's side. Tyler's face was pale, more so than he'd ever seen him. And yet, when Walter touched his skin, it burned as though from a high fever. "You don't look so good," he said, trying to lighten the situation.

The dragon arched his back, pushing up from the ground. His teeth ground together as scales formed up and down his arms and legs. Steam began to rise from his neck and chest. A low growl filled the air as he fought against the acid coursing through his senses.

Not sure what was going on, or what would help, Walter did the first thing that came to mind. He ran back to the

Lake and emptied one of the ammunition cans, then filled it with water. Hurrying back as fast as he could, he dumped the liquid over Tyler's head.

Tyler gasped again as the water hit his body, his jaws separating top from bottom. Some of the liquid spilled into his mouth as he opened it. His eyes flew open. "Callum!" he called out, not sure if his brother would hear him, or if his spirit would even come.

For some reason, he felt it more likely his brother would answer his call than that Kern would. And since the Nurrim was likely meditating, he thought it the more likely Callum could help him. The sensation he felt reminded him of touching the knife Daphne had thrown on the Mountain. Only this was much stronger in nature.

"Greetings, my brother. I believe your thoughts may be correct," Callum said as he materialized in front of the dragon lord. "It is good the poison does not flow in your veins." His human form was still translucent, tinged slightly with moonlight. It made him look more like a ghost than something tangible. "You were wise to call me."

Tyler tried to sit up but couldn't as another wave of acid seemed to rain across his body. "What's happening to me?" he asked through teeth trying to elongate in his mouth.

Callum's phantom form wavered momentarily as he stood in thought. "It is as you thought. The pain you are feeling is that of poisoning from Revenant blood," he finally confirmed. "And yet none has entered your body. Most curious. I have never seen anything like this before. I wish I could be more helpful but this is beyond my knowledge."

Walter watched helplessly. He wasn't sure what was going on, or who Tyler was talking to. But he hoped it wasn't a sign that things were worse than he'd observed. Tyler wasn't the hallucinating type. He contemplated going back to the shore for more water, just in case.

Tyler's eyes went wide as an image flashed through his mind. He was back in the Mountain, searching desperately for Anwen. He was clawing chunks of fallen rubble away from her fragile form. He was holding her lifeless body in his arms. Then he was bending over her. His hand pressed against her chest as he forced a part of his soul into her body, calling her soul back from death. "Anwen," he almost choked.

Callum's eyes widened upon hearing him speak her name. He could hear the thoughts running through his brother's mind. "You did, didn't you," he accused with a hiss. "You gave her a part of your soul. You know that practice is strictly forbidden!" He seemed to gather himself together, like someone trying to become as small as possible. "Giving your soul to a *mortal*." He said the last word as though it were an epithet. "How could you?"

Tyler closed his eyes, the image of Anwen's pale, dead face floating behind his eyelids. It was more painful than the Revenant poison's sensation. "She was dying!" he gasped.

"Better you had let her die!" Callum responded, pulling further way. "This is a curse you have brought upon yourself, brother. What she feels, you will now feel. What you feel, she may even feel. And if one of you dies, the other dies. Did you never wonder why such an act was forbidden?"

The pupils in Tyler's eyes narrowed to pinpricks as Callum's words sank in. *What she feels, you will now feel. If one of you dies, the other dies.* The words echoed over and over again as his body became even more rigid. *Did you never wonder?*

Seeing the realization sink in, Callum closed his eyes in pity. It was foolishness to fall in love with a mortal. It had been similar foolishness that had presented the rather unfortunate consequences in the first place. And that foolishness had ended in tragedy when that mortal had died. It was why one dragon sharing his or her soul with a mortal was considered one of the highest of taboos.

"She will not live forever as we may," Callum continued, his voice only a little more gentle as he hung his head. "When her life is over, so is yours. You have condemned yourself, brother. You have signed your death warrant. And there is nothing I or any other can do about it." With that, he dematerialized, returning to the Mountain and his sleep-frozen body. His departure left an uneasy mist behind.

"Tyler?" Walter wasn't sure if he should come any closer or go for more water like he'd contemplated getting earlier. Was his friend having some kind of spiritual experience? Or was it the obvious pain talking? "Tyler?" he asked again. He had not seen any other entity near his friend and couldn't help but wonder.

The dragon clenched his teeth once more, his lips pressed firmly together. Closing his eyes in anguish, he gave voice to the chaos inside his heart. His scream didn't go far. "Anwen," he choked, hitting the ground with one fist. "Why did Kern never tell me?"

Images flashed behind his closed eyelids. Kern, the great Nurrim, leader of the dragons. At one time he had a mate. She had been the mother of all other dragons. Mother to all dragons of silver scales. The faint stirrings of memory shifted inside his mind. He had never actually met his mother. She had given birth to many. And her offspring had given life to many more. Tyler had been one of the last, before she had unexplainably died. At least that's what he'd thought. Up until now.

Quiet whispers now reminded him of how his mother had fallen in love with a mortal. Rumors spread of their love and how the Nurrim had pronounced on them his blessing. He had given her freedom from their union. And then their Mortal Enemy had attacked the outlying settlement her love had tried to create. The man had died. His draconic wife died in tandem, falling from the sky as she raced to rescue him from harm. Perhaps she had been foolhardy, as Tyler had been, and given part of her soul to that mortal man.

Kern had been upset for many years after her death, never taking another mate. Though he'd sanctioned the union with the mortal, she had been his favorite. Not even after his older children offered their own offspring did he take a mate. It wasn't until Anna Magus had come along that he'd loved another female. It was no wonder the pairing had been considered taboo. She was mortal and all feared he might give her a portion of his soul, just as his previous love had to another mortal.

Tyler opened his eyes, registering the night sky. Looking around, he realized Walter was there, staring at him. He'd likely tried to get his attention for some time. "Anwen," he breathed, still feeling the acidic pain piercing through him. "We must return to the Island and find her. I fear she is trouble."

Walter took a step back. The dragon sounded almost desperate. But whether it was from pain or for some other reason, he wasn't sure. He glanced up to the sky and noted the position of the moon. Morning was slowly creeping upon them. At least his friend hadn't made a full transformation, staying mortal size, though his skin was covered in scales. "Can you stand?" he finally asked.

Gathering his willpower, Tyler tried. Walter had to help him. Even with his support, he felt weak and useless. His friend had to half carry him to the raft. Once inside the boat, he flopped next to the canisters and boxes. "Just give me a moment," he said in response to Walter's questioning gaze.

Five minutes later, he had gathered what felt like his remaining strength, insisting he help paddle the raft across the water. It took just about all he had to not let out another cry of pain. If he felt this much, he reasoned, how much more must Anwen be feeling? And if these sensations were coming from her, what was causing them? At least he'd managed to halt his transformation. They didn't need the Mage Circle storming the Lake as well.

FIFTEEN

ANWEN FELT MORE THAN EXHAUSTED. The desire to scream increased with every minute, but she tried to hold on. She could not rely on the others for everything. Some things had to be done on her own. She had to be strong. She kept repeating that to herself, over and over again.

Daphne flounced to a reclining position. She took great joy in observing the mortal shell of the woman she haunted. Her determination was truly commendable. She wondered just how much more the girl could take. The pain would eventually subside. But there was no telling when it would flair up again. She relished in the idea that it would debilitate her as she tried to wake the sleeping dragons. In fact, she was counting on it.

This was one more point towards her victory. The dark mage may not have been able to complete the Ritual, but this was almost as good. And if she could cause the soul scars to flair, it would cause that much more chaos when the time came to reopen the gates.

Overhead, the sky began to lighten as nighttime came to

an end. With the increasing light, the pain finally began to subside. Anwen was more than a little relieved. She felt completely drained. Her body refused to move from her prone position on the forest floor. Her breath came in short gasps as she tried to reach for the canteen that lay several inches from her hand. Despite her best efforts, her fingers would not move at command.

Daphne contemplated her nails as the light filtered down. "Daylight," she mused. "Guess that means someone will come looking for you soon." With that, she returned to the shadows of Anwen's mind, content to wait on developments.

Anwen gave up on her efforts to reach the canteen. Instead, tears glistened in her eyes. She couldn't help but whimper at the phantom pain spikes that still lingered.

Tyler felt the pain leave as they reached the Island's shore. And with that, his scales began to disappear. All the same, he felt exhausted in a way he'd never felt before. It was worse than feeling drained of energy. It almost felt as though a part of him had been ripped apart and scattered to the winds. Or at least thrown to the ground like littered trash.

Walter jumped from the raft to pull it up onto the beach. Once the rubber had beached, the dragon all but rolled over the inflated walls of the craft. He then lay in the sand, feeling the sun against his skin. It was almost a relief to feel the fine grains press up against his back, reminding him he was alive.

Seeing them from further up the slope, Courtney dropped the wood she'd set out to gather. "Hey," she waved as she romped towards them. She came to a halt upon seeing Tyler lying like death warmed over in the sand. "Looks like you had quite the night," she commented, wondering what had happened. She took in the scene, including the black rubber raft half filled with military gear.

"One might say that," Walter responded as he made sure the boat wouldn't drift back into the lake. He tied a long line to a protruding rock., prepared for that purpose.

Courtney blinked in confusion as she watched, not sure how to take his comment. Deciding to wait for an explanation, she continued to close the distance between them. "Hope you don't mind me coming to help," she said. "I figured you could use it. That and I wouldn't mind a break from Margo's insane training." She quickly glanced behind her to make sure Anwen's mother wasn't within earshot.

Tyler rolled over and propped himself up with an elbow. "The help is appreciated," he smiled. "But if you don't mind, I think I'm going to quickly cool off in the water." With that, he stood a bit shakily and headed into the lake.

Walter watched his friend, giving him a once over to make sure the previous symptoms had not returned. He didn't fear the dragon drowning. Tyler was an excellent swimmer and had the lung capacity of an elephant. Perhaps he just needed to cool down. "Right," he said, turning towards Courtney. "If you'd be kind enough to help me haul some of this up past the tree line, I'd appreciate it."

Not sure what had just happened, Courtney reached to pick up one of the ammunition cans offered her. She kept an eye on Tyler as he plunged under the water. "What's going on?" she asked, not sure she wanted to know.

Glancing towards the lake, Walter shrugged. Steam hissed up from where Tyler had entered the water. "Long night. I guess he just wanted to wake up a bit. I'm sure he won't be long." He lifted up the canister and handed it to her, amused as she strained under the weight.

"What in the world do you have in these things?" Courtney complained as she tried to handle the metal container. Her arms strained against the weight.

"Explosives ain't light," Walter commented with a chuckle. He picked up two of his own canisters to carry. "Shall we?"

Tyler dived deep under the lake's surface. The drop off he'd located was several dozen yards deep and he relished in it. With open eyes, everything was tinged a blue color. And the cool water was more than helpful in restoring his energy. He'd always loved the water, even though he had not been born a water dragon. There was something pure about the liquid that felt a little like home.

It was nice to not have to worry about the others for a few minutes. At least for the most part. Just as he started to relax, the thought of Anwen shot him back to the surface. Even though the pain had stopped, he still did not know what had caused it. Had it really come from Anwen as his brother had hinted? And if so, why? He had to find out.

Using strong strokes, he swam back towards the Island. He'd moved further off than he'd originally intended. The beach he and Walter had landed on sat a good ways away, not that it bothered him. He knew the Island like the back of his hand. Soon, he came upon a small section where the rocks dropped sheer from the landmass. He sprang upwards and grasped the rough top, pulling himself onto the shelf. Water sluiced off his body as he stood and oriented himself.

From across the way, he could see the Mountain rising majestically. If the mages were still there, they made no sign. Satisfied, Tyler turned towards the island's center. Thankfully his scales had returned to flesh on his body before Courtney had met them on the beach. He still felt a lingering pain from the forced partial transformation.

But if he focused, he could distinguish a second palpitation in his chest that he thought came from Anwen. If the double pulse was indeed a reflection of her heart beating, he knew the recent trauma was over. The rhythm was too calm to mean anything else.

Feeling reassured, Tyler turned his senses towards camp. Nothing seemed out of place there. He let out a sigh of relief. And yet, there was a niggling thought that wondered what had distressed Anwen. He turned towards her grove and headed out.

The undergrowth was dense, as untouched now as it had been a hundred years ago. The foliage had taken advantage of the passing time. It had woven an even more complex path than what had existed before. Trees protruded in areas once bare. It made Tyler take a more circuitous route than he'd planned on using.

The sound of giggling stopped him halfway to his destination. Pausing, Tyler looked around but couldn't sense anything unusual. He took another step and the giggling came again. Whatever gave voice to the sound was young. He could tell that much. And was likely female as well.

It was next to impossible for another mortal to be on the Island. As such, he reasoned the giggling child must be draconic in nature. Or at the least, was somehow related to them. Speaking in the dragon tongue, Tyler focused on his surroundings. "Reveal yourself." The command was met with more child-like laughter. "Come out and I will do you no harm."

Some leaves rustled in a low bush and Tyler focused in on the movement. Walking as quietly as only one dragon-born can, he moved towards the foliage. "I know you're out there," he continued, speaking as one to a spooked animal. "Show yourself."

Having reached the shaking bush, Tyler parted the branches. What he saw caused his mouth to fall open. A young girl, no more than three or four years of age, stood near the central stump of the plant. She smiled with brilliant blue eyes close in coloring to his own. Her dark red hair contrasted sharply with her white dress. The color of her clothes made her skin seem rosier than it might have otherwise seemed.

"Hello," Tyler ventured, bending down to her eye level. "Who are you? Are you lost?"

The girl shook her head and put a finger to her lips. The look on her face made her look a bit puckish as she smiled. "Shh. Mommy's sleeping."

Tyler quickly looked around but still could not sense or see the presence of any outside his small party. "Where is your mommy?" he asked. "I'm sure you've made her worry. Why don't we go find her?"

The child's countenance seemed to light up like a firework. "She's over there," she pointed with her left hand, indicating some place to Tyler's right. It was further in from the shore.

Looking in the direction she pointed, Tyler tried to see past the trees but couldn't. "How did you get here?" he asked, returning his attention to her. But when he turned back, he realized she was gone. "Hey!"

The faint hint of giggling came from the direction she'd indicated. Tyler all but leapt towards the sound. He leapfrogged up the incline, following the infectious giggles. But no matter how fast he moved he couldn't seem to catch up with her.

Finally, Tyler had to pause, a bit winded from the chase. Looking around, he recognized the Bounding Circle that encompassed the Sacred Grove. "Where are you?" he asked the air, not even sure if he'd gone in the right direction.

Several yards inside the ring, a large stone protruded from the ground. The child moved out from behind this stone and stood next to it, arms down at her sides. "It is the Hour of the Mage," she said, now looking serious.

Tyler looked directly at her, realizing for the first time that he could almost see through her. It was as though she was like Callum or Kern, but he dismissed the idea. He did not recall any children among the dragons. Leastways, not any this young. "Who are you?" he asked again.

The child smiled. *"Then come those dragon born, Mages of the land. And one to rule them, from a foreign realm. Skills to learn or defy, while fire rains from the sky. She of dragon soul to mend, else all dragon kind shall end."*

Tyler stared at her. "Where did you learn this?"

Movement from the trees called his attention away from the girl before he could get an answer. From behind one of the larger trunks, a young woman appeared, almost as if she'd walked out of the living wood. Tyler couldn't move, let alone look away as he followed the woman's progress towards him.

"Well met, Daemyn Durand," the woman said as she stopped just inside the boundary circle. She was as translucent as the girl who ran over and gave her a peck on the cheek before running off into the trees. "It has been a long time."

"Kaida Magus," Tyler breathed in disbelief. "How is this possible? You have been dead for centuries."

Kaida inclined her head as a gesture of respect, her knees bending slightly as she bowed. "The flow of time has been disrupted. Both the past and the future are coming together. Unless things are set to rights, the Flow will continue to erode. '*She of dragon soul to mend, else all of dragon kind shall end*'."

Tyler watched the dragon mage with intense eyes as her red hair flared out like living flames. "I have heard this saying before today, but I do not remember from where."

Kaida's eyes burned like molten amber. "Strange that you cannot. You were there when it was given. But seeing through a mortal's eyes for so long has likely dulled you. It is a prophecy from long ago. And now its time is upon us. My father knew this day would come. Just as he knew that by becoming one with my mother, he might risk the future of his kind."

Tyler felt as though a heavy weight had fallen on his shoulders. "Knowing this, why did he not turn her away?" he mused. But he already knew the answer and could not blame the Nurrim for it.

The first dragon mage shook her head, her hair fanning out around her. "It was for the same reason you shared your soul with another. For love. True love is pure, without fault or blemish. It accepts all and magnifies the light within. But, as with all things, there must be an opposite."

The dragon bowed his head in understanding. "Fear. Love's true opposite is fear. Fear and envy."

Kaida smiled. "As a mortal, I came to understand both emotions. I saw them, as did my progenitors. Hate and distrust came from them. And it is fear and envy that has brought us to where we are now."

Tyler had to acknowledge her wisdom on the matter. "Yes. Fear and the desire to control that which is feared. And, over time, that fear became hate, envying what they could never have. Forgetting the gift they were given was more than most ever receive."

Kaida nodded. "Yes. As such, balance was lost. For there must be a balance between fear and love. Between the Darkness and the Light. And that, as you are well aware, is young Anwen's task. Kern knew her destiny from the moment she was conceived. And that is why he did everything in his power to conceal her, even from you. Until the time was right."

Thinking of Anwen, Tyler couldn't help but let his thoughts take their own course. He mused on the possibilities. "He must have used his gifts to hide her. It wasn't until I read her grandmother's journal that I really began to wonder who she was. Though her coming to the Mountain was certainly unusual enough to peak my curiosity."

A sudden stab of pain brought back the night's happenings to mind as he went down to one knee. But, unlike the night before, the pain did not last. "Anwen," he called out, breathless from the sensation. "She was in pain." He looked towards Kaida, his eyes liquid gold.

Kaida looked solemn as she nodded. "I heard what Callum told you about Soul Sharing. It would seem there are more serious repercussions for that act of love. If I were among the living, I would partake of the Sage's Fruit and look into the future for you. But I cannot."

An image of the square-stemmed plant entered Tyler's mind. He could almost see the velvet-like leaves, green on top but yellow on the underside. The local mages called it by the more common name, Diviner's Sage.

In the past, several mages had used its unique properties to glimpse into the unknown. The process was risky and had left many blind or insane. It took one with a strong gift to handle the force of the visions the plant induced. And most who thought they had that gift ended up not having it. That's part of what made it was so dangerous.

"What I don't understand is why that pain would return," Tyler confessed. "I felt her heart at rest. She was calm not that long ago. I purged the poison from her soul. It shouldn't have come back. Not unless…" he trailed off, looking into the distance with a sudden pensive attentiveness. "I need to go to her. She may be in danger."

Kaida reached out a hand. "She will be fine," she assured. "Anwen is not in any immediate danger. As I said, the lines of time are blurred. We are connected by blood. Just as wounds may scar the body, so might darkness scar the soul."

"Soul scars," Tyler breathed. "Is it possible?"

The dragon mage nodded. "The darkest of tools can scar even the purest of hearts. No matter what countermeasures are used to stop them."

SIXTEEN

JOSEF STOOD IN THE SMALL clearing just past the Endless Chasm. In frustration, he kicked at the low scrub sitting closer to the canyon wall. He'd been over the path what felt like hundreds of times. And still there was nothing, no sign that Daphne had been there. But he somehow knew she'd been there. With a growl, he aimed his boot at another clump of foliage. Only this time he hit something that rang with a dull clunk. Curious, he bent down to retrieve the item he'd hit, realizing it was a dagger.

With a sharp intake of breath, he pulled back. A drop of blood spilled from his finger where the sharp blade had pierced the skin. He sucked on the wounded appendage as he bent to retrieve the knife, hefting it in one hand. "This was Daphne's," he told the air. How many times had he seen her playing with this blade, or another like it? She'd made them under her uncle's tutelage. There was no mistaking it.

The dark metal seemed to burn in his hand, though not unpleasantly. He gripped the handle more tightly, and then pocketed it. Something had definitely happened to his fiancé in this pass. He was on the right track. If only he knew which way to go from there. Making a quick decision, he headed back down the path towards the village. The Ruined City held nothing else for him, but other places might.

Margo welcomed Walter back to camp with fried eggs and sausages. She tried to not look at the conspicuous pile of boxes and metal cases he and Courtney had brought up from the beach. Sometimes it was better not to know, she decided. "Where's Tyler?" she asked as she sipped a cup of coffee.

Walter glanced up from his plate of food and looked around. At least an hour had passed since the two had returned from the mainland. But, knowing Tyler, he was probably off mulling over events. "Don't worry," he assured. "He'll come back when he's hungry. Chances are good he's just dozed off somewhere."

Raising an eyebrow, Margo decided not to comment. Courtney had already reported that the dragon hadn't quite acted his usual self on the beach. She couldn't help but wonder why. With an inward sigh, she let the matter drop. It was better to not meddle in the affairs of dragons. Not that she feared he would eat her, but she would rather not risk the wrath of an almost deity. Even if he was relatively levelheaded.

Courtney watched the exchange between the two adults, not sure what was going on. After having helped carry several loads worth of weaponry and who knew what else, she was glad for the rest. But, now that she thought about it, Tyler had looked a bit odd. It was almost as though his skin had partially scaled over, like he couldn't decide which form to take, mortal or dragon.

Margo set down her cup and stood from her stump. "You're probably right," she said as she brushed off her pants. "In that case, make sure you leave something for him to eat when he returns." Turning to Courtney, she picked up the canteen by her side. "Time to get back to work."

"I was afraid you'd say that," Courtney said with a sigh.

By the time Tyler reached Anwen's little grove, she had fallen asleep. He stood several yards away, contemplating her prone form. She looked exhausted, and no wonder, he thought. Cautiously, he moved closer, bending down to touch her forehead. The contact didn't so much as disturb her slumber.

"What a pair we make," he mused as he sat down next to her, legs crossed underneath him. "I wish things were different. If only we could go back in time, before the Mage War, things would be different. But times are changing. I'm sure even normal mortals can feel it."

Lying down, he faced the sky, shading his eyes from the light filtering down through the trees with one hand. "I'm afraid of what the mages are planning," he admitted. "There are far more of them than there are of us. But I'm even more afraid of losing you. Either way, we don't have much time. Damned if we do. Damned if we don't. Wake the other dragons or die trying. Don't wake them and all dragon kind ends, maybe even the mages. Not that they'd listen to that." He sighed heavily.

Weariness caught up with the dragon and he closed his eyes. "I'm tired, Anwen," he confessed. "I'm tired of hiding. Tired of being alone. So tired." Without thinking, he moved his hand towards hers. As sleep overtook him, his fingers laced with hers. It created a similitude of the bond their souls now shared.

Madame Millard paced in front of her tent. Only the rising majesty of the Mountain by Tarragon overshadowed her. Things were going much more slowly than she'd anticipated. Another group of Fallen had been dispatched to find the Keeper, but without any results. This time she'd sent a few mages along, but even they had returned with empty hands. It was almost as if the group she sought had disappeared, but that was impossible. Even if they were dead, the Fallen would be able to find them.

The mage grabbed the first person to cross her path and raked her long nails down his arms. Blood trickled from the deep scratches as she pushed him away. "Why!" she demanded. "Why can you not find one stupid, little girl?" They were all useless, she decided. There was only one person she trusted to get the job done. Why she hadn't thought about contacting her before was anyone's guess. But now that her need was dire, she had to make a decision.

"Find me Kira," Madame Millard yelled with an icy voice, her arms thrown wide to show her frustration.

Several mages ran to obey her command, knowing the tone she used meant someone might die before the end of the day. Unless her whims were fulfilled.

Courtney wiped sweat from her brow. Today's lesson had definitely been more complicated. She wasn't sure if that was a good or bad thing though. It would be easy to assume that since she was being given harder challenges, she was improving. But it was also possible that Margo was just pushing her because they were running out of time. And she was so sore.

She leaned against a nearby tree stump. What with all the intense training, and helping Walter haul his goodies to camp, she was exhausted. The break was more than warranted. Part of her wondered if they'd have a chance to eat some lunch before continuing. If nothing else, she wanted the chance to catch her breath.

Margo walked a circle around Courtney's resting place, contemplating her student. "In battle, the enemy won't care if you're tired," she lectured. "They won't care if you're hungry, dying, or even dead. And if you don't give it your all, you will be dead."

Courtney tried to control her breathing as the sweat ran down her face. The sun was quite warm, despite the overshadowing trees surrounding the clearing. "I thought you wanted me to conserve my energy and use it constructively."

Pausing in front of the teen, Margo nodded. "In an ideal world, that's how it should be. But both you and I know those of the Mage Circle fight dirty. And there will be more than unfair odds against us. We won't have the luxury of taking our time. That's why you must treat each attack as if it were your last, because that's what it might become if you don't."

The blonde-haired girl nodded as the concept clicked. "I still don't like it," she said under her breath. But she understood the reasoning behind it. Madame Millard had a reputation of being ruthless, as well as many who followed her. They feared the master mage's retribution more than they feared for their lives.

Margo smiled, dirt smudged across her face from their previous exertions. "You don't have to like it. But you do have to deal with it." She moved a few paces away, picking up a convenient stick as she moved. The branch expanded into a spear without so much as a spoken word from her lips. With lightning-quick speed, she turned on her young companion.

Courtney somehow managed to evade the older woman's attack by falling on her rump. Backpedaling, she managed to use another tree to stand. She then transformed a piece of deadwood into a weapon. Her efforts produced a blade that was nowhere near as long or as elegant as Margo's spear. But it was functional and that's what mattered.

The Kaida didn't give her much room to maneuver, coming in fast and hard. Using the long shaft of her weapon as a pole, she vaulted over Courtney, only to quickly pivot around. With her free hand, she thrust forward, sending a wave of energy towards the girl.

Not expecting this line of attack, Courtney was hit full on by the wall of wind. The energy knocked her back to the ground, sending her skidding several dozen yards. She lay stunned from the unexpected force and felt Margo's spear pierce her shoulder as a result. Adrenaline sang through her as she grabbed the nearest item at hand and threw it.

Hot cinders peppered Margo's body as she rolled to one side. "That's more like it," she panted as she regained her footing. Brushing a few sparks out of her hair, she edged more carefully forward as Courtney got back on her feet. "Now let's see how far you can go." With that, she lunged forward once more.

SEVENTEEN

NIGHT HAD CLOSED IN WHEN Anwen opened her eyes once more, only to stare at the stars and branches overhead. It took a moment for her to realize someone was holding her hand. Feeling the pressure of unknown fingers, she turned to see who they belonged to.

Tyler lay next to her, unmoving, his fingers still laced with hers. His light hair needed a trim and a good wash, she noted. There were funny flecks of green and brown in it, like leaves, though she doubted that's what they were. Either way, she thought he looked quite handsome. Despite that, she couldn't help but wonder what he was doing there. According to her mother, she was supposed to train alone.

She didn't remember him joining her after the bout of searing pain caused by her dreams. But she didn't remember much of what had happened after that either. Moving carefully, she withdrew her hand from his. Tyler didn't even stir. She rolled to one side, groaning slightly as she did. Every part of her ached, but it felt good to move. With a little more effort, she sat up and looked around.

Starlight filtered down through the trees. The moon was nowhere to be seen. Despite this, Anwen was surprised to find she could see as clearly as though it were day. A light mist seemed to waft around the trees, but nothing else was out of place.

The sound of giggling drew her attention towards a strand of three close-growing trees. A small head with deep flame-colored hair peered from behind the furthest tree. The child waved almost shyly as she moved a little further into the open

"Follow me?" the girl asked as she seemed to reach for Anwen with one hand.

Anwen felt inexplicably drawn towards her, like a needle to a magnet. She moved to stand. Without so much as thinking, she followed the little girl away from the glen. Before long, she was heading further towards the center of the island. "Wait!" Anwen called out as the child momentarily disappeared from view.

The young girl reappeared from behind a small tumble of rocks. "Shh," she whispered with one finger to her lips. "Daddy's sleeping."

Not sure who the child was talking about, Anwen only nodded. There was something ethereal about the girl in the white dress. She almost seemed to glow like a star and Anwen felt more than willing to believe almost anything she told her. "Who are you?" she asked, using a quieter voice.

The girl giggled with a secretive smile. She then turned and continued up the incline leading to the center of the Island. Scrambling to keep up, Anwen almost lost her footing when some rocks broke free from the soil. She managed to break her fall by pressing flat against the ground.

"Almost there," the child said as she looked down to check her progress. "Not much further."

Anwen scrambled back up the slope. "Where are we going?" she asked. The child didn't say anything so she continued on. After several minutes of climbing in silence, she had her answer.

Recognition kicked in as Anwen came to a halt. They were standing just outside the circle marking the beginning of the Sacred Grove. Goosebumps prickled up and down her spine as she remembered the last time she'd been to this place.

The child paused to look back, skirting the embedded stone. "We won't go in there," she assured as she moved parallel to the curved line. "Uncle wouldn't like it."

Somewhat appeased, Anwen again followed. She didn't want a repeat of the last time she'd entered that sacred circle. The recovery time had been long. She noticed a swirl of energy reach out to the girl from inside the boundary. Soul energy. She remembered seeing a similar swirling of light when Tyler had first brought her to the Grove. The only difference was that this girl's seemed a mix of purple and white.

"This way," the child encouraged. She now headed towards a mass of thick undergrowth a few yards away from the boundary line. She parted thorny branches as if they were silk curtains. "In here."

Anwen hesitated. The idea of going into such an enclosed space left her feeling anxious. Especially since she didn't know what was in there. But when the child motioned from inside the foliage, she couldn't say no. There was something familiar about her, like a scent of home. Stepping carefully, she moved towards the thick growth. As she pushed the first tangle aside, she scratched her hand on a thorn.

With an outward sigh, Anwen decided there was nothing for it and pushed past the next set of brambles. More thorns sunk their claws into her clothes and skin, drawing more blood. She ignored the scratches. Instead, she followed after the lyrical sound of giggling coming from further in. Pushing past the last few branches, she broke into a small meadow no larger than a country cottage. She took a step forward, and then back, noting the ground was boggy.

The girl stood in the middle of the vegetation, which reached well past her waist. "Come," she smiled as she beckoned Anwen over. "Here." She pointed to an unusual plant growing among the moist patches.

The top of the plant reached almost to her shoulders. Brilliant green and yellow leaves branched from hollow square stems. Violet flowers burst from the top of the plant. What almost looked like white feathers pushed through the petals. The flowers reminded Anwen of snowdrops. A most unusual but pleasant smell came from their silky flesh.

The young girl pushed a long stem of the plant towards Anwen. "It is the Hour of the Mage," she said.

Anwen blinked in confusion. "What do you mean?" she asked, moving closer to touch the velvety foliage. The earth squelched underfoot, but the matting of many plant roots kept her shoes dry and her footing firm.

The child plucked a good handful of leaves from the plant. "Grandfather said to give you this." She held out the handful of vegetation.

Taking the offering, Anwen held the bundle of green with uncertainty. "Your grandfather?"

The girl nodded. "He said it be good for you. Said you should chew it. Like this." She pantomimed eating the greens.

Anwen examined the leaves. They definitely reminded her of some kind of plant one wasn't supposed to ingest. "You want me to eat this?" She raised her eyebrows, wondering if this child wasn't pulling her leg after all. She had no idea what this plant was or what it would do to her. Most plants in the wild weren't considered safe to eat, and yet that's what this child seemed to want her to do.

The red-haired girl nodded emphatically. "Grandfather said it's like medicine. But tastes better."

Anwen didn't like the sound of that, but her stomach grumbled at the prospect of any kind of food. And, for whatever reason, she felt she could trust this girl. Maybe it was because everything felt like a dream. After all, the child hadn't led her through anything dangerous. Brambles were hardly a hazard, just annoying. Perhaps it was all right to continue to trust her. Maybe she'd wake up in a little while, realizing it had all just been a dream after all.

With only a twinge of misgiving, Anwen placed one leaf into her mouth and bruised it with her teeth. The sap that escaped was not unpleasant, though she couldn't place the flavor. It was rather exotic in taste. Feeling no adverse effects, she popped the rest of the leaves into her mouth and chewed. The resulting juices made her mouth water, mixing with the sap. It left a faint buzzing feeling on her tongue. Finally, she swallowed the mouthful and turned back to look at the girl, but the child was gone.

Anwen whirled around, half expecting the imp to be behind her, but there was no one there. Letting out a heavy sigh, she turned towards the way out. She wondered if the girl had left while she was contemplating the leaves. Her mother's instructions surfaced in her mind. They reminded her of the ritual fasting she was supposed to undergo to finish her training. She shrugged it off. It was too late now anyway.

Several scratchy minutes later, Anwen emerged from the brambles. But the child was still nowhere to be seen. "Where are you?" she called out, heading in what she thought was the most appropriate direction. It was hard to tell which way she'd gone since there weren't any footprints on the ground.

Courtney washed blood from her skin as she bent over the stream. Margo had been almost brutal in her training and she felt totally drained. But she was not the only one nursing bruises and puncture wounds. A bit further down the stream, Margo washed dirt from her own injuries. The girl couldn't help but feel a small sense of satisfaction at that.

She'd improved so much already, Courtney decided. Her previous training session hadn't produced quite as many injuries on her partner. But the reverse could also be said of her. She had more injuries than she'd had the previous session as well. Margo was pushing her harder and harder.

Pulling her hair back, Margo plunged her upper body into the cool water and let it just course over her. The stream afforded several pools deep enough for a somewhat decent wash. She came up with a splash, shaking water everywhere. "I hope you know basic healing spells." She inspected the wounds that had closed up all across her skin. Some would leave scars, but at least they weren't anything major.

Courtney watched the older woman, noting the absence of puncture marks. "How did you do that?" she asked in awe. She knew healing spells could be tricky. She'd only tried one or two minor ones in the past, with little success. But then she'd only heard them and not actually had someone show her how they worked.

Margo pursed her lips. "I suppose that answers my question. Let's see if you have enough energy left in you to learn how." She strode over to Courtney. Water trailed from her skin as the knee-deep water tried to throw her back under. The liquid sluiced off her clothes as she walked.

Courtney watched her progress from her spot on the stream's bank. Despite being a decent swimmer, she'd chosen to remain closer to the shore. Maybe she just wanted to have her space. Or maybe it was because she still felt a bit intimidated by the older woman.

Clothes still dripping, Margo settled down next to her companion. "When invoking a healing, the trick is to remind the flesh of how it was before it was injured. Most wounds will respond with the right kind of encouragement. Sadly, not all wounds can be healed. While we have the power of dragon kind, ours is limited, diluted from the natural source. But, if we do what we can, most of the time it's enough."

Nodding that she understood, Courtney focused on one area of her body. To be safe, she kept it small. She didn't want to meet with failure. The trick, she supposed, was to see what is and remind the flesh of what was. Just like anything done with the true power of the mage, things could not be coerced. Unless one wanted to be like those in the Circle.

"That's it," Margo encouraged. "Listen to the elemental song. Then nudge the discordant tones back into their proper frame." She closed her eyes as if listening intently to some music only she could hear. She nodded, not needing to look to see the small scrapes on Courtney's skin close over.

Courtney couldn't help but feel a bit pleased by her efforts. And it did take an effort of will. Darkness had its own way of doing things. Anything against the natural order tended to pull towards that darkness. It was a struggle to send it back to its rightful path.

Margo gave her shoulder a quick squeeze before standing up. "When you're finished tending to your wounds, it will be time to return to camp," she informed. "We still have to make dinner, unless you want to keep practicing that is." The resulting groan her announcement made only brought a smile to the Kaida's lips.

Tyler woke with a start. For the briefest of moments he felt a sense of disorientation, but it quickly passed. Pushing up with one hand, he looked around the small glen. His heart gave a sudden pause when he realized something was amiss. "Anwen."

Scrambling to his feet, Tyler looked around wildly. He hoped she'd only gone on a quick personal errand. But, after inspecting the area further, he realized she'd been gone for some time.

Heart thudding in his chest, he searched the ground for any signs of a struggle but didn't find any. He did find a set of footprints leading away from the area though. They were calm and measured in pacing. Whatever had led her away from the glen did not apparently mean her harm. Or at least she hadn't thought it would.

Deciding it best to follow the tracks, Tyler practically flew forward like a deer in flight. Above, faint moonlight filtered down through the trees. It created an almost silver path that only he could see.

EIGHTEEN

ANWEN STUMBLED AND SLID DOWN the good-sized slope she'd been trying to navigate. She somehow lost all track of time as she lay there, staring heavenward as a sudden bout of laughter filled her. She rocked back and forth where she lay, arms hugging her torso. Fallen leaves and dirt caught in her hair and clothes.

The strange taste of the sap lingered on her tongue as the giggles erupted from deep within her belly. Lifting both hands above her face, she stared at the pale skin that covered them. Dark branches stood out against the morning sky overhead, still drenched in only starlight.

The shapes of the branches blurred at the edges. They were replaced with the outlines of stone buildings hewn from the mountain ranges. Anwen shook her head and the giggles subsided. The world seemed to spin around her. It almost felt like she was floating above the ground. The earth felt as though it slid underneath her.

"Deep within these halls they sleep," a voice seemed to whisper as the view blurred once more.

As the sky began to show the first tinges of sunrise, the Mountain reared up in front of her. She felt as though she were standing looking at it instead of lying on the ground.

"Only one may enter the Keep," the voice continued, echoing as if from far away now.

Suddenly Anwen found herself back in her childhood home. She was in the nursery where a dragon-filled mobile slowly spun over the crib. Inside the bed, a light-haired baby burbled, reaching for the wings and tails above her. It didn't seem to matter that she would never reach the fluttering fabric. Just reaching was enough.

A young James Porter peered down at his daughter, eyes soft. "Someday, little one, you will fly with dragons." His smile was warm and filled with a love so profound it made Anwen's breath hitch in her throat.

Margo Porter entered the room, an apron around her hips. She carried a wet dishtowel in one hand, which she used to wipe the excess water from her skin. "You're supposed to be putting the baby to bed," she admonished. Her hair was longer, pulled back in a messy bun. The wrinkles of time had smoothed from her face, making her look years younger than Anwen was used to seeing.

James turned to his wife. "Stories are an essential part of bedtime," he reminded. "Besides, they're not just stories."

Margo's expression softened as she leaned against the door frame. "She's too young to be able to remember those stories later," she said.

Mr. Porter shrugged. "Maybe. Maybe not. Only time can tell that tale." He gave the mobile a spin. The motion sent the miniature dragons dancing over the reaching child inside the crib.

The scene shifted.

James Porter sat at a drawing table, pencil in hand as he sketched out the rough silhouette of a mountain range. He looked a bit older than before. There were a few strands of grey mixed in with his darker hair. A few more wrinkles creased his face, but the same vitality remained in his eyes.

"The City used to be here." James placed a finger on the drawing. A two-year-old Anwen peered over the top of a kitchen chair pulled close to the table. "Right between these two points. That's where our family used to live."

A look of awe crossed the young girl's face. "And Mountain?" She bounced up and down on the chair. Her little feet occasionally left the wooden surface each time her body rose from the surface. Her tiny fingers clung to the back of the chair for balance.

James pulled out a fresh piece of paper and began drawing again. A sort of path curved around the paper, stopping at what had become a straight line. "The Gates," he said, indicating the drawn wall. "Someday one of us will go and unlock them."

From behind the pair, Margo entered the room. Her hair was pinned up on her head in a bun like the one from before, only more tidy. One or two wrinkles had formed around her eyes. A few silver hairs peeked through her crown of red-shot brown hair. Despite this, they were hard to see without direct light shining on them.

Without so much as announcing her presence, she walked over to her child. She bent to place her lips near her daughter's ear, then whispered words in a strange tongue. She then kissed her daughter on the crown of her head and moved to take her husband's hand. "Kern wants us to keep those memories locked away," she said as James looked at her, questions in his eyes.

"Are we to stop telling her about her heritage as well?" he asked. A line of disapproval creased his brow. "Is she not to know her duty as one of our family? Can we not tell her anything at all?"

Margo nodded solemnly. "It's for her protection," she assured. "She must not know who she is or what she can become. Until the time is right."

Anwen gasped like a fish out of water, the scene muddying around her. Were there other things Kern had not wanted her to remember from her clouded past? But why were they coming to light now? And protect her from what? From others learning who she was? She supposed that was possible. All the craziness hadn't started until she'd come across Tyler. Tyler, who had somehow known what she really was even when she hadn't.

But that wasn't quite right either. Because her father had been murdered in cold blood when she was still just a child. Kern had protected her from the same fate, hiding her from her father's killer. It wasn't until she'd strived to fulfill his dying wish that things had started to come to light.

Wind seemed to howl around her, whipping dust every which way. *"Find the Heart and speak the Word."* The same voice from before intoned into the darkness. It spoke with an authority that could not be denied. *"Only then will your voice be heard."*

The dust began to take form, light flickering like an old film reel spinning at the end of its run. The Mountain loomed overhead. The Gates stood wide open to receive her. Almost as if someone had hit fast forward on a movie, everything sped up. Anwen found herself rushing through various passageways at breakneck speed. She felt like she was riding a roller coaster. Up, down and around she sped.

Finally, the dizzying pace subsided. She found herself in the large gallery she'd seen only in dreams. The living crystal at the center pulsed like a beating heart, just as it had when she'd seen the Master Key made. But instead of the massive space being empty, row upon row of various dragons stood as if frozen in stone. Moments after she recognized what she was seeing, she was moving backward. At the same pace as before, she found herself retracing the breakneck ride in reverse. Once outside, the massive stone doors closed in front of her.

Anwen felt breathless as she stood outside the Gates. Slowly, she turned from the barred doors and started down the path back to the Ruined City. Firelight greeted her as she reached the courtyard below. The ruined amphitheatre remained empty, despite the flicker of flames from beyond.

Tents were set up like a small city in the main square, with some of the old structures used as temporary housing. There were more tumbled buildings than before. They opened up the secondary courtyard to the main one. Anwen realized the buildings that had hidden the amphitheatre from view were completely destroyed. Only rock and dust remained.

A tent, far larger than the others, sat near the dry fountain in the secondary courtyard. Several Fallen stood guard at the tent's flap. Anwen drew back into the shadows but they didn't seem to notice her. The sound of muffled talking came from inside the canvas walls but she couldn't tell what was being said. Part of her wanted to move closer to hear what was going on. Another part told her to stay back.

From the ancient path, a small group of people marched forward. No one challenged them as they passed into the tent city. A few even joined them as they headed towards the main tent where Anwen stood. They stopped just outside the entrance, oblivious of their silent observer.

The tent flap was suddenly thrown open. Anwen took a few quick steps back into deeper shadow as Madame Millard strode out. "Ah," the master mage said. Smiling, she held out her arms in welcome to the hooded newcomer standing in the midst of the small group. "Kira. Thank you for returning under such short notice. I would not have called you had our need not been great." The overweight woman ushered the group inside the canvas confines. She dropped the flap once all were inside.

Everything swam in Anwen's vision, like someone had swirled their hand in a once clear puddle. When her vision cleared, she was staring up at a sky full of stars. Light was creeping across the sky, turning midnight blues to a lighter shade. The trees framed the opening to the sky.

Anwen felt as if every fiber of her being was vibrating. She closed her eyes. She still felt like she was floating above the ground. Despite this, she could feel every grain of dirt pressing against her skin. For the briefest of moments, she wondered if she'd gone mad.

NINETEEN

TYLER TILTED TO ONE SIDE as a most unusual
sensation overpowered him. He had to put out a hand
against a tree trunk to steady himself. Despite that, he felt
almost giddy. It reminded him of the one time he'd tried fire
whiskey in mortal form. It was not an experience he'd
wanted to repeat.

Stumbling, he went to the ground. The whole world
seemed to spin above him and he closed his eyes to try and
block out the sensation. He lay there for what felt like an
eternity until the sensation passed. When he opened his eyes,
Tyler realized the night had almost ended. Sunlight began to
color the sky a brilliant red. He still felt a bit lightheaded
when he stood.

As his head cleared, his thoughts returned to Anwen.
Had something happened to her to cause his own symptoms
just now? He doubted the sensation had occurred because of
anything he'd done or not done.

Fearing he knew not what, Tyler retraced his steps until
he picked up her trail once more. He paused for a moment

when the tracks doubled back on themselves. But he was able to pick up the fresher trail a few paces further on.

It did not take long to find the incline where Anwen had rolled down in an almost drunken haze. Seeing her at the bottom, he slid down the slope, sending up a shower of dirt behind him. "Anwen," he called out, his breath catching in his throat as he realized she wasn't moving.

Upon reaching her side, Tyler noticed her eyes were closed but she was breathing. Her pulse felt slow but steady against his own. It was almost as though she were asleep. He touched her shoulder, calling her by name.

Anwen's eyes opened, but there was something off about them. It took Tyler a moment to realize what it was. Her irises were liquid amber in color. And even though her eyes were open, they didn't seem to focus on what was around her.

The faint scent of something he didn't quite recognize wafted from her skin. Bending closer, he inhaled deeply, taking in the fragrance. After a few moments of contemplation, he was able to identify it. Salvia divinum. Diviner's Sage. But how she'd come across the plant was beyond him.

Anwen slowly sat up. Her eyes still shone gold in color as she turned towards Tyler. "I can see you," she said, one hand reaching out to almost touch him. She pulled back just before making contact. Her fingers traced outlines of color normal eyes could not see.

"That's a good thing," Tyler responded. Something in her tone was different, he decided. Something had obviously changed. He just wasn't quite sure yet what it was. "How do you feel?"

He'd seen the after effects of many who had partaken of the unusual plant. But none had had symptoms quite like this. No one's eyes had ever changed color. And their aura had not changed either.

Anwen hadn't so much as blinked as she stared at the dragon, eyes wider than usual. "No. I can *see* you," she said.

"I see you as a dragon. And as a man. But I can also see every part that composes your body, down to the smallest particle. I can see you."

Tyler's eyes widened at this declaration. It's what they'd hoped for. Sort of. But not like this. Not with the help of the mage's sage. Perhaps as a last resort, but not before all other means had been tried. The dangers were too great.

Margo's method had focused more on hearing the eternal melodies of each particle. Her gift worked best when in harmony with nature. Apparently Anwen's worked by sight of the elemental. It was only a little like how dragon abilities worked.

He reached out to touch her with an almost hesitant hand. Heat radiated from her skin long before his fingers touched hers. "Anwen," he started, almost as if in command, but had stopped short.

Anwen moved to stand, arms down at her sides as she stared ahead, ignoring his reaching hand. "I can see the trees," she continued. "And the particles that make them. They're the same. The same as the ones that make up you and me. Like small planets circling miniature suns. I can see the smallest details." Her eyes widened in awe. "It's beautiful."

Tyler stepped forward to stand beside her. Sometimes the plant had allowed such vision, but the cost was usually high. More than a handful with similar sight had gone blind from the experience. That was why it was better for mortals to "hear" everything rather than see it. He only hoped there would be no such resulting repercussions in this instance.

Concentrating, Tyler tried to reach out to the part of his soul that resided within hers. His Soul Gaze was met with an aura of brilliant golden light, entwined with hints of red and blue. Silver flashed throughout, like a protective cage made of lightning. It seemed to dare anyone to try and displace it.

Anwen turned towards Tyler. The morning sunlight glinted off her auburn hair like little sparks of fire. She closed her eyes and leaned into him, her lips meeting his. Both their hearts thumped like drums in perfect harmony. Despite that, Tyler stood frozen in shock. The kiss was brief but oh so sweet as she pulled away. "You taste like summer," she observed with a wistful sigh.

Tyler felt rooted to the ground, his eyes wide at her rather unexpected advance. "Um," he managed, looking at her. "Thank you?" Her eyes had returned to their normal coloring, he noticed. That was a good sign. Perhaps she wouldn't go blind after all.

She laughed a giddy, childlike laugh, and then spun around. "I feel like I could rewrite the entire fabric of the stars," she declared as her arms flared out from her sides. "I could just float up to them and bring them down here."

Tyler grabbed her, stopping the mad twirling. "Hold on there a bit," he advised. "This is the plant talking, not you. Come back down to earth, Anwen."

Anwen collapsed into his arms, still giggling. "How can I when I feel so high?" She reached one hand upwards as if to grab the sky.

Staggering a bit under the unexpected weight, Tyler maneuvered so he wouldn't drop her. "High is right. There's a reason using that plant is discouraged. How much did you take?"

Smiling a bit crazily, Anwen held up her hand, pointing to her closed palm. "About this much? She said to eat it because it was like medicine." Another giggle escaped her lips.

"Come on, little one," Tyler said in an almost fatherly tone. "You need to sleep this off." Sweeping her up into his arms, he headed back towards camp. Judging by the size of she'd indicated, Anwen had consumed at least a dozen leaves. But who was this "she" Anwen was talking about? He had no idea and that bothered him. Certainly Margo would not condone the plant's use. Especially not this early in the scheme of things. But if not Margo, who?

"Wow," Anwen said as her relationship with the earth changed. "I can feel your heart beating. It's got a nice rhythm. Reminds me of drums." She snuggled up against his chest, arms around his neck. Her feet dangled from his strong arms.

Tyler rolled his eyes but continued walking. There was only one thing to do, let the plant's unique qualities run their course and hope for the best. He wasn't sure how long that would take though. Usually only a leaf or two was chewed. Then, once the sap had been ingested, the quid had been spit out. He'd never heard of anyone who had just wantonly chewed up and then swallowed so many leaves before.

Anwen let her head lull against his shoulder. "I feel like I'm rocking in a giant hammock," she declared. "It's nice. Back and forth. Back and forth. Like a little baby in a bassinet."

He briefly wondered if this was how she'd behave if she were ever became drunk, then dismissed the notion. Tyler wasn't sure he wanted to find out. "What am I going to tell your mother?" He looked down to see her reaction but realized she'd dozed off instead. He let out a small sigh. "Anwen, you're going to be the death of me."

Walter sat several feet away from the campfire. He had one of the many boxes from his storage locker pulled close. He wiped his brow as he paused in his work. Then he carefully poured a mixture into a small glass container. The glass resembled a holiday ornament. He'd combined various powders with some thick liquid to create a rather explosive concoction. Several other such balls lay in a small pile next to him, already filled and capped.

Margo sat across the fire pit, warming her hands in the early chill. "Do I even want to know what those are for?" she asked as she watched him cap yet another orb. He'd been working for at least an hour or so on the mixture. And all that time, he'd carefully measured out various ingredients.

Smiling, Walter set the sphere down. "Let's just say they'll make a lot of noise and cause a lot of confusion when they shatter," he answered. "And, in larger quantities, cause a lot more chaos." He'd thought about bringing the plastic explosives, but had decided against it. He'd heard and read too many tales about the mages to risk having an electric timer they could mess with.

"Sounds entertaining," Margo finally replied. She turned at the sound of Courtney crawling out of their tent. The girl emerged into the light through the low doorway. "Good morning, sleepy head. It's about time you woke up. I was almost ready to come in after you."

Courtney yawned as she stood and walked over to the crackling fire. "I feel stiff all over," she complained as she took a seat next to Anwen's mother. "Is the coffee ready?" She reached for the metal pot sitting next to the flames. She remembered to grab an insulating cloth just before touching the hot metal. "Smells good." She reached for a mug and poured a cup.

The sound of twigs breaking caused Courtney to pause just as she was about to take a sip. All eyes turned towards the direction of the sound. She fumbled for her bone knife while Margo reached for a kitchen utensil. Walter hefted one of his exploding balls, ready to throw it.

Tyler pushed through the trees and strode into camp, causing them all to relax. Margo noted he was carrying Anwen in his arms. It took her a moment to realize he was coming from a different direction than where the girl was supposed to be. She couldn't help but wonder at that.

The older woman stood, putting her utensils and plate down before striding over. "Morning," she greeted, looking pointedly at his full arms. "Looks like you've had a busy night."

The dragon paused as Margo came up and greeting him. He resettled Anwen against his chest as she'd managed to slide a bit during the trek back to the others. "Morning," he returned. "I figured it was time for the lost lamb to return to camp," he explained at the questioning looks sent his way. "If you don't mind, I'm going to put her in her tent so she can sleep in peace."

Margo moved to let him pass, watching as he moved to the larger of the two tents. He had to duck to go inside, but somehow managed to not drop the sleeping figure in his arms. Less than a minute later, he was exiting the canvas confines and heading towards the fire. Groaning, he picked out a mug from their collection. He then went to pour himself a cup of the dark beverage simmering on the coals. "That's more like it," he said with a contented sigh.

Courtney picked up her own cup, having put the knife back in her pocket. "I thought Anwen was undergoing special training," she commented. She glanced towards Margo over the lip of her mug. Part of her wondered how the woman was going to take this development.

"She was," Tyler replied before taking a sip of the rich brew. "I'm taking matters into my own hands now."

Margo looked like she might protest but settled back on her seat. "I thought we were in agreement with my methods," she admonished. Part of her wondered where the dragon had been during the previous day but didn't dare ask. It was sometimes hard to remember that this young-looking man was more than he seemed.

Shrugging, Tyler put his mug down. "Certain events made it necessary for me to intercede on your methods," he replied. "Somehow, Anwen discovered a spread of salvia divinum. Whether it was out of hunger, or something else, I'm not sure. Anything's possible. But she pretty much ate a whole handful of the leaves. At least she didn't eat the flowers along with them. We can thank the stars for that."

Anwen's mother bit her lip as she contemplated what Tyler had just told her. "Salvia divinum? Are you sure?" Her fingers tensed as she gripped the edge of her seat. She'd never seen the plant herself but had heard of its unique properties. And the adverse side effects.

Tyler nodded. "Quite sure. And to some interesting results, I might add. I found her after she'd gone through the initial effects. I don't know how it affected her in total, but I have some guesses. What I do know is that it brought on some interesting results." He then began to tell them what had transpired after he'd found her lying at the bottom of the small hill. "I don't know what visions she may have had, but it would be interesting to find out."

Courtney watched Margo as she seemed to pull within herself. She glanced over to Walter who had gone back to filling his glass orbs. Dragon and mage magic didn't have much to do with him. She didn't blame him for at least pretending to not pay attention. He was good at it, if he truly was pretending the disinterest he showed.

"So, until she wakes up," Tyler continued, "there's no way of knowing what effects it might have on her. Permanent or otherwise. I'm hoping for the best, but we do need to be prepared for other possibilities."

He was fairly certain Margo knew what he meant. Anwen might still go blind from the sudden opening of her Soul Sight. And while it wasn't necessarily a bad thing, it hadn't quite been the older mage's aim. But, if Anwen retained her sight, both body and soul, it was a far better prospect than they'd dared hope for.

Margo stood from her spot, looking pointedly at Courtney. "If you've finished, we have more training to do."

Courtney groaned.

TWENTY

JOSEF HADN'T HAD MUCH LUCK finding any further clues. Not even along the long mountain trail leading back to the village. Finding the dagger had been his only success, and even that wasn't enough. The small wound he'd received from the darkened blade had closed over. But it continued to sting. Maybe it had become infected. He hadn't exactly used the usual antibacterial solutions on it. Nor had he kept it clean by using a bandage.

Now back in the village, he went to Daphne's house. No one was home, as they'd all gone up the Mountain. Her mother had died in childbirth years before. Her father was a minor mage. Not for the first time, Josef wondered why he hadn't been born one as well.

After trying all the doors, he decided on more drastic measures to get inside. He broke a small window next to the front door, ignoring the thorny vines that grew around it. Within seconds, he was inside the one story structure. Already knowing the layout of the house, he headed directly to Daphne's room.

The bed was neatly made, with several small pillows tossed near the headboard. All the clothes were hung, coordinated by color, or were stacked in dresser drawers. A small vanity sat next to the wardrobe, with a smattering of makeup and perfume on the wooden surface. Nothing was out of place.

Josef began searching the room, throwing things at random. He wasn't sure what he was looking for but knew he'd find something. It felt like a fire was consuming him from the inside out. He had to find something, anything that could confirm the idea growing in his mind. That interloper, Anna, wasn't it? She had to be responsible for Daphne's disappearance. Her, Courtney, and Tyler.

The sound of the backdoor opening caught him off guard and he quickly ran to hide in the wardrobe. Had Daphne's father come home? Or was someone else there? Either way, he didn't want to be discovered. And if it was a thief, he could at least surprise them so he hid.

Rustling fabric and footsteps sounded in the hall. Then someone pushed the bedroom door open. There was a lengthy pause before whoever was there continued into the room. Josef felt as though he were sweating bullets as the noises continued, growing closer.

Another pause sent his heart racing. Had they gone? Were they still there? Who were they and what did they want? Was it a thief taking advantage of the owner's absence? Or was it something more sinister?

The door of the wardrobe began to open so he pushed back behind the clothes. The person on the other side of the door smiled. "Found you," she said as she pulled the door all the way open and parted the clothes to reveal her prey.

The afternoon waned as Tyler sat, staring at Anwen's motionless form. After conferring with Walter, they'd both decided the girl was dehydrated. That was something Tyler's abilities couldn't fix. Luckily, Walter had packed his medical kit. From that, he'd produced several saline bags and the tubing to go with them. They'd had to improvise a stand, but that had been easy. After that, the veteran had decided to give them some privacy.

Touching Anwen's skin, Tyler was pleased to find her temperature had gone down. Perhaps the effects of the plant were finally wearing off. He wasn't sure though, as they didn't seem to share them any longer. Maybe only the stronger sensations and emotions were shared, he mused. It was also possible the connection wasn't as reliable as he'd been led to believe.

He contemplated those moments after finding her. Why had her eyes glowed like a dragon's? Soul Sight allowed an individual to see the different auras of individuals. But Mage and Dragon Sight were completely different. Dragon Sight was a special ability of the dragons, allowing its user to see down to the elemental level. Few mages ever attained anything close to it. Their version remained a healthy medium between the two. Their mortal frames weren't made to withstand the higher levels of the ability.

But Anwen seemed to have exhibited signs of Dragon Sight. And it just wasn't possible. Unless the part of his soul inside her had resonated with the salvia divinum she'd eaten. It was possible, though decidedly not likely.

Anwen groaned in her sleep. "Only one," she mumbled. "Only one."

Her skin was so soft, Tyler thought as he brushed a strand of hair from her face. "It's probably a good thing you sleep so much," he mused. "I have a feeling it might be a tradeoff for the double heritage you have."

He touched his lips, remembering the brief kiss she'd given him. Had it been her true intention to kiss him? Or had it been something induced by the plant? He wished he knew for sure. He could still remember how she'd tasted, a cross between vanilla and sunshine.

To his knowledge, no one from the Kaida's direct line had ever married one of the Keeper lines. It would be interesting to see how things would play out. Tyler couldn't help but wonder how a relationship with her would work out. Once the others had awakened, would it be forbidden? Or would Anwen be accepted with open arms?

With a start, Anwen sat up, her heart pounding. "We have to hurry," she announced as she stared ahead. "We're running out of time." She moved to push off the blankets covering her.

"Easy now," Tyler admonished as he gently took her hands into his. "We still have time."

Shaking her head, Anwen turned to look at him. It had been rather odd to see the colors and swirls of atoms that composed his body. She could still see after-images of that strange phenomenon. Part of her wondered if it wasn't all just a dream.

With impatient hands, she pushed Tyler's hands aside and moved the blankets "No. We don't have time. I have to get inside the Mountain no later than two days from now. If I don't, it will be too late." She impatiently pulled the I.V. from her arm. In her haste, she didn't even bother to staunch the flow of blood from the puncture that remained.

Realizing she wasn't to be reasoned with, Tyler grabbed a gauze pad. He insisted on applying it to the needle mark before leaving the tent so she could dress. Once outside the canvas enclosure, he turned his attention to the fire. Seeing it had all but died down, he let out a brief burst of flame to relight the deadwood. By the time Anwen emerged, he had some broth heating over the crackling flames.

"That smells good," Anwen commented as she sat next to him. "I feel like I could eat a horse."

Tyler smiled at that. It was a good sign. Sometimes those who partook of the Sage's Fruit lost interest in eating. It was another dangerous side effect of the plant. "Back in the tent," he hazarded, "it sounded like you mean to enter the Mountain alone." He took up the pot and poured her a cup of the broth.

Accepting the drink, Anwen nodded. "Yes. I do." She took a careful sip from the mug. "Do you know these words? '*Deep inside these walls they sleep. Only One may enter the Keep. Find the Heart and speak the Word. Only then will your voice be heard.*'"

Tyler contemplated the fire as he tumbled the words in his mind. "Where did you hear that?" It sounded like a prophecy, but not any he'd heard before. At least not that he could recall.

Anwen peered into the distance as she held her mug. "In my dreams. After the little girl gave me the plant, I dreamed. There were some strange dreams. Some of them felt like memories. Then, there was a view of the Mountain where I saw Madame Millard and her camp. She welcomed someone named Kira. Do you know who she is?"

Thinking back on all the villagers, Tyler's expression went vague. He knew everyone who lived in the village, and those associated with it, past and present. After a minute or so of contemplation, he shook his head. "No. I don't think there's anyone associated with the mages by that name. At least none that I know about. That doesn't mean to say there isn't someone outside my sphere of influence with that name."

With a sigh, Anwen took another sip from her mug. "I wonder who she is."

Josef stared, his jaw slack, not sure if he believed his eyes. "Daphne?" Somehow he felt silly for hiding. It didn't take much to realize no one else was stupid enough to break into a mage's house and hide in a bedroom closet.

The dark-haired girl smirked as she stepped back so he could get out of the wardrobe. "I hope you're planning on cleaning up this mess," she said. She indicated the chaos he'd created with a sweep of her hand. "You know I don't like my things out of place."

Josef sheepishly picked up a bra and stuffed it back into the appropriate drawer. "I thought something had happened to you," he managed as he paused to face her. "You've been gone for over a week. Where were you?" He wanted to shake her but didn't. That wasn't how their relationship worked.

Kira smirked to herself. This was going to be easier than she'd anticipated. "Of course I was gone," she replied, flipping her hair to one side. "I was doing something for my aunt. I'm sorry I couldn't send word but I had to keep silent. It was necessary to find out more about that Key Keeper who opened the Mountain." The lies came so easily, she mused.

Feeling tired, Josef sank down onto the bed. "I thought the worst when I found your knife on the mountain path," he confessed. He pulled the blade out and handed it to her. "I thought you were dead. And when the Mountain shook…" he trailed off.

Kira took the knife and fiddled with it. A slight stain adorned the blade. Blood. She smiled in satisfaction. If the small wound on Josef's finger was any indicator, she felt sure the blood was his. Running her finger against the blade, she felt the skin part enough to let the blood well up. A slight smile touched her lips before she transformed it to a look of shock. "Ouch!"

Josef jumped up in alarm. "What is it? Did you cut yourself?" He reached for her hand. "Let me see."

A thin red line graced her finger, with some blood ebbing from the deeper part of the cut. Josef took the wounded appendage and sucked the blood off, not even thinking about what he was doing. It tasted rather sweet, if he thought about it."Better?"

Laughing to herself, Kira nodded, batting her eyelashes. "Yes. Thank you." She removed her hand from his and traced the wounded finger down his cheek. When she removed her finger, the cut was gone. Mortals were so gullible. Not even that stupid Madame Millard, her so-called aunt, was as smart as she thought herself to be. "Come," she said. "They need us in the Ruined City."

Josef took her offered hand like a lost child. Inside, he felt a strange sense of chill begin to spread through his body.

TWENTY-ONE

COURTNEY PUSHED LOOSE STRANDS OF hair from her face. Not for the first time, she wondered why Margo had asked Walter to observe them. She didn't like others watching her get her rear handed to her in a basket. It was humiliating. But, at least she was doing better.

"Again," Margo instructed as she raised her blade once more. This time she wielded a metal weapon in the shape of a rapier. The point was sharper than a pin, with the sides honed to razor sharpness. She was far from playing anymore.

The blonde raised her modified bone knife and charged. With her free hand, she stooped to scoop up a pine cone and threw it. The spiny brown nubs spun out like shrapnel as they sped towards their target. Courtney yelled as she thrust ahead with her blade.

Margo's eyes went wide as she realized what the young mage had done. She pivoted to one side and reached down for a handful of dirt. The small grains flew out like a fine mist, colliding with the flying thorns. Despite the counter-attack, several fragments made it through, embedding in her flesh.

From the outskirts of the meadow glen, Walter winced. "That's gotta hurt," he said to the air. He was slowly realizing why Margo had invited him to watch. This was a mage battle at its finest. It was easy to feel a new appreciation for their abilities. Not only did the two women fight with physical weapons, but they seemed to create new ones out of thin air. Instinctively, he knew he'd never win against them if he was on his own.

Hearing the sound of crackling leaves, the veteran turned to look behind him. He relaxed as soon as he realized who was approaching.

Tyler nodded in greeting. Anwen walked by his side. They both strode as if with a specific purpose. "They still at it?" he asked as soon as they reached the veteran.

Walter rolled his eyes. "For hours. If I didn't know any better, I'd say they were trying to kill each other. They're pulling out all the stops. And I mean *all* of them."

Anwen took a step forward to peer around her companions. She blinked in surprise to see the two combatants going at each other with such intensity. "I never knew my mom was that flexible," she commented as she watched the sparring match.

Letting out a low chuckle, Walter put a hand on her shoulder. "Full of spice, that one," he said. "Like a momma mountain lion. Wouldn't want to be on the receiving end of that ferocity."

Anwen bit the inside of her cheek as she watched the spectacle. The two combatants almost seemed to dance around each other. Except that each movement seemed to bring the cling of striking weapons. Or a flash of blood as it flew from a freshly opened wound. "I don't blame you. It's kind of scary to watch."

Tyler cleared his throat. "We need to interrupt their little match," he announced. "Anwen has something to tell everyone."

Glancing wryly at the combatants, Walter shrugged. "Your funeral. Personally, I'm staying as far back as possible while still getting a good show. I just need a soda and some popcorn."

Smiling mirthlessly, Tyler moved out into the meadow, ignoring Anwen's protests. "Watch and learn," he said as he walked away. He strode with surety. When he reached the vicinity where the two mages sparred, he paused. Taking note of their positions, and fighting styles, he went in, moving like a viper.

Anwen tried to follow Tyler's movements with her eyes but couldn't. They were just too fast. She blinked a few times, as if her eyes were at fault, instead of blaming her brain's inability to keep up.

Margo felt something suddenly connect with her chest like a battering ram. It sent her flying. Mustering what strength she had left, she somehow managed to use her hand against a tree to spring into a roll. She landed half a dozen feet away, winded and in pain.

Courtney found herself being flipped over by an assailant too fast for her to see. She had a brief moment of euphoria before she landed with a thud on her back.

As both women turned towards this new attacker, they paused. Shock showed on both their faces. But it was Margo who was the first to recover, though she was sure there were a few broken ribs. "Impressive," she wheezed as she stood. "I didn't even see you coming."

"That's not fair," Courtney gasped as she let her body relax with her exhaustion. She received a smile for her complaint.

Seeing the danger had passed, Walter and Anwen moved to join the others. "Very nice," Walter commented as he patted Tyler on the shoulder. "If I hadn't seen it with my own eyes, I wouldn't believe it. Not that I could follow your moves. Do all dragons fight like that?"

Tyler couldn't help but grin as he went to help Courtney to her feet. "Sorry for the abrupt interruption, but Anwen has something to tell us." He turned towards the auburn-haired girl. "Isn't that right, Anwen? Follow me back to camp?"

The wind rustled the branches of the trees surrounding the small clearing. The fire burned bright in its pit, though the five campers did not sit around it. Instead, they surrounded a makeshift table Tyler had fashioned out of one of the many stumps in the area.

Walter sat next to Tyler and Anwen. The veteran had pulled out a map of the area from one of his many packs. "Not the most accurate," he apologized, "but it will have to do."

Tyler found some transparent paper. With it, he sketched out a rough but accurate layout of the Ruined City. "Those buildings are gone now," Anwen corrected him, pointing out the flaw. He made the correction.

Margo finished tending to her and Courtney's wounds while the map was completed. Both had sustained many wounds thanks to the intensity of their sparring match. "You did well today," she complimented the other mage. She finished coaxing one last scrape to close over. "Very creative. Keep that up and we might have a fighting chance."

Hearing that, Walter looked up from the sketch. He wasn't one to give false hope, though the girl had fought like a tiger. "I just hope we can take them by surprise. Otherwise we might be in trouble. I have a rough estimate of how many mages live in that village and the numbers don't look good." If they were going up against as many mages as was indicated on the map, surprise was their best weapon.

Tyler nodded over the new outline. "And you're sure that's all the changes? Including all the tents and mages you saw?" He glanced over at Anwen for confirmation.

Double-checking the layout, Anwen nodded. "Except for here." She pointed to the area where the Ruined City met the main path. "There was a guard posted there too." Part of her felt surprised to remember such details but she chose not to question it.

The dragon made the correction. "Okay, I think we're ready," he announced. As the others turned their attention back to the map, he set a small light orb floating just high enough for all to see. Even though the fire gave some measure of light, it wasn't quite enough.

Courtney eyed all the X's on the page with a grim face. It looked like the whole village was on the Mountain. "They're not taking any chances, are they?"

Margo pursed her lips. "I take it most of the upper level mages will be near this point." She pointed to the largest mark indicating where Madame Millard's tent sat. "Keep the more powerful and experienced mages close to the Gates. That way they can rush in when they open. But far enough away to give us a false sense of confidence."

Walter rubbed at the stubble on his face. "Makes sense to me. Means we'll have to have a pretty good distraction to keep them from getting there before we do." He eyed his box of goodies.

Seeing him look at the homemade explosives, Tyler smiled. "I propose we split into two groups. The first group will travel the main path to the City and use whatever means necessary to distract them. The second group will go the back way up. Whoever goes in this group will make sure Anwen reaches the Gates and gets inside."

He glanced around to make sure everyone followed his reasoning. "I think the groups should be as follows: for group one, Courtney, Walter, and Margo. Group two should consist of Anwen and myself."

Margo raised her eyebrows at this. "Why don't I go with Anwen instead? I agree that each group should have at least one strong offensive player. But wouldn't it be better for two women to slip past the other mages? Unless you plan on masquerading as a female. Most upper level mages tend to be women."

Tyler inhaled sharply, about to protest when Anwen spoke up. "I think mom's right. From what I can see, the second path is easier to navigate, even if it is hidden. If you can distract the others, we can reach the Gates. Mom can keep watch while I go inside."

Her mother sucked in her breath, giving her daughter a rather incredulous look. "Alone? Now that I won't allow. Who knows what dangers you may find inside?"

Anwen locked eyes with her mother, matching her will against the older woman's. "Yes, alone. According to my dreams, a mage cast the spell that put the dragons to sleep and only a mage can undo it."

Margo shook her head. "I'm not about to let you do this on your own. It's too dangerous."

The look Anwen flashed her gave the woman pause. "I cannot go against what I've been told. I must go alone."

Tyler stood abruptly, upset with the argument. "The next thing out of your mouth will be something like 'let me go instead. After all, I'm a mage too.' Am I right?" he looked at the older woman. "But it doesn't work that way. You know it. I know it. We can't always hold Anwen's hand. Her vision. Her future. She has to do this on her own."

Margo looked like she was about to protest again but held her peace. It would not be wise to risk further angering the dragon before her. Especially not now that she knew what he was capable of doing.

Watching the exchange, Walter poked at the fire, sending up embers. "I think Margo's right. She should be the one to go with Anwen. Out of the two of you, Tyler can create the most powerful distraction. But someone has to watch Anwen's back and keep an eye on the Gates. That would be you." He pointed at Margo.

The plan made sense, Courtney decided. "Won't our major obstacle be getting the other party into the City? Not to mention you once told us we need you on the path to keep from getting lost or dying." She thought back to that fateful trip only a few weeks ago. It felt like an age had passed since this whole quest had begun.

Shaking his head, Tyler pointed to the map. "If I know anything about the Mage Circle, they'll want the Key Keeper to reach the City. I'm willing to bet the guard posted at the entrance is there only as a lookout. I don't think we'll have any problems reaching that point."

"Yes, but wouldn't it be a shock if they got a dragon instead of the Key Keeper?" Walter countered. "That'll keep them busy for sure. At least long enough for Anwen and Margo to slip behind their backs and open the Mountain gates."

Tyler couldn't argue with his logic. Well, he could but he knew he'd lose. Walter was right. "Fine. I'll go with the main group. Margo can go with Anwen. But Anwen still goes inside the Mountain alone."

Margo sat back in resignation. "I have only one question. How will Anwen find the right room, or whatever it is, to wake the dragons? It's not like she's been there before. And if memory serves, the halls of Tarragon are meant to be confusing to those who do not know them."

"I'll know the way when I see it," Anwen answered as all eyes turned to her. She suddenly felt as though a heavy weight had fallen on her shoulders and she let out a hesitant little smile. "I hope."

After more planning, everyone finally broke up for the night. The sun had long set and dinner had been consumed. Stars shown down on the Island, illuminating the campsite with an ethereal glow.

Anwen snuggled into her sleeping bag but sleep would not come. On either side, both her mother and Courtney were sound asleep. She could hear the sound of their quiet breathing as confirmation of their slumber. She stared at the peak of the tent, wondering why sleep fled her.

Before her eyes, the specter of Daphne appeared,

lounging casually in the air. "Think you've got it all figured out, don't you," she stated. "But what are you going to do when my aunt and the others catch you? They'll just make you do what they want anyway. So why bother?"

Shaking her head, Anwen rolled to one side so she needn't look at the dark-haired ghost. "We won't fail," she countered. "I'm not the same anymore. I've changed."

Daphne moved back into her field of view, peering over Courtney's sleeping form. "Oh, that's right," she said with heavy sarcasm. "You have Soul Sight now. But you can't control it. Nor does it mean you can control your abilities just because you can see molecules and auras. And that will make you blind. Tyler clearly hasn't told you everything."

"Nice try," Anwen retorted. After she'd tried to explain her visions, Tyler had told her about the plant she'd eaten. He'd also mentioned the Soul Sight and the basics of how it worked.

The specter shrugged. "Basics don't mean you know how to control an ability. It takes years to learn that kind of control, which is time you don't have," she smirked. "Besides, the Circle has a secret weapon."

Counting to ten, Anwen let out her breath. "Leave," she said. "Tomorrow's a big day and I need sleep. Besides, I don't believe you."

Daphne gave a mock salute as she began to fade from sight. "Good luck with that. You'll need all the help you can get." With that final thought, she vanished.

From Anwen's other side, Margo peered over at her daughter. She only turned her head slightly to see through half-closed eyes. Her eyes opened wider as her daughter closed hers. Something was obviously going on, and not in a good way. But, as Anwen at least feigned sleep, she closed her eyes once more to let dreams claim her. There was nothing she could do about it now. The wheels were already too far in motion to stop.

TWENTY-TWO

AS THE SUN ROSE, MADAME Millard smiled. Her niece returned that smile with one of her own. Only a small handful knew about Kira's true identity. And, just as the master mage had planned, the majority had accepted her as Daphne. The two were all but identical. Only those of the Inner Circle knew the truth.

She applauded herself for following their mother's advice. Hide the one. Let the other be the public face for both. Now the wisdom of those words had come to fruition. Daphne had been a skilled mage. Kira was better.

Lounging in the master mage's tent, Kira idly stroked the skin of a Fallen. "You should have seen his face," she gloated. "It was like he'd seen a ghost. And insuring his loyalty? A walk in moonlight. I almost feel sorry for him." She laughed giddily.

Madame Millard shook her head but smiled with pride. After all these years researching the darkest of spells, her lost niece had returned. She could allow a few indulgences. "Did you find the spell?"

With an idle hand trailing along the Fallen's rough hide, the younger mage sat up from her pillows. "Of course," she purred. "But this will be more difficult than the Ritual of Obliteration. We're not seeking to destroy a soul, but to steal one," she reminded. "And don't worry about the Mage Moon. It won't affect the Ritual in the slightest."

The master mage impatiently brushed the reminder aside. "And you know for sure the Kaida is coming here?" It was beyond her wildest dreams for such to happen. Having the Key Keeper was one thing, but the Kaida as well? She could almost jump for joy. It was better than Christmas.

Kira smiled at her overweight aunt. "My spies confirmed it. They saw her get off the train at Blaucii Station. She only had a one way ticket. She's here. Somewhere. I'm sure it won't be long before she shows her face."

Madame Millard steepled her fingers together. "Excellent. Be sure you have everything prepared. We must not waste a moment. If she is as wise as her forbears, she will know the time grows short, one way or another."

The bleak scenery flashed by as Margo navigated the old truck along the path Walter had described. How the others planned on reaching their destination, she didn't know. And, at the moment, she didn't care. The desert mirrored her thoughts, dry and weathered, as old as the hills around them.

Sitting in the passenger seat, Anwen stared out the window. She couldn't help but mull over her conversation with Daphne. What was the secret weapon she'd mentioned? Did it really exist? Or was it a ploy to undermine her confidence? If so, it was working.

Every now and again, Margo glanced over at her daughter, wondering what was going on in her head. It was hard to guess. The little one-sided conversation she'd overheard the night before was more telling. She had tried to contact Kern to ask his advice, but with no result. Perhaps it was too close to the time for him to respond, his soul rejoining his more physical form.

"It's okay to be nervous," Margo finally said, trying to consul her child. Her distress washed over her like ocean waves.

Anwen looked up from her musings. "Hm?" She absently looked away from the window to peer at her mother's face. The intrusion was not unwelcome, her thoughts less than happy ones.

Keeping her eyes on the fading path, Margo didn't notice the look of confusion on her daughter's face. "There's no shame in it," she amended. Noting the gas gauge, she slowed the vehicle until they came to a stop. "Almost out of gas," she explained. "We'd better go on foot from here."

"I'll be fine," Anwen said as she left the truck's cabin, closing the door behind her. She went around to claim her bag from the back. Hefting the pack over one shoulder, she felt the Master Key's chain bite into the skin under her shirt. She'd almost forgotten its presence, having grown used to wearing it.

Watching her, Margo felt something had changed. "Look at you," she exclaimed as she joined her. "You're all grown up." Moisture glistened in her eyes.

Anwen rolled her eyes. "Really, mom? Can we not do this right now?" She pulled away from the hands her mother had placed on her shoulders.

Margo sniffled a little. "I know. I know." She gave her daughter a quick hug before pulling away. "It's just that you've grown so much over the past few weeks."

Shaking her head, Anwen strode down the path, taking up the lead.

Tyler looked out across Lake Wyvern from atop the Sacred Grove. The highway swept past the path leading to the Ruined City and the Gates. And beyond even that, Anwen and her mother journeyed towards the far side. He could almost imagine where they were now. Chances were good they were halfway across the small expanse of desert. If he'd calculated correctly.

Turning back towards the Grove, he noted the presence of Kaida Magus. Her body was just as translucent as before. Despite this, she somehow seemed more present than in previous encounters. For the briefest of moments, he glanced towards the direction of their camp. Part of him wondered what the other two were doing.

"We meet again, Daemyn," Kaida said as she walked out from among the trees. Her footsteps made no mark on the ground, nor did her passage make any sound. "Perhaps for the last time. I take it you did not impart our last conversation to any others?"

The dragon shook his head. "It is mine to bear," he answered as he sat on a convenient stone. "Let the others worry about what they know."

Kaida shook her head. "As self-sacrificing as ever, I see." Her long skirts swirled around her as a gentle breeze combed through the trees. "You may indeed be one of the Council, second only to the Nurrim, but even you have limitations. Nor are the others so weak in their mortality. You could do worse to trust them."

Tyler pulled at the grass. He plucked a handful or two, only to send the fragments scattering in the breeze. "Old habits die hard," he replied. The wind teased his hair and clothes, causing the fabric to ripple like the quiet surface of a pond.

The woman knelt down on one knee to look him in the eyes. For all his relative height, she overshadowed him when he sat. "Then, perhaps you are the more blinded by it. The others know their limitations. They have yet to realize their true strengths. I fear the same fault lies in you. Remember, you are not alone."

The breeze picked up, scattering leaves in the air, making it necessary for Tyler to cover his eyes. When he looked up, Kaida was gone. He expected no less from the first mage.

Child-like laughter filled the air as the wind peaked again, then subsided.

"Love you, daddy."

Tyler started at the young voice; sure he'd heard it before. But before he could remember from where, the ground rumbled underneath him. With wide eyes, he put one hand to the stone.

Tomorrow, the earth said.

"Tomorrow," he replied.

TWENTY-THREE

JOSEF SWAYED AS THE MOUNTAIN shook, but didn't seem to notice. His eyes appeared glazed over as he stared ahead. If any were to touch his skin, they would complain at how cold it felt. But no one did as he stood inside Kira's tent. No one dared enter without permission. Such was the privilege of being related to the master mage.

Kira strode through the flap of the tent. She threw aside gloves and the knife she'd retrieved from Josef in the village. They weren't necessary for anything more than show. "Slave," Kira called over to the male teen.

Josef moved to stand at attention, his body rigid under her command. He would obey any command she gave him, even if it meant taking his own life.

"You are to take watch at the City's entrance," Kira ordered. "Send those there back to camp. If anything happens, pierce your hand with this." She threw another, smaller blade at Josef. The knife hit the ground in front of him and stuck there, the stiletto thin point scoring the ground like a needle. "I will know when you do and will let the others know our foes are upon us."

Josef mindlessly bent to retrieve the knife and pocketed it. With a stiff bow, he turned to face the entryway, ready to follow his orders.

Kira held out a hand to stop his immediate departure. "One more thing. Act normal or your life is forfeit." Her expression brooked no argument and none would be given. He was hers and she knew it.

A cruel smile crept up her cheeks after he left. What the other mages didn't know--well, it just might kill them. Especially when she played her final card.

Walter checked his watch for what felt like the umpteenth time. The glowing numbers only told him what he already knew. Tyler was late.

The sun had set over an hour ago and the sky was dark. If all had gone according to plan, they'd already be on their way back to the mainland. But something had apparently held Tyler up. Maybe it was the earthquake they'd felt earlier. Maybe it was something else. Whatever it was, he was late.

Both Walter and Courtney had loaded the raft early on. They'd only packed the necessities. And, if all went well, they'd get the rest of their gear later. If they survived. He knew the two conditions were not necessarily synonymous no battle came without casualties.

They'd taken the morning hours to finish preparations. The afternoon hours were spent resting. They were to set out once the sun set. With luck, they would make good time, the road remaining unwatched. Tyler had taken Anwen and Margo across to the truck in the wee hours of the morning. He'd returned only to disappear again soon after.

"Sorry I'm late," Tyler said from behind Walter, making Courtney jump. He wore dark clothes that blended into the night. With a cap on his head, his light-colored hair seemed to take on a darker tone.

Courtney was tempted to thump him on the head, but resisted. She remembered the faster-than-thought attack from yesterday's sparring match with Margo. "Don't do that!" she hissed instead. "I'm nervous enough as is without you popping out of the woodwork."

"Let's go," Walter said, reminding them both of their mission. "There's plenty of time for apologies later."

With a bit of an effort, the three friends pushed the rubber raft into the water and climbed aboard. Walter and Tyler pulled strongly on the oars. Their efforts sent them skimming across the reflective surface. Looking towards the Mountain, Courtney shivered. Anwen and her mother were up there. Somewhere.

The hours seemed to melt away as they reached the further shore. They landed at the small fishing village ruins Tyler had shown Anwen weeks before. From there, it was relatively easy to reach the road, even with all of Walter's gear. With only the stars to guide them, they crossed the silent highway without incident.

Tyler allowed a break at the old picnic tables so they could eat something. Then, giving them all a sip of the precious Dragon Meade, they roped up and headed up the trail to the Ruined City. Though the path was fairly even from the start, it could become treacherous at night. For obvious reasons, he allowed little light to guide them. Instead, he chose to rely on his memory and Dragon Sight to lead them.

The going was slow. It became even slower as they reached the Endless Chasm. After careful consideration, Tyler persuaded the path back together. There were several areas where chunks of rock had broken free from the wall. Inching along like ants, they all finally made it to the wide expanse past the steep drop-off. They took their second break there.

Overhead, the moon had come and passed out of sight, though it had not brought much light. Tyler maintained a ban on the use of light orbs so they wouldn't give away their position too soon. Theirs was a mission of secrecy, surprise their best weapon. And the timing was crucial.

The second real difficulty occurred as they reached the Consecrated Hall. Walter had been so overcome with memories from his days serving in the military that he'd been unable to move. Tyler had to step in and act as a buffer between the man and the stone's effects on him. Their pace picked up past the obsidian walls.

Once they'd passed the lattice-sealed tombs, Tyler called for their final halt. The sun was slowly crawling upward. They took another rest just before reaching the large archway to the City. Using a charm of concealment, they blended in with the dun-colored stone.

Just as Anwen had said, no one seemed to be in sight. Despite this, they all knew there had to be someone watching the path. It went against the grain of the Mage Circle to not have some kind of sentry posted. They would have one if for no other reason than to alert the others of visitors.

"Now we wait," Tyler whispered. He hunkered further down in the small hollow they'd found for shelter. He glanced briefly to the left where the stone archway was barely visible around a fold of rock. He felt a presence over there, though he wasn't sure from what. It didn't quite feel like man or animal.

Josef lay on his belly over the archway that indicated the entrance to the Ruined City. Something told him few people looked up. As such, he had taken the opportunity to place himself in the highest position possible. It had been easy to convince the other two who'd been guarding the archway to leave. They'd seemed more than happy to do so, not that it mattered to him. He'd been given an order. He was only happy to obey.

The hours had passed by without incident. Night had come and gone, and yet he still lay on the stone, looking down towards the path. It was what Daphne wanted. It didn't matter that it was uncomfortable, or that he was chilled through to the bone. All that mattered was what he'd been told to do.

As the sun began to rise, there was a faint squabble of stone down on the path, but nothing had come of it. At least nothing he'd seen. But, despite his desire to fulfill the order given him, his mortal frame still had its own needs. Eyelids heavy with sleep drooped closed.

The smallest vestiges of his mind rebelled the order, knowing something was wrong. The enveloping cocoon of cold soothed those protests away, burying them deeper inside. A mere mortal's will was nothing when compared to the poison in his blood. But mortal still, and so he slept.

TWENTY-FOUR

ANWEN LEANED HEAVILY AGAINST THE enclosing walls of the secondary path. Tyler had been right about it being easier. What he'd forgotten to mention was that it was a lot longer and more winding. The only real advantage she could see was that there were no sheer drop offs or ways to get lost. Taking a swig of water from her canteen, she looked towards her mother.

Margo surveyed the path ahead, lifting her own canteen to her lips. They'd camped just past the head of the trail late the night before. Neither had talked much during the hike to the trail head. The older mage wasn't sure what to say. Should she admit to listening to that one-sided conversation? Should she let it be?

Now they were almost to the top of the path, waiting for events to unfold. If they'd navigated correctly, they should have only a turn or two until they reached the City. It wouldn't take more than a few minutes to reach the protrusion of rock that hid the space. But what would they find when they got there?

Looking up, Margo tried to gauge the time. She'd never put much stock in watches but wished she'd had one now. Were the others in place? Had they made it up the path unharmed? Had someone fallen on the way? She wished she knew. "We might move a bit closer," she finally said as she looked back at her daughter.

Following her mother's example, Anwen moved further up the path. They were now within a turning of the City. She rubbed clammy hands against her pants, hoping they would stop shaking. "I think I can safely say this is the most nerve-wracking thing I've ever done," she confessed.

Margo smiled with compassion and took her daughter into her arms. "Whatever battles you are fighting inside--whatever struggles you are facing--just know I have faith in you." She pulled away just enough to look into her eyes. "And remember that you were born for this."

Taking a step or two back, Margo reached for the chain she carried around her neck, pulling it out. The ring she'd fiddled with back at Walter's home dangled from the end. The green gem flashed in the light filtering down into the tunnel-like area. "Your grandmother gave this to me when I turned seventeen," she said with a reminiscent smile. "That's when I knew she was dying."

Anwen looked at her mother with concern. "Mom, are you trying to tell me something?" Horror welled up at the idea of losing her.

Margo took the ring into her hand as she undid the chain's clasp with the other. "I won't coddle you with the idea that there isn't the possibility. We are heading into danger, have been this entire time. But it's where our fates have led us. It's never wise to go against prophecy. People have tried. It didn't end well."

With a sigh, Anwen looked to the ground. Hadn't Tyler said something similar? Or was she remembering things that hadn't happened? A few tears leaked from her eyes. "I don't want to lose you," she confessed. "I finally feel like

I'm beginning to understand you. And what do you do? Talk like you won't make it back alive. You just can't do that, mom."

Holding the ring out to her daughter, the mage only smiled. "We only have so much time given to us in this life," she reminded. "And if it is up to the fates that I am taken, then so be it. But if not, I *will* want this back. In the meantime, you may need it once you get inside the Mountain." She pressed the circular object into Anwen's hands. "This is a relic of the Kaida line. There was only the one made. It is a sign that you are the true and only heir to that title."

Clutching it fiercely in her hand, Anwen hugged her mother with all her being. "I'm not going to say goodbye. I'm not ready for that yet. And who knows," she sniffled, "maybe we all come out of this alive."

Margo stroked her daughter's hair. "Just remember who you are. You are the last Key Keeper. You are my daughter. And somewhere out there," she gestured towards the City," is a dragon who is madly in love with you."

Anwen had to laugh as she sniffled. "How do you know?" Despite her skeptical remark, she felt a warm glow flow through her. The brief image of kissing him came to the surface and she turned slightly red at the memory. Had he kissed her back? She wasn't sure.

Shaking her head, her mother let out a low chuckle. "When you've lived as long as I, and have seen many others in the same circumstance, it's easy to tell. Believe me. He would move heaven and earth for you."

A sudden explosion filled the air, making the ground quake. The loud sound of people crying out all at once filled the air as confusion reigned in the City. "That's our signal," Margo announced as she grabbed her daughter's hand and squeezed it. "Get ready."

Walter counted down the seconds. In one hand he held a

glass ornament filled with his homemade mixture of explosive powder and goo. In the other, he held his watch. His job was to create the initial chaos that would call the mages towards the high-reaching arch. Having reached the appropriate mark, he tossed the crude grenade and ducked. Despite his assurances to Margo that they wouldn't do much, he knew better. Those orbs packed a wallop and he didn't want to be caught in the aftermath.

Not that he had to worry about that. But the resulting flash of light was more than enough to dazzle the eyes of any who looked that way. He resisted the urge to let out a little victory shout as the first tent burst into flames. If that didn't cause confusion, he didn't know what would.

From her location near the top of the arching stone, Courtney held on for dear life. The ground rumbled underneath her, making her perch more than precarious. Whatever Walter had packed into those small balls of glass was potent. She found herself more than ecstatic to not be on the receiving end.

She saw various mages run around like panic-stricken insects drawn to a flame. Except that it was far from comforting as another tent caught fire, then another. She almost giggled but kept it in as she pulled out the orb Walter had given her. She definitely had a new appreciation for the small glass spheres. But now it was her turn.

They'd all decided Courtney could do the most damage if she were somewhere up high. They hadn't seen any guards. As such, Tyler had figured it was the best place for her to enact the next step of their plan. Divide and cause more chaos.

Not even all the way to the top of the arch, Courtney had settled herself as securely as possible. She made sure to still have a decent view of the courtyard inside. Counting down from the initial explosion, she threw her orb with all her might. She added a push of wind behind it to lob it as far into the middle of the tents as possible.

Courtney didn't wait for the explosion before lunging for the next handhold to the top of the archway. "It's a good thing I'm not afraid of heights," she muttered as the blast filled the air with light and sound. The percussive force sent debris upwards in the main square. She had to momentarily shade her eyes as she reached the top of the natural formation.

As soon as her vision cleared, Courtney realized there was a slight flaw in their plans. She wasn't alone.

Josef woke from his stupor at the first concussive blast. Shaking his head, he turned towards the cries of the internal sentries. They were running towards the chaos. Someone had infiltrated the City.

With a feline grace, he vaulted to his feet. The knife Kira had given him came to his hand as if he'd called it. He couldn't see who was behind the explosion, but knew it wasn't part of the plan. And he couldn't let that happen.

He held the blade steady with one hand, ready to pierce his flesh. Then a second blast rocked the ground, sending violent shivers up the stone archway. The knife fell from his fingers. It clattered towards the far side of the foot-wide arch. His eyes went wide in panic. His breath heaved at the possible implications should he lose that knife.

For a brief moment, his true self tried to assert authority over his body, telling him this was all crazy. He shouldn't be there. And why was he so obsessed with a knife? But then the magic binding his soul took over again and he went after the blade.

Struggling up the remaining bit of stone, Courtney let out a gasp. Her opponent was going for a weapon. It only took her a moment to realize who she faced. And for that brief moment, she hesitated. But, knowing what was at stake, she made to ram into the older teen. They couldn't have him interfering with their plans. "Hey guys! I'm going to be a bit busy!" she yelled as she almost tripped on a rock.

Tyler bit back a curse as he followed Walter under the arch. Just in case the villagers hadn't figured out his true nature, he'd opted to stay in his mortal form. At least for the moment. There were plenty of male mages. He just hoped they'd buy the guise for now. It was too soon to pull out the big guns.

But the important point right now was to make sure no one realized they were there. And for that cause, he cast a glamour around himself and Walter as the two entered the main courtyard.

Just as Anwen had described, the stone structures were in a less presentable state. The pillars lining the walkways had been knocked down. The apparent goal had been to widen the courtyard, though most of the tents didn't start until a bit further back. And now a good eight of those tents were on fire, thanks to both Courtney and Walter's efforts. The mages were scrambling to put out the flames. They seemed completely unaware of the two figures who all but marched right into their midst.

Walter nodded to Tyler, a prearranged signal to drop the glamour as he continued on into the string of tents. With all the confusion, he easily blended in with the others. Unlike in a military campaign, he'd opted not to wear the traditional attire. Instead, he wore something that would blend in more with the mages around them. But, if he had to, he could shed his outer layer of clothes to reveal camouflaged long johns.

Disguised as one of the male mages, Walter made his way into the center of the tents, pretending to go for supplies. But when he reached the designated area, he didn't help his supposed compatriots. Instead, he set another tent on fire with a lighter. Then he threw another sphere, aiming towards the far wall. That accomplished, he blended in as best as he could until he could find another place from which to lob his homemade bombs.

TWENTY-FIVE

ANWEN SUCKED IN AIR BETWEEN her teeth and counted to ten, trying to make her pounding heart slow down. The second explosion happened what felt like only a matter of seconds behind the other. The third was their signal to move. She just hoped the others were doing okay. From the sounds behind the façade, she was sure things had gotten a lot more hectic out there. It reminded her of what happened when someone kicked over an anthill. Chaos everywhere.

Her mother continued to hold her hand as she silently counted out from the last explosion. When the third rumble filled the air, she let go of her daughter's hand to rush forward. Margo covered her face and hair with a scarf to try and hide the obvious hints of red. She only had to glance sideways once to confirm Anwen had done the same. "Just try to fit in with the chaos," she reminded, hoping no one else could hear.

The press of the crowd seemed focused on heading towards the initial outburst. Going against the flow would only make them stand out all the more. With a nod, Margo led her daughter in a rather odd zigzag line. It made it seem as though they were following the press of the mages. But, in fact, they were going against it.

Ducking to avoid the notice of one of the higher up mages, Anwen kept close to the wall her mother had led them to. She recognized where they were, not from past experience, but from her dream vision. Things had changed so much that if she'd relied on memory alone, she felt sure she'd be lost in a moment. Nothing looked the same. At least someone seemed to know where they were going.

A sea of tents rose up before them, with people running around them like spooked horses. Many rushed towards the main entrance of the City. Others seemed to be gathering defenses. It was like an insect hive on high alert. How on earth were they to get through this, she wondered

Madame Millard was about to sit down to a cup of tea when the ground shook under her. The tea slopped up the inside of her cup from the unexpected shaking, staining her shirt. Not sure if it was one of the mages trying to get into the Mountain again, or something else, she rose to her feet. "What's going on out there?"

At the sound of her voice, the two guards posted outside her tent all but tore the flap open in their haste. "Someone has attacked the front of the camp!" one cried out. "They're calling for everyone to head in that direction to help."

The master mage thrust past them into the open, wondering what they were talking about. From her vantage, she could see the smoke billowing from near the City's entrance. "Find out what's going on down there!" she ordered.

Before either guard could rush to obey, a second blast shook the stones around them. More smoke billowed up, but from further in. The woman looked about ready to burst a vessel as her face turned a motley color. "Get down there! Now!"

Kira emerged from the neighboring tent, her expression neutral as she glanced at her aunt. "Looks like they're a little early," she observed. "You know what we have to do."

Madame Millard nodded. Leave it to the others to sort out. They had bigger fish to fry. And if she knew anything, she knew exactly where to find them.

Still on the sandstone arch, Courtney somehow managed to avoid falling flat on her face. It was a feat made necessary after tripping on a small protrusion. She pulled out her dragon knife and asked it to extend into a spear. "Stop!" she called out to the once familiar boy. Her breath came in short gasps from her efforts to stop him.

Having realized who he was, she'd tried to ram him, but that had failed epically. She'd managed to send the two of them rolling in different directions. It was a narrow thing managing to avoid falling from the high structure, but she'd somehow managed it. And, for that brief moment, she thanked Margo for her intense training. It had paid off.

But when Josef turned towards her, she realized something was wrong. His eyes were too glazed over to be normal. Something solid dropped in her stomach as she realized why. It was mage work of the darkest kind.

Josef lunged for the thin knife that had fallen from his grasp no more than a minute before. All he had to do was pierce his hand with it and his Daphne would come. That's all it would take. It was the only thought in his head. He reached for the blade, only to have it knocked aside by Courtney's long spear. He turned on her like a feral cat. "Witch!"

The knife clattered down the rock wall, landing next to Tyler. He reached to pick it up but quickly stopped as the metal superheated, causing his skin to burn. He hissed in pain. Instead of taking the blade, he kicked it away. It went skittering along the stones and out of sight.

Caught off guard by Josef's behavior, Courtney found herself thrown back onto the rock. As she landed, the third explosion ripped through the air. Rock crumbled underneath her as Josef launched himself at her like some wild beast. "Josef!" she called out. "Stop this!" Her blade shrank back to knife form as she tried to ward off the boy's attacks.

Josef snarled as he clawed at her face, trying to reach her throat. "No one gets between me and my Daphne," he hissed. "No one!" He grabbed her wrists with one hand so he could reach past them without further trouble. He tried to pin them above her head as he panted in her face with an acrid breath.

Courtney managed to free her arms and pushed back. She thrust at his chin to try and gain some leverage against his massive weight. "Stop it! This isn't like you!" She wondered what had happened to the mild mannered boy. If Daphne hadn't claimed him, she might have been tempted to try and twist him around her own little finger. But no. That was before she'd met Anwen and learned that Tyler was a dragon.

Growling, Josef retaliated by raking suddenly longer than normal nails across her face. Blood splattered from his claws as Courtney's face bled. The feral look in his eye increased as fur began to form along his skin. His bones began to elongate, becoming heavier as they changed.

With heart thudding like crazy, Courtney couldn't help but watch with wide eyes. Was this how a Fallen was formed? Was the Mage Circle so depraved they'd transform a mortal into one of their creatures? A living one at that? Her face stung where the claws had gouged her. A small part of her mind focused on fixing the damage while she tried to figure out how to get out of this situation.

Josef's teeth elongated in his changing mouth. They dripped saliva that burned as it hit the mage's skin. He continued to claw at her, held back only by the failing strength of her arms. If only he could get his teeth next to her throat, then it would be over and he could go find his missing blade.

With a scream of pain and rage, Courtney focused her energy into the knife she still held in one hand. Turning it to just the right angle, she willed the blade to extend. With a rush of air, the blade changed shape, pushing the creature from her, and toppled him over the side. There was a thud as the half Fallen hit the ground below.

Breathing heavily, Courtney took a moment to focus on closing her wounds. She silently thanked Margo for teaching her the basic art of healing. Shaking, she took to her feet and prepared to send out her barrage against the growing mass of mages below.

Tyler almost felt like he was wading through a dream. In that state, he used his abilities to maim and sometimes kill the mages milling around him. To him, it as though the crazed villagers moved around him like molasses. His nature made it more than easy to flow around his foes like quicksilver. He didn't want to kill any more than he had to. The majority of the mages were not truly bad. But there sure were a lot of them.

Off to one side, Walter lobbed another of his homemade bombs, sending up a series of glass shrapnel and fire. The distraction this caused gave Tyler all the advantage he needed. He swept through another group of mages like a hot knife through butter. They were so distracted by the chaos that he incapacitated them with ease.

Knocking one mage to the ground, Tyler ducked to avoid another one of Walter's homemade bombs. It sailed through the air, narrowly missing his head. The glass orbs were small enough they weren't too noticeable. Their coloring was also less obvious than the ornaments he usually used on his holiday tree.

Tyler took a moment to look ahead. Seeing past the others with his Dragon Sight, he hoped to catch a glimpse of Anwen and her mother. With luck, they'd made their way to the Gates by now. Whether it was because of some kind of interference, or something else, he couldn't see them. But he could feel Anwen's heart beat pounding out with his and knew that, at least for now, she was safe. He prayed it would stay that way.

When Madame Millard seemed less inclined to join the others, Maggie Mintaw took over. Let the master mage do her thing, but Maggie would be the one whose lauds would be sung over the centuries.

"We're obviously dealing with a decent-sized group," Maggy told her compatriots. "They want to divide us by throwing everything in chaos. We must not let them."

The other mages of the Inner Circle nodded in agreement. Their people were running around like mindless zombies, with no one leading them. That had to change.

"You will take charge of your individual districts and bring order to this chaos!" the elder mage demanded. "And I will personally join you while our more cowardly leader hides in the hills."

Cries of agreement and outrage filled the small gathering. They broke into their respective groups as Maggy waved them off. Order would be brought to the fight below. They would find those who dared defy the Circle and make an example of them. And if they found the Key Keeper or the Kaida among the mix, well, their reward would be more than ample.

TWENTY-SIX

AT ANWEN'S SUGGESTION, SHE AND her mother ducked out of sight. They hid behind the last stone structure standing outside the amphitheater courtyard. Peering out at the moving mass of people down in the main courtyard, she felt glad they had. Even more mages were headed towards the far entrance, leaving the path to the Gates more open. But was it a trap? Or had the others created that great of a distraction? It was hard to tell.

Margo watched the villagers with discerning eyes, calculating and reasoning their behavior. They'd passed the master mage's tent without incident. They'd made sure to keep as far back from it as possible. The Fallen Anwen had seen there in her dream weren't visible and they both wondered at that. Perhaps they had joined the fray.

"Put the ring on," Margo instructed her daughter, realizing she'd only put it in her pocket. "I don't want you to lose it in the melee to come."

It didn't take much to realize her mother's advice was sound. Anwen did as asked and slid the green-gemmed circle onto her finger. She felt tingling as the stone came to rest just above the final knuckle. "I haven't seen Madame Millard," she whispered. "Shouldn't we have seen her?"

Margo shook her head. "I don't know. But we should be cautious. She might not have fallen for the ruse." She planted a kiss on her daughter's forehead. "May the dragons protect you." Looking around one last time, she pulled at her daughter's hand. "Let's go."

Dashing past what had once been an alley, the two reached the ruined half-oval of the amphitheater. It was there that Anwen had seen her possible future in the Dust. They both turned away from the broken columns and headed towards the winding path to the Gates instead.

"Get the key ready," Margo huffed as they ran. "You must get in as fast as you can. I'll close the doors behind you, though they won't be locked. I'll try to delay any who come near for as long as I can."

Nodding, Anwen pulled the chain from around her neck. She clasped the folded wings of the dragon-shaped key in her hand. Dust pounded underfoot as they ran on, winding up the Mountain path for all they were worth.

Overhead, a shadow swooped past the sun, though neither turned to look and see what had caused it. The goose flesh on the back of their necks was more than enough. Just ahead, the Gates looked like silent stone sheered smooth. Though unsealed, they stood firmly locked against those who would intrude beyond them.

Lunging forward, Anwen thrust the key into the hidden hole they'd found only a week or so ago. With a quick turn, light flowed around the cracks, outlining the double-doors. With one final turn, the doors flew open, spewing compressed air outward.

"In! Get in!" Margo shouted as the shadows outside the massive hall darkened. She thrust her daughter forward as Anwen removed the key, not giving her a chance to pocket the crystal. With a great bout of concentration, she willed the doors to close behind the teen. Her daughter was now alone inside.

The massive slabs of rock shuddered at the Kaida's command, leaving no trace of an opening behind. Margo turned as the dust settled, knowing it wouldn't take much to open them now they were unlocked.

A deep growling sound came from the path leading back to the City. "Hello, cousin," she said, steel in her eyes. "I knew you would come."

Courtney looked down at the destruction below. Tyler and Walter had done a fantastic job of making a chaotic scene. But was it enough? She reached for the pouch she'd managed to keep secure during her fight with Josef. Inside, she found one of the many pine cones she'd stashed there.

With an indrawn breath, she held it aloft like she was about to pitch a ball for a game. "Here goes nothing," she whispered and hurled the object over the fighting mass below. Just as on the Island, this one exploded into thousands of splintery shards. Those shards sped towards the fleshy targets below.

Screams ensued from those hit by the fiery projectiles. Some went down as they hit more vital spots, such as eyes or spaces between legs. Others danced around as their clothes erupted in flames. Courtney lobbed a few more, adding to the panic before ducking out of sight.

The blond imagined this must be what it felt to be in a war zone. But, despite that, she felt a sense of euphoria at being a part of the force creating the chaos. If what Walter had told her was true, she'd need to change positions soon. That or she'd have to find a way to make her pine cone projectiles appear to come from a different location. It was too bad she didn't have some kind of animal to bear her to a different location.

Keeping in mind the need to maintain some semblance of sanity, Courtney slid down the archway. She aimed to land near the outside edge of the City, more to the left where a tumble of boulders lay. There, she could hide from preying eyes. Most of the mages were occupied with the insanity from the tents. She even saw a few Fallen in the mix.

Courtney braked at the last minute, preventing a potentially disastrous situation. Another mage had rushed to the gates. She'd probably thought to bottle the potential of more enemies entering the City. But she'd come about at the completely wrong time.

With a yell, Courtney launched herself at the woman, tackling her to the ground. She rolled to her feet in an instant, lashing out as the mage fought back. She didn't know the woman's name. She just knew she was from the village.

The mage fought back, pulling her own weapon to bear. It looked like some kind of spiked club. She wielded it like a baseball bat, swinging with a speed any normal mortal would kill for. Her movements sent Courtney dancing to avoid getting hit.

"Man, what I wouldn't give for that simulacrum now," Courtney said under her breath. "Sure would make this easier!" With that, she threw herself at her opponent with a frenzy. She could not afford to lose.

Looking up at the sound of Courtney yelling, Tyler narrowly avoided being hit by a flying object. It was another one of Walter's orbs as it sailed past. The dragon couldn't help but notice his friend as he followed the path back to his hiding place.

He kicked at the legs of his nearest foe. This sent the mage to her back as he moved to distract their attention away from Walter's position. The veteran was doing well for himself, but he'd stayed in one place too long, gathering a bit of crowd.

The somewhat grizzled mortal threw another of his homemade grenades and ran for cover. He rolled and ducked as necessary to stay out of sight. But the press of people was making it difficult. And knowing his location had been compromised didn't help matters. He took the risk of smashing another bomb almost at his own feet to create more confusion so he could get away.

Several of the glass shards embedded in his arm. He let out a low grunt as he dropped behind one of the toppled buildings to catch his breath. Smoke rose from all around him, making it harder and harder to see. But even with the melee of people around, he felt sure none were of the higher ranks. None of them were fighting on the level Margo had.

But their screams sent his mind reeling back to the combat he'd seen years ago. It was something no one ever really got over. And it took an effort to draw his mind back to the present.

Tyler spotted his friend and created a whirlwind of dust and stone to cover him. The dirt devil swept the lower ranking mages and Fallen away from the area. He rode the center until he could drop neatly down by the man. "You okay?" he yelled over the maelstrom.

Walter nodded as he checked to make sure none of his other toys were damaged. "Do you think Anwen's made it inside yet? I could sure use a break!"

Letting his eyes lose their focus for a moment as he concentrated, Tyler nodded. "Yes. I think she's inside. But I sense something out of place. I can't say just what though." He refocused on the scene around him, his expression grim. "I don't like it."

TWENTY-SEVEN

MADAME MILLARD STOOD SEVERAL YARDS back from the closed gates. She now wore the ceremonial robes of the Inner Circle, made from enough cloth to make a small tent. The rich purple fabric fluttered around her. A twisted smile ripped her face as she smirked. "After all these years," she said. "After all this time, you finally return. It is just as prophecy foretold."

Margo looked rather unimpressed as she placed both hands on her hips. "And which prophecy are you referring to? After all, there are a great many."

"This one." The matriarch's eyes seemed to glaze just a bit as she began to recite. "*Open once, a spell undone. Open twice, for the Dragon Born. Open thrice, an era to end. Open all, the Kaida return by the light of the Mage's Moon.*"

Resisted the urge to roll her eyes, Margo considered the woman before her. "Ah, you mean that prophesy. Well, I guess it's come at least partially true. The Gates have been opened twice now. And here I stand, one Dragon Born. But then, aren't you one too?" She gave her a shrewd look.

A twisted smile spread across the older woman's lips. "Ah. You would see the irony, wouldn't you? By the way, where is the Key Keeper? I know you couldn't open the Gates on your own. Not even my best mages have been able to do that. Where have you hidden the Porter girl? The Gates cannot be sealed with her inside."

Shrugging, Margo said nothing. Instead, she reached towards her pocket where she kept a bone knife similar to Courtney's. It was an older blade, one she'd kept hidden for many years, even from her husband. Until the time was right. "It is the Hour of the Mage," she finally replied. "Who knows what that means for the girl? Perhaps the mages of long ago have spirited her away where neither of us will find her."

Madame Millard waved an impatient hand. "You speak nonsense, just as your grandmother did. It's a pity she left our valley with your mother. We would have welcomed you both into the Circle."

Margo resisted the urge to laugh. The only way they'd have accepted her into their society was as either a slave or willing participant. There was no way either would have happened. She knew her mother and her grandmother would have ended the line rather than let that happen.

"I believe you came here with more of a purpose than to just goad me into a fight," Margo pressed as she moved closer. "Or are you really as defenseless as you look?"

The dark mage frowned at those words. "Defenseless? How dare you! When I have finished with you, all will know me as the master of all mages! I will pass on the title of Kaida to its rightful owner! And together we will rule over all the dragons!"

Margo Pack stared at the proprietress. "You're mad. You know as well as I where the rightful line ends. And if the Mountains will that Line to end for good this night, then so be it." With that, the Kaida lunged towards the master mage, her blade elongating into a shape of a sword.

Anwen knelt in total darkness. The moment her mother had closed the doors, she'd felt cut off from everything she'd ever known. It was so dark she couldn't see, wondering why the Soul Sight she'd had earlier wasn't working. Quelling a momentary bout of panic, she took in a deep breath. It took a moment to remember to give herself a count to one hundred before doing anything else.

As she counted, she noticed it was not quite as dark as she'd first supposed. It was almost as if the barest amount of light made the air shimmer like the fuzz on a television, only much darker. She reached out a hand, trying to see if there was anything in front of her. As she passed her hand in front of her face, she could almost make out the shape of her fingers. They were tinged with a faint glow.

The secret to using your abilities is to realize everything is made up of matter.

For a brief bout of time, Margo had tried to instruct her daughter on the basics of mage skill. Considering they'd been walking up the winding path to the City, it hadn't gone well. But Anwen tried to remember everything her mother had said anyway. As well as everything she'd heard the others say about it.

When I make my bone knife grow, I just ask it to and it does, Courtney had told her when she'd asked.

Was that the key? To ask? She remembered hearing one of the reasons those of the Circle had become corrupted. It had something to do with forcing matter to form to their desires, instead of asking. Was that how the Fallen were created? From forcing nature against itself? But how did any of that apply to her now?

Everything was made of matter, she reminded herself. Even light. Thinking about that, she reached out again. She tried to grasp the little particles that floated before her vision. "Glow," she said, wondering if that would work. "Please glow."

The faintest of light orbs formed in front of her. It shed enough light that she could make out the floor around her for about a yard or two. Was it enough? She felt almost giddy at the small success and wasn't at all sure she could improve on it. Daphne had been right that it would take more than a basic knowledge to master her craft. She thought she heard a faint hint of laughter at that thought.

But was it really enough to see where she was going? The main hall was vast. She remembered that much. But, perhaps if she looked around a bit more…. She looked down and saw the dusty ground disturbed by their initial footprints. Maybe if she followed them, she could at least find her way across the vast expanse that was the front gallery. From there, she would have to hope her dream from before would come back and help her.

Courtney grunted with exertion. The mage she fought didn't want to go down. She let out a yell of outrage when her opponent got through her guard and managed to throw her to the ground. This wasn't supposed to happen, she thought. How on earth did she get involved in a one-on-one death match with an older mage? Okay, it was a silly question, but she still couldn't help but ask the ether.

With a bit more effort than she'd care to admit, the fledgling mage flipped back to her feet. She moved just in time to avoid being impaled by the other mage's conjured spear. This was getting old and fast. But at least this woman didn't have quite the skill level Margo did. There was at least that.

"I'm getting sick and tired of people picking on me!" Courtney yelled as she reached for one of her pine cones. In a fluid motion, she threw it at her opponent. She pivoted on her heel at the last possible second to shield herself from the blast.

The pine cone exploded like a grenade. Tiny thorns raced out in all directions. Like hundreds of little darts, they pierced everything in their path. Both mages screamed as the projectiles embedded in their flesh. For

Courtney, they hit her back. But the other mage was not as lucky. Her entire front area was peppered with red-hot spikes, including her face.

Concentrating, Courtney willed the thorns in her back to escape harmlessly to the ground. Despite her efforts, the wounds stung like nothing she'd ever experienced. She could well understand the reactions of the mage before her as the woman crumbled to the ground in agony. But she had no time to try and soothe over the pain. The others needed her.

Not bothering to look back at the mage writhing on the ground, Courtney vaulted over a low stone. She raced like a panther to find the rest of her friends.

Chaos reigned below as Kira stood atop a shelf above the closed Gates. They were all pathetic. She could see exactly what Courtney and her friends were doing. Divide. Distract. And hopefully buy enough time for their precious Kaida to do something heroic. It wouldn't work.

Kira began her preparations. Fate was on their side, or her side, rather. To capture the soul of the Kaida would surely end dragon kind. It was a goal she and her associates had worked towards for a really long time. It was a pity the stupid matriarch of that so called Mage Circle would have to go down with them. She had been a useful tool.

Standing almost majestically above the Gates, she swept her arms out in a wide circle. While Madame Millard kept the Kaida distracted, she could enact all the appropriate rites without any trouble. And with the other mages distracted down in the City, she feared no interference.

Overhead, the sun shown down, pelting across her slender shoulders. But she didn't notice as she pulled out the ritual dagger and raked it across her left palm. Dark blood oozed up from the long gash. She let it gather in her hand until she could transfer it into the chalice at her feet. With the requisite amount of fluid, she bound her wound with a tight cloth and bent over the cup.

Chanting strange words, the contents of the goblet began to froth, as though coming to a thick boil. Now standing, Kira completed a complicated set of whirls around the area. She used her movement to inscribe a circle with eerie light flowing from her fingers. Energy partially drained, she slumped to the ground. She needed to rest until it was time to move to the next part of the ceremony.

After what felt like forever, Anwen stood before the five massive archways that led off to different parts of the underground city. The far left was the one she and Tyler had taken when they'd come that first time. The one just to the right of that was the one they'd come back out of. Or so she assumed from the multiple sets of prints leading away.

Pacing in front of the collection of open spaces, Anwen felt more than intimidated. She paused, trying to remember which one the dream vision had taken her down. Why couldn't she remember?

Shaking her head, she turned towards the far right opening. Was it this one? It might be that one. They all looked the same, which definitely didn't help matters. Why couldn't she remember?

She felt a slight tugging behind her eyes and turned to the next over, just to the left. It was almost as if a waft of air had come from that vast hallway and whispered, *"This way."* Somewhat encouraged, Anwen moved towards the dark opening. Her weak orb followed just above her head like a lost balloon.

Dust kicked into the air as she walked. Small stones skittered ahead as the path began to descend and curve. Several passages opened up on either side but she continued down the main way. Coming to another crossroads, she stopped to assess her location.

Ahead, there were seven different choices, minus going

back. Each branched off the slightly oval chamber she'd entered. Various figures were carved above each doorway. Unfortunately, she couldn't make them out in the faltering light.

Closing her eyes, she tried to retrace the steps from her dream. Had she come across such a room? It was hard to tell. "When in doubt, stop and think about it," she told herself as she settled into the dirt to meditate.

TWENTY-EIGHT

MARGO STOOD WITH HER BONE blade at the ready, waiting to see what Madame Millard would do. So far the woman only seemed to be full of boastings. When she'd lunged for the other mage, the woman had merely side-stepped the attack. "Didn't you come to try and persuade me to join you? Or, maybe, to seek my life? If either be the case, there is only one way. Raise your weapon."

The overweight woman sneered. "Very well, then," she responded as she reached into the inner pocket of her robes. "If that is how you wish it to be, I am more than happy to oblige." With the speed of someone half her size, the upper mage lunged towards Anwen's mother. Her intent was clear. She wanted blood.

"That's more like it!" Margo encouraged as she moved to counter the woman's efforts. "Show me the skill others boast so much about. I've been dying for a good fight for some time now."

Madame Millard let out a cry of rage. "You dare goad me? You left us! You forsook us! And now you expect us to just bow down to you because you return to the Mountain? Never!" She lashed out again, holding her blade as one accustomed to fighting in close quarters. Dark stains glared out from the polished surface.

But Margo only laughed. "Who is goading whom?" She parried the other's blade, moving to circle around the enclosed area. While there was room for a good-sized dragon to stand, the space was small for a duel. "Besides, your kind forced us out! With your thirst for vengeance on a wrong never committed! It's your greed that has become your undoing."

Her words seemed to spark a maniacal fire inside the master mage. "You will regret those words!" She lashed out with her weapon, moving at a much quicker speed.

Things were starting to get quite warm, Walter decided as he raced to another hidey hole. Most of the tents were on fire, and yet the mages still came. And he'd run out of glass grenades. Not having packed any guns, he went to his next weapon of choice, a sling shot. "Man, this takes me back," he said to himself.

Off to one side, Tyler seemed to flow like quicksilver, though even his pace was slowing down. Whether from fatigue or a desire to conserve his strength was anyone's guess. And he had yet to transform into his true form.

One mage moved to cut off the dragon lord, sneaking up on him from behind a protrusion of rock. Walter saw him and launched a quarter-inch marble. The glass orb hit the man in the back of the head with enough force to knock him forward.

Tyler spun to knock the mage off his feet. He offered a brief salute of thanks before moving back into the melee. The time to transform was coming, but his thoughts were still preoccupied. Something smelled foul on the air. It was a stench he'd only smelled once before, he was sure. But despite that recollection, he still couldn't remember what had caused it.

Out of the corner of his eye, he saw a female mage try to sneak up on his friend. With a motion so smooth it almost couldn't be followed by mortal eyes, he picked up a stone from the ground. With the rock in hand, he threw it. The projectile hit its target with deadly accuracy.

Walter took that opportunity to run for different cover. Part of him wished he'd thought to bring a pellet gun but he hadn't. Instead, he let fly more marbles, wondering how long his supply would last.

Somewhat restored from her previous fatigue, Kira stood from her crouched position. She held the cup in one hand. The contents had turned to a dull red powder. She smiled in satisfaction before setting it back down. Then she rummaged in her volumous pockets. She pulled out a small ceramic bottle with a cork stopper.

"Ashes of the fallen," she intoned as she removed the soft wood from the bottle's mouth. Tipping the open end over the chalice, fine ashes poured into the bell end of the vessel. She stirred the two powders together with one finger. The resulting mixture was a dark muddy color.

Once more, Kira held the goblet high in the air, intoning words in a strange tongue. Thunder seemed to crackle through the air, though there was no lightning. Looking below, she saw the occasional explosion from the main courtyards of the Ruined City. She only hoped the extra noise her spell-casting created would be ignored. Perhaps they'd consider it part of those pyrotechnics down below.

When she lowered the chalice, the contents had solidified into something like coal. She took the lump and tossed the cup aside. Its purpose was fulfilled.

Anwen continued to sit with her eyes closed. Thinking back on the dream, she tried to remember the route. How had it gone? This was becoming more than annoying. It was a problem she had to fix and fast.

"Maybe you should just give it a rest already," Daphne's voice bubbled up in the darkness. "I will give you points for that pathetic display of magery. Or do I dare actually call that orb a light?" She laughed as her ghostly image came into being.

With a heavy sigh, Anwen opened her eyes. "Daphne." She ground her teeth just a little. "Don't you ever get tired of bugging me? Surely you have better things to do."

The specter shrugged as she paced the oval chamber, leaving no prints behind. "I have all the time in the world, something you don't have. My aunt has already begun her preparations for the final outcome. Neither you nor your friends can escape it. Just accept it already. You've lost."

Drumming her fingers, Anwen tried to recompose herself. "Not yet," she replied. "I have until midnight."

Daphne snorted. "Midnight? Hah! You have until the moon rises. And that will be way before midnight. Besides, do you really think you can find your way through this labyrinth before then? Or that your friends will keep off the full might of the Circle? I don't think so. Give it up already. The Gates aren't really sealed. Once they figure that out, it will all be over."

Anwen did her best to ignore her, closing her eyes against the ghostly image. Unbidden, the thought of Kern came into her mind. "Grandfather," she pleaded, not sure why she was calling out to him. "Help me."

The ghostly mage snorted. "The Nurrim cannot help you now," she taunted. "You're done and just don't know it. Now let me show you some real magic." The mage began some kind of incantation. But before she could finish, a rush of wind filled the void. It sent Daphne's incorporeal body into the dark recesses of space.

The breeze continued to flow through the chamber. It scattered Anwen's light orb like embers in a fire. The air drew those embers towards the furthest doorway, like flotsam caught in a stream. And there they remained, as though held by some net against the storm.

Anwen looked up in time to see a different swirling mass of energy sweep down towards that passageway. She ran to follow. It was like trying to chase lightning, but she did her best. Following the flow of energy, she passed many other open doorways, along with a few pitfalls.

After madly chasing the light, Anwen slowed down as the energy flowered up into a frenzy of light above her head. The reflected glow showed that she'd reached some kind of anteroom. On the other side of the maelstrom of whizzing atoms, a set of double doors stood, waiting to open.

As Anwen moved towards the doors, the energy around her coalesced into the form of a dragon lord she knew all too well. She stopped to stare at the humanoid form. "Kern," she breathed.

The dragon lord bowed slightly, his long robes brushing against the floor. *Well met, Fair Little Dragon*, he said. *I bring you to the doors. Beyond this point, you are truly on your own. I will not be able to help you. In truth, it has taken all that I have left to help you. Unless you succeed, I will be no more. Remember the words given you on the Island. The Word will come to you at the right moment.*

The simulacrum began to fall apart in front of her, like falling rain. She ran towards the scattering energy. Reaching out her hands to touch him, she came up with empty hands. The Mountain trembled.

TWENTY-NINE

COURTNEY FELT HER FOOTING SLIP as the ground suddenly quaked. She lost hold of her last pine cone as she tried to grab at any protrusion that could save her from falling.

Hitting the hard stone, she let out a shriek. Something snapped. Pain flared out along her right arm and shoulder as she rolled down towards the open area of the main courtyard.

All around her, mages fell to the ground and covered their heads and ears. It was as if some kind of supersonic sound had brought them to their knees. From the masses, one Fallen stumbled free. It sniffed towards the far wall where Tyler had kicked a dagger at the beginning of the battle.

The blond mage watched the creature as it snuffled around with its nose, unable to stop it. It somehow found the weapon and took it in its teeth. It settled the blade between two crags of stone so the sharp end pointed upward. With an almost manic look in its eyes, it thrust its paw down onto the blade.

A scream of pain and rage filled the air, causing Kira to smile. It was about time. She turned towards the sound of the anguish and saw a pillar of swirling ash. She knew the ash had once been Josef. A sacrifice had to be made, after all. And since Daphne was dead, there was nothing left for that boy to live for. It had been a kindness really.

She bent back down, scribbling symbols on the stone shelf she'd stood on through the whole ordeal. The circle was almost complete. She finished it with a flourish of scrawls and ancient lettering. When she was finished, she moved back, taking care to not smudge the lines.

The whirlwind of ash continued to move upward. It coalesced into a flying funnel of energy as it moved across the sky. It no longer touched the ground as it flew towards her. It drew the attention of the two mages fighting just below her.

Margo stared in horror as the dark matter centered on the shelf above her and her foe. Why had she not noticed the girl's presence there? "No!" She put her hands out in defiance, her blade falling from her fingers.

Anwen stumbled into the door as the Mountain shook. Something had happened outside; she was sure, though she didn't have any idea what. Under the press of her weight, the doors creaked open, dumping her onto the floor. Dust flew up into the air as she hit the ground. The fine particles made her cough and it took some moments before she could bring it under control.

When she looked up, she gasped in surprise. There was no need for a light orb here, not that she was sure she could conjure another one anyway. Energy pulsed like a lamp, spreading uneven light across the expanse. Standing, she accidentally sent a stone skittering across the floor. The resulting echo filled the vast space before her.

Massive pillars held up the ceiling where the living crystal pulsed like a heart. The still forms of dragons lined the length of the seemingly endless hall. There were more than she'd be able to count in a lifetime. And she felt there were even more that she couldn't see beyond those there.

With wide eyes, she stood and stepped further into the space before her. It almost felt like the floor was vibrating underneath her as she moved. The air was thick with expectation. Was she supposed to go to a specific place in the chamber? Or did it matter?

Deep inside these walls they sleep. Only One may enter the Keep. Find the Heart and speak the Word. Only then will your voice be heard.

Taking a deep breath, Anwen continued forward. She headed towards the massive crystal in the center. It felt like it would take forever to reach it.

From the ruins of the buildings in the main square, Walter peered out. The quake had rattled him but he'd managed to stay upright. "What happened? What's going on?" he called out to Tyler.

The dragon lord faced the peak, his expression grim. "I fear the mages are playing their last, dangerous card. This does not bode well." He looked towards the base of the Mountain, lower down from the main gates. "Anwen, you must hurry. You're running out of time."

Something had changed, and he wasn't sure if it was in a good way or not. Then his attention was pulled in another direction. A pillar of ash swirled upwards from near the stone archway. His eyes widened in horror at the realization of what had happened. But he could not bring himself to feel anything more than pity for the soul whose life had been claimed.

He turned his attention back to the Mountain peak and his heart almost stopped. Someone stood above the Gates. Someone who looked a lot like Daphne. He shook his head in denial. "No. It can't be."

Walter moved to look in the same direction his friend did. Though his eyes were not as good, he could still make out the outline of someone standing atop the stone. "Can't be who?"

Tyler only shook his head in denial. "It can't be her. She's dead."

The veteran moved to join Tyler but stopped. Several of the mages were coming out of their shock. And while he wanted to be by his friend, he knew someone had to keep the enemy busy. "Go," Walter urged. "Do whatever you need to do."

But before Tyler could so much as think about going and stopping the girl, Mr. Millard moved into view. "I know what you are!" he called out to the teen. "And even if you try to stop what's going on up there, you won't make it in time."

The dragon lord focused his attention on the man. This was the person responsible for Anwen's father's death. This was the man who had hunted down Keeper after Keeper. Not only had he hunted them down, but he'd killed them for no other reason than to keep the Mountain sealed. This man had caused enough death and suffering.

White hot anger filled his breast. "It was you!" Tyler's eyes took on a steely quality as he stared the man down. "You will pay for what you have done to Anwen." With that, he launched himself at the male mage.

Kira crowed in triumph as Josef's ashes spun inside the circle she'd made with blood and dragon ashes. And now the ashes of a mortal were trapped inside, compressing into a long, thin shape. The blackened material absorbed the circle. It seemed to draw the material into itself as the metallic darkness glowed like a heated forge.

There was nothing anyone could do to stop her now. The spell was all but complete. No more incantations were necessary at this stage. The ashes need only continue to harden. They compressed themselves like folded steel in a forge. And the resulting weapon could strip the soul from any living flesh.

From below, Margo shielded her eyes against the glare. She felt the energy surging around the dark shaft. "What have you done?" She turned to her cousin who stood staring in shock. She took the woman by the robes and shook her. "What have you done?"

But Madame Millard seemed incapable of answering the question. Let alone having a coherent thought. Her eyes were fixated on her niece as the girl raised her arms in victory over the masses below her. "Kira," she breathed with unbelieving eyes. This wasn't how the spell was supposed to go. Something had definitely gone wrong.

THIRTY

ANWEN FELL TO THE FLOOR OF the chamber, which vibrated more and more with each step she took. Soon her entire body was vibrating. It made the air shimmer and shake, tiny molecules of matter dancing around in the odd light. She almost felt like she was being taken apart and rebuilt from the inside out.

"Find the Heart and speak the Word," she whispered as she drew closer to the crystal. All around, stone-like statues of various dragons kept a silent watch of her progress. Despite their presence, she felt small and alone. "I don't belong here," she told herself. "What can I doing anyway? Maybe Daphne was right."

Thinking about just turning around, the image of her mother entered Anwen's thoughts. From there, the words she's spoken outside the Mountain came to mind. *Just remember who you really are. You are the last Key Keeper. You are my daughter.*

Anwen looked down at the ring around her finger. The green gem seemed to sparkle in the low light. *You are my daughter.* Tears leaked from her eyes as she thought about everything that had led up to this point. As the images flashed through her head, her clenched hand tightened.

"No," she declared. "Mom's right. I am more than just some person who stumbled into a bad deal. I am the last of the Key Keepers. I am the heir to the Kaida name. And somewhere out there is a dragon who I'm madly in love with. I won't let it end here!"

With this declaration, Anwen strode forward. She headed directly towards the area she remembered from her dream. Once, a long time ago, a sword had been forged there, from the crystal that once more hung around her neck. Her footsteps echoed around the chamber as she moved, dust kicking into the air.

Having reached the place where the forge had stood, Anwen paused to look around. The tingling in her bones continued to grow stronger. She felt as though the hairs on her head were standing on end. She was almost there.

Walking further, she noticed the largest of dragons turned towards the crystal. He appeared to be composed of white marble, but there was no mistaking the majestic curves and lines. This was Kern. And to his left stood the silver-green dragon she'd come to think of as one of his lieutenants. She had arrived.

Tyler felt the inner urge to transform growing. He didn't need his Dragon Sight to realize what was going on by the Gates. A dark aura flooded the area. But he couldn't do anything about it as Mr. Millard attacked him like a mad man.

Looking off to one side, he could barely see Courtney as she lay against the stone floor. She was still trying to defend herself, even though he could tell she was hurt. Walter had disappeared, but he heard the sound of one of his projectiles hitting home. How much time had passed since he'd silently called out to Anwen to hurry? A few seconds? Several minutes? Hours? He wasn't sure.

With the press of Mr. Millard's attacks, he found it hard to concentrate on much else. Tyler's anger rose to surface. "Enough!" He let out a mighty roar as he picked up a shard of rock and asked it to transform according to his needs. With a well-aimed throw, he pinned Mr. Millard to the ground with the stone spear. The man's blood spilled to the ground from the wound in his chest.

"To the Gates!" Tyler cried out as he flew into the crowd of recovering mages. He didn't look back

Anwen couldn't help but look up in awe as she stared at Kern's immobile face. Even trapped in stone, there was something regal and majestic about the Nurrim. And his size. It was more than enough to make any mortal quake. Even her dreams of him hadn't prepared her for the reality of his dimensions.

"Speak the Word," she reminded herself in a whisper. "What's the Word, though?" She looked around, as if it might be written somewhere. But there were no words written that she could understand.

The Word will come to you, Kern had said. But where was the Word?

"Calm your mind and listen. Having Soul Sight is not nearly enough. You must still be able to listen and hear."

Tyler had told her that after she'd told him about her dreams and the continued oddity with her vision. She knew he'd been telling her something important. *Calm your mind.*

Taking a deep breath, Anwen closed her eyes. *It is the Hour of the Mage*, a tiny voice said from her memories. Who was that child? Focus. She tried to quiet her thoughts.

Daphne would have rejoiced over their being so scattered. But then Anwen came to a realization. Daphne didn't exist. She was only a creation of her fears. She only existed if Anwen let her. She had power over her and her own mind. Anwen could be anything she wanted to be. And she wanted to be at peace.

Opening her eyes, Anwen felt something strange inside. It was almost like mirth bubbling over, but ten times more powerful. Nor did she feel the desire to laugh. But it was a glorious feeling, one she'd definitely never felt before. It was warm and free.

A blue glow shone from the chain around her neck and she pulled out the pendant. The key dangled in front of her eyes as she stared at the glowing crystal. Had she looked at herself in a mirror, she would have realized her eyes were alight with a golden hue.

The blue crystal clinked against her mother's ring as Anwen clasped it in her hand. She removed the chain from around her neck. Green light flashed from the circle around her finger. That light mingled with the light from the key shining through her fingers.

Anwen turned back to face the Nurrim, the key held high in one hand like a torch. Unbidden, words came to her mind. "Enhad ma taneen. Enhad!"

The sound of rumbling filled the air as the ground shook. Anwen was thrown to the ground. Dust and stones seemed to fall like rain. She had to cover her head to keep from breathing it in. Curled in fetal position, she did not see the stone statues begin to move. They shook off an outer layer of rock and precious stones.

Roar after roar filled the massive chamber, echoing through the vast cavern. The sound was so loud Anwen felt as though her ears would never hear again.

THIRTY-ONE

KIRA STRODE FORWARD AND TOOK the massive spear she'd conjured from its place in the air. The ashes and blood had come to rest, creating the massive weapon. The sound of thunder filled the sky as she took hold of the spear, twirling it in one hand. Lightning flashed down from the sky.

A cruel smile cracked across Kira's face as she moved towards the shelf's edge. As she moved, her body began to transform. Dark scales formed up and down her arms and legs as they extended in a disjointed way.

At the sound of thunder, Margo turned from the solemn woman she'd been shaking. It seemed as though the sky had darkened significantly in the last few seconds. A massive shape towered up from the rocks, grotesque and unnatural. The elongated limbs were something out of nightmare. The creature's head looked as though it came from the deepest pits of hell, with eyes that glowed a livid red. And in its hands, a massive spear of black ebony sat poised, ready to be hurled into the air.

"Puny mortals," Kira's voice issued from the creature's mouth. Only it didn't sound quite like Kira's voice anymore. It was deeper, darker, and seemed to echo around the stone City, or what was left of it. It was almost as if her soul had been wrenched from her body and was forcefully put into something else. The agony of a thousand deaths echoed in her words. "You thought to use me. And now you are the ones to die."

Hearing those words, Madame Millard trembled. Hesitating, she looked up with horror as her face went dead white. Her knees gave out from under her and she went down. "Deceiver," she whispered through a voice suddenly much older.

Laughter filled the air as Kira tilted her head back. More lightning flickered across the sky. "Who was trying to deceive whom? I have always been what I am. But you were too stupid to understand or realize what you were dealing with. And for your ignorance, you will die. Along with the Kaida. Once I have consumed your souls, I will destroy the dragons and balance will be restored."

Margo shielded her eyes, her own knees feeling weak. She turned towards the pathetic woman who shared blood with her. "How could you not have known? You idiot! Do you know what that is?!"

The master mage trembled with fear. "It's a…It's a…" she stuttered, trying to utter the word. Her blood ran cold at the thought, but she finally got it out. "A Revenant."

Tyler felt the world fall away from him as the ground trembled below. But before he could make any true sense of what was happening, he saw lightning rip through the sky. Towering over the Gates stood one whom he'd learned to fear. His heart felt cold as he realized what the creature was doing. It was the darkest of magic, beyond the capacity of a mortal mage. He'd never seen such a ritual practiced before but recognized it from descriptions out of the ancient books.

White-hot anger burned inside him once more, causing the air to ripple with the heat. Those mages who had swarmed to stop his progress to the Gates fell back as the temperature increased. With a mighty roar, Tyler transformed into his dragon self. Pushing off, he flapped his massive wings to gain altitude. The upsweep of his wings sent mages and debris flying around him. They meant to harm Anwen and her mother. He would not let them.

"Enhad, Kaida."

The words seemed to echo in Anwen's head as she cowered. Was the ground still shaking? Was the loud rumbling still going on? She couldn't tell. Her entire body felt numb.

"Enhad, Kaida."

The words came again and she stood, eyes now open. Her knees felt a bit weak as she stared at the massive head in front of her. "Kern?" Pins and needles seemed to race throughout her body. It felt as though the circulation had been lost then restored.

The white dragon looked grim as his multi-facetted eyes stared into hers. "We do not have time for you to cower, Fair Little Dragon," he admonished. "There are others who are in danger. Climb onto my back and we will be off. It is time to go into battle."

Looking around her, Anwen realized the whole room was filled with dragons. They were all brushing off dust or preparing to fly. She turned back to the Nurrim as he moved so she could mount his long neck. She quickly pulled the chain back around her neck, letting the key fall against her chest.

"Hurry, Little Dragon," Kern urged. "We do not have much time if we are to save the lives of those you love."

Setting her misgivings aside, Anwen stepped up and swung her legs over the first ridge. Trying to settle herself more securely, she almost fell as Kern pushed off from the ground. Rising majestically, he circled the pulsing crystal mass in the center of the chamber. And then he plummeted towards what looked like a small opening at the far end of the cavern.

Anwen couldn't help but scream as the air rushed past her. She'd never traveled so fast in her entire life. It was hard to not think they were going to crash, becoming a greasy spot on the stone walls. But Kern dropped through a large archway that more than accommodated his wingspan.

Flying past various openings, they sped towards the entrance. Anwen didn't dare look, ducking her head against the large spines as she held on for dear life. Would they make it in time? She wanted to be sick.

Down in the main courtyard, Walter made his way to Courtney's position. He couldn't tell just how badly she'd been injured but knew she'd be out of the game. It was difficult to reach her as he tried to dodge not only the mages but now dragon fire as well. He was running out of ammunition and still the mages came. Vaulting over some tumbled stone, he managed to pull the young mage towards a crag of rock.

Courtney hissed as her arm and shoulder were jogged, but she didn't complain. "Give me a sling," she gasped. "I can still fight."

Walter examined her arm and shoulder, shaking his head. "It's no good. I think you've broken more than a few bones. Probably tore some muscle in there too. Unless you know how to fix that kind of damage, you're probably not going to do much else."

Courtney tried to shake her head but stopped as the pain threatened to make her vomit. "What about Anwen? And Tyler?"

Walter did what he could to try and set her arm, wishing he'd brought some kind of painkillers with him. "I saw Tyler transform and fly off towards the Gates. Seems there's something major going on over there." He looked behind him to see a few mages headed their way. He pulled out his slingshot and fired off the last of his marble projectiles. "We need to retreat," he insisted. "Let the others handle things from here!"

The ground shook underneath them, sending boulders cascading down from the cliffs above. Walter pulled Courtney aside in time to avoid having her legs crushed under a tumbling stone. Screams ensued from the main square. The rocks continued to plow downward into the courtyard. They smashed tents and anything else in their way.

"Let's go," Walter yelled over the din. He hoisted Courtney up to her feet, pulling her good arm around his broad shoulders. "If we can reach that secret path the others used, we might be able to make it out of this alive."

Helping as much as she could, Courtney pushed along. She called out warnings as more stones fell around them. There seemed to be something wrong with the other mages. They now cowered in what looked like fear, but the two had no time to really consider what was going on around them. They had one priority, and figuring out what frightened the others wasn't it.

The Revenant raised her spear even further as she prepared to hurl it towards her victim. "Kaida! You're soul is mine!" With one swift motion, the spear left her disjointed fingers. It flew like the wind towards the space in front of the Gates.

At the last possible moment, Madame Millard jumped in front of Margo, her arms spread wide as if to shield her. The long spear pierced through her heart as Margo was knocked to the ground under the overweight mage. The weapon glanced off the stone beneath them. Thrown off course, the ground cracked the spear shaft as the dark shape hit the stone beneath the two women. It splintered, then shattered into a million pieces.

THIRTY-TWO

"OPEN YOUR EYES, LITTLE ONE," Kern admonished as he flew at breakneck speeds. "You need bear witness to what unfolds."

Anwen opened her eyes as she felt the upsweep of Kern's wings. He seemed to hover in the air as she looked over his arching neck. She was just in time to see a massive spear speed downward from the far side. Had she looked, she would have realized they'd come from an entrance far down the Endless Chasm. And while the others raced towards the City, Kern headed to the Gates where her mother had stayed behind. "Mom!" Her sweaty hands slipped as Kern banked to one side and she felt herself slipping. "No!"

Kern charged forward, heading towards the creature towering over the Gates. "You dare approach the Gates of Tarragon!" He brought his claws to bear when only halfway across the Ruined City.

Anwen couldn't maintain her hold any longer. She slid from his scales, falling towards the stones below. Just as she thought she'd hit the ground, she felt something close around her. It reminded her of the time she'd fallen off the Mountain into the Endless Chasm. Looking up, she realized that, once again, Tyler had saved her life. Holding onto his claws, she focused on the direction where Kern had flown. "Mom! I need to go to her! Please!"

Sensing her fear, Tyler changed course and sped towards the Gates. He dropped her at the head to pathway leading up to the Gates before going to joining his brother and the Nurrim above them. Anwen ran ahead, the key banging against her chest as she moved. "Mom! Mom!" Tears hit the ground as she ran.

With pounding heart, Anwen rounded the last bend to see her mother lying to one side. Margo's face and shirt were covered with blood. There was a long gash down her arm. "Mom!" Anwen dropped down by her mother's side, cradling her head in her arms. "Oh, mom," she sobbed.

It took Anwen a moment to realize Madame Millard's body had pinned her mother down. She tried to push the heavyset woman aside. It took a lot more effort than she'd thought possible. The woman was solid, even in death. But she finally managed to free her mother from the other woman's remains and pulled her into her arms.

Margo coughed as the pressure was released from her crushed ribcage. Blood dribbled from her lips. "Little one," she half whispered as she stared skyward, a look of wonder in her eyes. "You did it. You did…it…" Her eyes went glassy as her body went limp, growing heavier in Anwen's arms.

Anwen pulled back a little, staring in horror. "No," she shook her head, voice hoarse. "No. Mom! Mom!" Tears rolled freely down her face as she pulled her mother back up into her arms, but Margo was gone. "No!" Her anguished cry filled the air.

The weight of her burden began to change and she looked down in horror. Her mother's body was glowing. Light shone from her like it was coming from behind shattered glass. Afraid, Anwen set her mother down and edged away, trying to distance herself. Her progress was stopped when she ran into Madame Millard's still form.

As she watched, Margo's body seemed to fly apart in a flurry of matter. That matter swirled around the enclosed area. It glowed a brilliant green, reminding Anwen of young plants in spring. As though comprised of thousands of tiny fireflies, the energy swarmed. It then converged around Anwen's shaking form. For the briefest of moments, it reformed into the image of her mother.

Unbidden, Anwen raised her hand as if to caress it. She thought she felt her mother return the gesture. As she raised her hand, the ring she wore flashed. The swirling mass of energy streamed towards the ring as if compelled by a magnetic force. The stone blazed with a blinding light that only intensified as the particles all but flew into it. As the last vestiges of energy entered the ring, the rest of Margo's body faded away, as if only a wisp of smoke.

Anwen clenched her fists as she bowed over the empty space. When she raised her head, an even more anguished cry ripped from her throat. Tears fell like rain, further blinding her.

Overhead, Kern charged at the creature that had once been Kira. His massive claws shredded at air as the Revenant moved out of the way. It sprouted massive wings, beating them back. Tyler dived in for the next attack, trying to come down from the opposite side. Kira only dodged, almost causing the two dragons to collide with each other.

The demon's laughter filled the air as they continued to attack. Every now and then, a chunk of what looked like dark stone flew from the Revenant's body. But it didn't slow her down. She reached out with large claws, almost sketching a series of dark lines down Tyler's flank. He managed to get out of the way at the last possible second, Callum coming to his aide.

The air was suddenly rent with the sound of Anwen's anguished cries and Tyler faltered. Kira took advantage of that moment to knock him from the sky. He went crashing down towards the stones below.

Hearing the loud thud, Anwen looked up to see what was going on. She couldn't help but cry out as Tyler's draconic form rolling down the Mountain's side. Her mouth twisted in horror as she stared through reddened eyes. As she peered upwards to see the other dragons, the Revenant filled her view. Pain sprang into life inside her body and she screamed as it paralyzed her. She fell to the ground in agony.

Kern had no time to turn and see what caused the anguish of his youngest grandchild. Kira made another swipe at him with her gnarled fingers. Talons raked upwards to pierce anything they could touch. He dove, tucking in his wings to sweep around her form. He reached out his claws at the last possible moment to tear across her back. Callum swooped in from the other side.

Tyler lulled to one side as he came to a stop down in the City. He stared at the sky as fire lanced through his body, raw fire. He let out a loud bugle of pain as his vision threatened to fragment on him. He panted heavily from his own efforts and the connection he shared with Anwen. She was in trouble and there was nothing he could do about it.

Anwen felt as though over a thousand volts of electricity were coursing through her body. Sweat beaded up all over her as she writhed in agony. Above, thunder continued to crash across the sky as lightning ripped through the stratosphere. Rain began to fall heavily to the ground, coating everything in slippery mud and tears.

From around Anwen's neck, the crystal key glowed like foxfire. The ring on her finger only added to the pool of light around her. There was something important about that light but she couldn't make her mind work. What was it about the light? It was almost as if it were trying to remind her of something. But what was she forgetting? The pain was almost too much to bear.

Images swam before her eyes. Memories that had been shaken lose when she'd eaten the Diviner's Sage. Images of Tyler. Images of Courtney and Walter. And her mother. What was so important about them?

Somewhere out there is a dragon who is madly in love with you.

The sudden recollection of those words jolted her and she lay still. With eyes wide open, she felt that same warmth from inside the Mountain began to spread through her body. Love? Was that the answer? Did Tyler love her?

She saw herself in the Mountain. Being crushed by the collapsed cavern that had claimed Daphne's life. And there was Tyler, pawing at the rubble like a man possessed. When he'd uncovered her body, he'd cradled her in his arms like she was something precious. And then she saw him lay her body on the ground as he gathered his energy into one point.

Light filled her vision, pure, white light so bright she had to close her eyes. *"What the Mountain gave to me, now I give to you."* His words echoed through her mind as the warmth increased. She felt as though her entire body was glowing. The energy that coursed through her subdued the pain from the soul scars.

When Anwen opened her eyes, she found she was standing. The crystal key was in her hand, only it had elongated into a sword. And she was shouting words she was sure she didn't know.

Lightning flashed around her like she was in a cage of the electric energy. One bolt struck the tip of the sword, arcing out around her as fire rained down around them.

Tyler felt the pain suddenly lift from his body and he rolled to regain his footing. Hearing Anwen's voice, he moved towards her but paused. A pillar of fire seemed to envelope her as she wielded the Keeper's sword, pointing it towards the sky.

Out of the corner of his eye, Tyler saw Kern, Callum and Kira also pause as though dazzled by the light. They clung to the craggy tops of the Mountain, mesmerized by the light display below.

Kira let out a screech of outrage as the pillar of fire spread out from around Anwen's standing form. For the first time in her life, she felt fear. "You will die!" She made to launch herself at the lone girl but stumbled. White-hot light stabbed through her, immobilizing her as Anwen pointed the blade at her. "No!" she screamed in defiance.

Kern took that moment to tear great chunks from her body. He sent them tumbled down like giant boulders that rolled across the City below. Seeing Callum attacking the creature from the other side, Tyler went to join him. The light continued to build inside the demon as they tore great blocks of stone from her decaying body. From inside her shell, red light coalesced into a pool where her heart might have once been.

"Turn away!" Kern called out to his kinsman as the Revenant began to crack like glass under pressure. He shielded himself with his wings as he fell to the ground. Tyler and Callum did the same.

With a sudden onrush of air, the Revenant exploded into thousands of shattered pieces. The resulting fragments rained down on the courtyards below. Dragons flung up their wings to protect each other. The flying debris came down like miniature comets invading the sky.

Screams of pain escaped many leathery lips as the hot shards stung and burned scales and hides. One dragon pulled Courtney and Walter under its protective wing. More debris reigned down where they'd been standing only moments before.

Overhead, the clouds seemed to lighten. They returned to a more normal state as the skies wept on the scene below. Tyler soared over the Mountain as he peered down at where Anwen stood. He landed on the path leading towards her. Noticing her arm wavering under the weight of the sword, he sprang forward to try and catch her. He transformed as he ran, reaching her as she crumpled into his arms, the blade falling to the ground.

Tyler's mortal legs collapsed under him and he sat down heavily. Anwen lay cradled against his chest, eyes closed. He pressed one hand against her wet hair, stroking it over and over again. "Please," he kept whispering over and over again. He could her heart beating slower than his more frantic one and held her all the more tightly for it. "Please!"

Anwen groaned slightly as she opened her eyes. "Tyler? What are you doing here?"

The dragon lord smiled as he loosened his grip. "We really need to stop meeting like this." He gazed lovingly down at her dirt-streaked face. "It's not good for either of our health."

Anwen couldn't help but laugh. "Yeah, I think you're right." She leaned against his chest, shaking as her laughter turned to tears, the grief moving to the forefront of her thoughts. "She's gone," she sobbed. "My mom! She's gone."

Tyler pulled her closer, bending over her to kiss her hair. "I know, Anwen. I know."

THIRTY-THREE

COURTNEY STUMBLED AS WALTER HELPED her over a stretch of loose stone. Wincing, she leaned against him even more. Under the escort of several smaller dragons, they made their way towards the Gates. There, Kern stared down at the path from the same shelf Kira had used. Both Tyler and Anwen were sitting against the wall as if someone had just tossed them there. "They're not…dead are they?"

Walter hobbled forward, favoring his left leg as they climbed the last stretch of the path. He let out a weary sigh of relief. "No. They're alive," he confirmed as he leaned against the enclosing stone. "They did it!"

Tyler looked up from holding Anwen and gave half a smile. "Looks like you survived, old duffer," he commented with affection.

Walter puffed up his chest as Courtney hung on. He was taller than her and she had to stand on tiptoes to not fall over. "Didn't I tell you once? Nothing's going to bring me down that easy. I'm a survivor. Though I will want some form of repayment by way of certain kinds of goodies, if you know what I mean." He winked.

Looking around, Courtney couldn't help but feel something was missing. Then it hit her. "Where's Margo?" She risked causing more pain by turning to look behind her.

"Margo's dead," Tyler said bluntly. "Daphne's twin, Kira--no, that Revenant killed her. And Madame Millard. The woman tried to save Margo at the last moment but failed. I'd like to think she wasn't as bad as she'd pretended. Her last act proves it."

Kern transformed as he came down to join them, wearing white robes that were somewhat worn. His face was filled with compassion as he looked on the small group. "You have all done well," he smiled. "I am sorry that lives were sacrificed to bring us to this point. I would have avoided it if at all possible."

He walked over to Courtney and gently touched her shoulder. She felt as though the pain had melted away under his soft probing. "The damage is not as bad as it feels," he told her. "With a few days, it will be fully mended. I will set it to mending, but you must let nature take its course."

Turning to Walter, Kern looked a bit more stern. "You took quite a toll on my City with your little explosions," he admonished. "And many of the mage line were injured or killed. But," and he smiled, "I am happy to report that those who remain have backed down and are waiting to learn their fate. Many of my kinsmen are seeing to their wounded."

The Nurrim left Walter's side and paced over to where Tyler and Anwen sat. He shook his head as he surveyed them. "Daemyn, Daemyn," he tisked. "You were always the one known for level-headed behavior and wise judgment. And yet you have done that which should not have been done. Do you understand the depths of your transgression?"

Bracing himself, Tyler nodded. "I accept full responsibility for my actions," he replied. "Anwen had no part in my decision. As such, please do not punish her."

Anwen looked up in surprise, not sure she understood what was going on. "No!" she protested. "Tyler didn't do anything wrong. He's saved my life more times than I can count. If you must punish someone, punish me."

Tyler looked back at Anwen, caressing her face with one finger. "You don't know what you're saying, Anwen. You have no idea the taboo I've committed."

She pushed his hand away. "Yes I do. I know what you did for me back in the Mountain. I saw it as I sat here, writhing in agony from the soul scars Daphne gave me. You gave me part of your soul. Maybe I don't know what all that means, but what I do know is you're now a part of me. And, by extension, I'm a part of you. What happens to one should happen to both. Don't you agree?"

Courtney all but stumbled forward in her surprise. "Wait. What?" She stared at Tyler like he was insane. "You didn't? Did you? But when?" She tried to think back and then it hit her. She gasped as she covered her mouth with one hand. "Back in the Mountain…. That's when…"

"Yes," Tyler confirmed. "When I found Anwen, she was already almost dead. In fact, she died in my arms. But I couldn't accept that. There was still too much for her to do, or so I told myself. But, to be honest, I did it for me. I gave her a part of my soul because I wanted her to live. I couldn't make myself want to live in a world where she didn't."

Kern raised one brow as he contemplated the couple in front of him, his hands remaining folded in front of him. "I see. In that case, you have passed the test. It is rare to see such devotion. Yes, there are many who say theywould give their lives to another. But few would actually attempt to do so, forbidden or not. I pass no judgment upon you."

Tyler bowed his head, resisting the urge to celebrate the reprieve. "I thank you, my lord Nurrim."

At that moment, another dragon walked up the pathway, also in mortal form. "Ah, Callum," Kern called out as he turned towards the newcomer. "What have you to report?"

The older male turned to his leader, ignoring Tyler and Anwen. "The mages have surrendered completely. They are gathered in the main courtyard of the City. Or what is left of it. The others await your orders regarding their judgment."

Nodding, Kern fingered his long white beard. "I see. Thank you."

Callum's eyes glinted as he frowned. "If you would like my opinion, I suggest they be destroyed for their transgressions. It is a fit punishment for turning against us."

Courtney gasped as Walter moved forward. "Now wait just a minute," the veteran protested. "What you're suggesting is genocide. Not everyone down there knew what they were doing. They were never taught anything different than what they know. You can't just condemn them because of how they were brought up. It's not fair."

Callum eyed Walter with disdain. "What would a mortal know about fairness? You are merely an insect in our path. It would be quite easy to squash you where you stand."

"That's enough," Tyler said as he stood. He rested a hand briefly on Anwen's shoulder, giving her a light squeeze. "Just because you had a bad experience in the past does not mean you need take it out on those around you. It is just as Walter said. These mages were never brought up to believe or know anything outside what the Circle taught them. A rare few," he glanced briefly at Courtney, "thought to question their ways. Judging them based on their upbringing and the beliefs handed down to them by their parents is not just. Have you no mercy in your heart?"

Before the other dragon could retaliate, Anwen stood.

Her legs were a bit shaky, but she placed herself between the two immortals. "I do not excuse the events of what happened," she began. "But I do know that Tyler and Walter are right. If you are too foolish to see that, I feel sorry for you. I don't know what your problem is, but it can't really be with these people. After all, you've been asleep for hundreds of years, long before they were even born."

The Nurrim smiled at his granddaughter's nerve. "Peace," he soothed. "There are other matters that are more important. The events of today will not go unnoticed." He glanced around at the ruins about them, reminding them of recent events.

"With the help of this Fair Little Dragon," Kern nodded to Anwen, "we were able to dispatch a Revenant. The others will not take too kindly to that. It would be wise for us to expect retaliation, in one form or another."

The small party looked around as Kern's voice rose on the last sentence. Around them, many dragons had come to witness the events. They clung to the crags around the path, leaving the walkway clear to those in mortal form. Their massive wings filled the air as they reached towards the heavens. Walter shifted a bit uncomfortably at the amount of dragons surrounding them.

"I agree," Tyler said as he looked pointedly at his brother. "With the fall of the Revenant once known by another name, we have likely angered the others. We should prepare for the time when they come. And we will need every hand that we can get to help us." The other dragons raised the voices in affirmation, their bugles filling the air.

Turning towards Anwen, the Nurrim bowed. "As Master Keeper of the Realm of Tarragon, I ask that you would open the doors one more time, Anwen Kaida Porter."

Anwen gulped as she looked into the golden eyes of the master dragon. "Uh, sure." She bent down to pick up the crystal sword. It shrank back into a key the moment her hand touched the winged guard. Walking solemnly, she approached the closed Gates as the others moved out of the way to let her pass.

As she raised the key to the keyhole, Kern turned to face the gathered masses. His vast sleeves trailed as he raised his hands into the air. "Under the light of the Mage Moon, let the doors to Tarragon be open once more. Let this signify the ending and beginning of a new era."

Anwen inserted the key and turned it to the rumbling of many dragon voices bugling in triumph

KEEP READING FOR A SPECIAL
PREVIEW OF

Tarragon
Dragon Bane

COURTNEY SURVEYED THE REMAINS OF their campsite. The tents had both been taken down and were stowed in their respective bags. The stones from the fire pit had been scattered, along with the ashes. Only a few impressions, and a pile of gear, were left.

With a sigh, she tucked a stray strand of blonde hair back into place. Walter had already carted his stuff down to the raft. All that she needed to do was carry down the rest of the equipment, but still she hesitated.

An eagle soared overhead, its wings spread as it caught an updraft. Courtney followed its progress until it dropped out of sigh over the crest of the Island. It was an area she hadn't explored, nor might she ever. That place was sacred to the dragons.

The crunch of footsteps on the rough ground alerted her to the entrance of her companion. She turned to watch him come up through the trees. The forested island had been home for a short while, but not it was time to return to the village.

"Still waiting?" Walter asked as he entered the clearing. He glanced towards the rise of land where Anwen and Tyler had disappeared hours ago.

Courtney nodded. "It's still unreal," she confessed. "It feels like it was only yesterday that I was sparring with Margo." She paused to swallow a lump in her throat. "And now she's gone."

Walter nodded as he rubbed at the stubble on his chin. He was in desperate need of a shave, but hadn't taken the time. "I know," he said as he placed a hand on her shoulder. "I'm going to miss her too."

Margo had a quite personality. Her fiery spirit was hard to forget, down to her almost stubborn way of doing things. And even though she was Walter's senior in age, he couldn't help but think of her as a feisty kid sister.

Picking up the two tents, Walter turned to go. "Come on," he invited. "They'll come when they're ready."

Courtney grabbed the last bag and followed the veteran back down towards Lake Wyvern. Overhead, the sun filtered down through the trees. The sky all but shown a clear blue, with the occasional cloud on display. The light made the trees seem that much more alive.

The sapphire blue water of Lake Wyvern lapped at the sides of the rubber military raft that was tied to the small jetty. It was not the same jetty they'd used that first time to cross over to the Island, but one that jutted out from where the tail of the Island would have thrust out. From above, the Island looked like the body of a partially submerged dragon. And at the top, there was the Sacred Grove, with its emerald-leafed trees.

Walter threw the last of the luggage into the raft and tied it down. "I think we're ready," he called out and the water started to bubble.

Two water dragons swam to the surface. Their scales were a darker variation of the water's color. Their serpentine bodies were sleek and wingless. Their eyes were wiser than mortal thought.

"You called?" one asked as it lifted its head from the water. "Are you ready to return to the shore?"

Courtney nodded dumbly to their guides. It was still strange to see real flesh and blood dragons, besides Tyler that was. Even that had taken some getting used to.

The two mortals stepped into the boat and took their positions while the other dragon wound the rope around its body. Water sloshed up onto the sand as the serpent spun to secure the rope. With a nudge from the first sea snake, the boat began to move, pulling away from the shore.

A cool draft of air filtered across the water as Courtney looked back. She fancied she saw a glint of silver from the crown of the Island, and then it was gone.

Anwen let her long hair flow freely in the breeze. It had been almost a week since the great battle, and her heart was still numb. Her light purple dress swept around with the wind as she stared ahead.

As was custom from the time before the Mountain was sealed, she raised the bone knife Tyler had lent her. With great ceremony, she slipped the blade between branch and trunk of one of the majestic trees. The small branch fell into her other hand, the smooth white bark almost warm against her skin.

With equal ceremony, Tyler took back the white knife and put it in his pocket. "Let that which was taken be returned to the Mountain," he intoned as Anwen presented the branch to him. He held the limb aloft so that the sun's rays ran the length of it.

Anwen felt a tear run down her face as she accepted the smooth stick back once more. "Rest in peace, mom," she whispered. When they returned to the mainland, the tree fragment would be woven into the lattice-covered niches on the path to the Ruined City. There, for generations untold, those of mortal blood who had sacrificed for dragon kind had been buried. She was glad she would not be the one doing the weaving.

A solemn assembly had been held inside the Main Hall of Tarragon for all who had died during the battle. A smaller gathering had collected to mourn the passing of Margo Kaida Pack, Anwen's mother. But, with no body, the actual burial hadn't taken place. This was the next best thing.

Most of the dragon mages had returned to their homes in the Village of Lindwyrm. Some had stayed in the City to help rebuild the once majestic structures they had helped to destroy. With the death of their leader, Madame Millard, they had taken the leadership offered by the dragons. And Anwen, as the Kaida, had taken charge of them, albeit reluctantly.

"I still wish Kern hadn't asked me to take charge of the mages," Anwen sighed as she wrapped her clipping in a silk sleeve. "There are more qualified people. Like Courtney." It didn't matter that Courtney was her age, still a teenager. She at least had more skill as a mage.

Tyler looked as though he was about to disagree but was distracted. It was almost as if he heard something but wasn't sure. "I'll be right back," he assured as he headed off towards the far side of the Grove.

Anwen watched him in surprise but didn't follow. Something about his expression told her he didn't want her coming along.

Tyler loped towards the section he'd heard the sound coming from. It was the same area where he'd met Kaida Magus before the battle. Upon reaching the large boulder by which the mage had stood, he stopped. But Kaida wasn't there.

"Hello?" Tyler called out as he peered around the trees. "Anyone here?"

The sound of giggling came from a small copse of trees just outside the stone line that marked the Grove boundaries. It was a child-like sound, both young and carefree. Tyler knew he'd heard it before. His suspicions were confirmed as a young child popped out of the trees.

Unlike the last time he'd seen this child, she wore a dark green dress that made her red hair even more poignant. "Hi," she said with a wave. Her fingers were as translucent as before, though the rest of her seemed more solid.

Walking slowly, Tyler approached her. "Hello," he greeted, squatting to be at eye level with her. "What are you doing here? Where are your parents?"

The child smiled a secretive smile as she put hands behind her back and twisted at the waist, back and forth. It had been the same question he'd asked her the first time they'd met. "They're busy," she replied. "Mawmaw's talking to mommy. Wanna play?"

Unconsciously, Tyler reached out a hand and ruffled her hair. It took a moment to register the odd sensation of not quite touching something. "Maybe some other time. Is your friend Kaida here?"

The little girl looked thoughtful for a moment, but shook her head. "Nope. But Mawmaw says I can play. You need ask Mawmaw?"

Tyler couldn't help but laugh. "You're persistent," he observed. "Alright, little one. What is your name?"

Her smile widened as she leaned closer as if to tell a secret. "They call me Emi," she whispered conspiratorially.

COMING 2018

GLOSSARY

Anwen Porter - Daughter of James Porter and Margo Pack, 17-year-old. Considered the last Key Keeper alive.

Blaucii, City of - City at the foot of the Drakonii Mountain Range, includes an Express station.

Bone Knife - A knife carved from bone (possibly dragon), usually used by dragon mages. Can be manipulated to change shape and size, pending on the need.

Bounding Circle – The stone boundary surrounding the Sacred Grove. It contains special wards and powers which protect the Grove and has the ability to make manifest the soul energy of any who pass near it.

Callum Durand - Older brother of Tyler Durand, one of the Dragon Council. A silver dragon with green undertones with the ability to change his physical shape.

Cascade Falls - A series of waterfalls at the furthest end of Lake Wyvern. Also the location of a small outpost.

Consecrated Hall - Located on the main path to the Ruined City, a corridor of black obsidian-like stone with white and blue veins of quartz running throughout the walls. Holds mysterious properties, including the ability to bring out memories of those who traverse its length, connecting them with the path on a spiritual level.

Courtney Willis - 17-year-old Fledgling dragon mage who grew up in the Village of Lindwyrm.

Crystal Chamber - A cavern found inside the underground city of Tarragon, where the Great Crystal, the Heart of the Mountain, is located.

Crystal Sword - A sword made from a shard of the Great Crystal, entrusted to the Master Key Keeper.

Daphne Millard - 19-year-old advanced dragon mage, a native of the Village of Lindwyrm.

Diviner's Sage (Salvia Divinum) – Also known as the Sage's Fruit, an herb that grows in a boggy climate, with brilliant green leaves on hollow stems. Violet flower bursts protrude from the top. Velvety in texture, the leaves are either infused with water to make a tea, or are chewed outright. The plant produces a sense of giddiness, along with visions and enhanced insight. Considered dangerous and must be used with caution.

Doc - A doctor living and practicing in the Village of Lindwyrm.

Dragon Born – One with dragon blood in their veins, usually referring to dragon mages

Dragon Council - A council body, usually comprising of twelve members, ten dragon lords, the Master Key Keeper, and the Kaida. Used to administer the laws of Tarragon and decide on any major course of Tarragon's citizens.

Dragon Mage - Any human (mortal) of dragon descent, with the ability to manipulate magic (matter).

Dragon Magic - the ability to manipulate matter through magic.

Dragon Meade - A special brew of Meade perfected by the dragons. Said to restore vigor and focus for limited spans of time.

Dragon Moon - The first full moon of summer, said to cause unusual abilities, or luck upon those blessed by the Mountain Spirits.

Dragon Moon Festival - A festival held in the Village of Lindwyrm to celebrate the arrival of the Dragon Moon.

Dragon Sight - The ability to see matter down to its basic elements of atoms, protons, and neutrons. The highest ability of Soul Sight

Drakonii Mountain Range - A mountain range located on the continent of Kekukani.

Dridi Inn - The only inn/hotel in the Village of Lindwyrm. Run by the Millard family, it fronts the River Drage..

Endless Chasm - A chasm along the main path to the Ruined City. The bottom has never been found.

Fallen - Considered a lesser demon, these are creatures/humans twisted from their natural state by a dragon mage or Revenant, and can take on the form of any animal. Used to hunt down Key Keepers by the Mage Circle.

Front Gallery - The first room past the Gates of Eternity, comprising a massive hall of stone, supported by stone pillars.

Gates of Eternity - The main gates, found inside the Ruined City, that lead to Tarragon.

Great Crystal - Considered "the Heart of the Mountain this crystal is both multi-faceted and grand in size. Comprising many different colors, the core is red and pulses like a heart. It is said to contain unique properties.

Great Exile - A period of time shortly after Tarragon was sealed from the outside where many were exiled from the Drakonii Mountains. Those exiled included all associated with the Key Keepers, as well as any dragon mage who defied the Mage Circle.

Hour of the Mage - A period of time when the abilities of dragon mages are amplified due to the movement of the celestial bodies in the sky.

Imugi Dragon - A type of water dragon without legs, often called a sea serpent.

Infirmary - the name of the hospital in the Village of Lindwyrm.

James Porter - Father of Anwen Porter, husband to Margo Pack. Murdered when Anwen was a young child. Was the last male Key Keeper.

Josef Forster - 19-year-old native of the Village of Lindwyrm, engaged to Daphne Millard.

Kaida, The - The title given to the master dragon mage, handed down mother to daughter in direct descent from Kaida Magus.

Kaida Magus - The first dragon mage, child of Kern Nurrim and Anna Durand Magus.

Key Keeper - One of mortal descent charged with the safely of Tarragon, and Keeper of the Keys to all gates leading to Tarragon.

Kira Millard - 19-year-old advanced dragon mage, native of the Village of Lindwyrm. Identical twin of Daphne Millard

Kern Durand - The oldest dragon and father to Kaida Magus. Also the head of the Dragon Council. A white dragon of immense age.

Lake Wyvern - A large, sapphire blue lake located inside the Drakonii Mountains. Holds the Sacred Isle.

Light Orb - An orb of white or yellow light composed of compressed matter, conjured by means of dragon magic.

Madame Matilda Millard - Proprietress of the Dridi Inn, dragon mage, lives in the Village of Lindwyrm.

Mage Blade - Any metal weapon infused with the blood of a Revenant. Usually used by dragon mages from the Mage Circle.

Mage Circle - A gathering of dragon mages bent on controlling or destroying all dragons.

Mage Moon - First new moon after the Dragon Moon.

Mage Sight – A form of Soul Sight, it allows the user to see basic components of a soul

Margo Pack - Mother to Anwen Porter, wife of James Porter. A dragon mage in hiding.

Master Key - The main key to the Gates of Eternity, kept by the Master Key Keeper, passed down through genetic line.

Master Key Keeper - The individual charged with the safety of the Master Key, inherited through genetic line.

Matthias' Last Stand - The even when all gates to Tarragon were sealed against the Mage Circle, before the Great Exile.

Matthias Porter - Ancestor of Anwen Porter, Master Key Keeper who sealed the gates to Tarragon.

Mountain, The - The Mountain containing the Ruined City and the main gateway to Tarragon.

Mountain Spirits - Reference to the sleeping dragons sealed inside the Mountains of Tarragon.

Mr. Millard - husband of Madame Matilda Millard, dragon mage, native of the Village of Lindwyrm.

Nurrim, The - Title given to the eldest dragon and ruler of the Dragon Council.

Old Mill - An old gristmill found on the River Drage near Lake Wyvern

Porter - The last name of the family charged with the protection of the Master Key.

 Quad - A grassy area behind the town hall in the Village of Lindwyrm.

Revenant - considered the true demon, they are the sworn enemies of dragons and were created at the same time as the dragons. They possess the ability to manipulate matter and can usurp the forms of other living creatures.

Ritual of Obliteration - A ritual utilizing dragon magic in a twisted way. It is used to destroy the soul of the intended target, erasing them from existence.

River Drage - The main river in the Drakonii Mountain Range. It feeds into Lake Wyvern.

Ruined City, The - A ruined city found in the Drakonii Mountain Range. Originally the home to Key Keepers and dragon mages loyal to Tarragon.

Sacred Grove - A grove of trees at the top of the Sacred Isle, home of the Sacred Shrine. Believed to be lost from time.

Sacred Isle - The largest of three islands located in Lake Wyvern, contains the Sacred Grove.

Sacred Shrine - A stone alter made from the same obsidian stone as the Consecrated Hall.

Simulacrum - A spirit being using material, such as dust, to manifest itself in physical form.

Sashamae - An herb with purple spiked flowers and long roots of a purple hue. Used to remove toxins by infusion in a tea or by using the oil/sap from the flower.

Soul Energy – The manifestation of the soul's aura

Soul Gaze – The ability to discern the aura of any living thing, the most basic form of Soul Sight.

Soul Presence – The manifestation of one's soul or energy through the fabric of time, felt only by the most skilled of mages or those dragon born.

Soul Sharing - The act of sharing part of one's' soul with another. Considered a taboo practice.

Soul Sight – The ability to look into view the aura of another's soul, also called Soul Gaze

Soul Speech - The ability to speak soul to soul.

Soul Tracing – The ability to discern the state of any being by tracing the soul wavelength of said being

Tarragon - The underground city of the dragons, found in the Drakonii Mountain Range.

Tawny Falls - A city on the other side of the continent of Kekukani.

Tyler Daemyn Durand - With the appearance of a 17-year-old, a dragon lord living near the Village of Lindwyrm, one of the Dragon Council. Brother to Callum Durand. A silver dragon with blue undertones.

Village of Lindwyrm - A mountain village in the Drakonii Mountain Range.

Vision Dust - A sand-like substance taken from under the Heart of the Mountain, used to facilitate visions.

Walter Watkins- A veteran in his mid to late 30's, former chief medic in the reserves, friend to Tyler Durand, lives in the city of Blaucii.

Woodruff (wild baby's breath)- a plant used as potpourri and, when mixed with certain other plants, as a detoxifying agent.

The Line of Porter

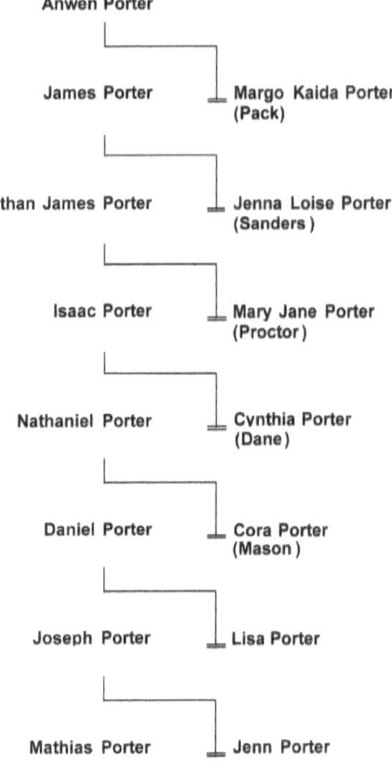

The Line of Kaida

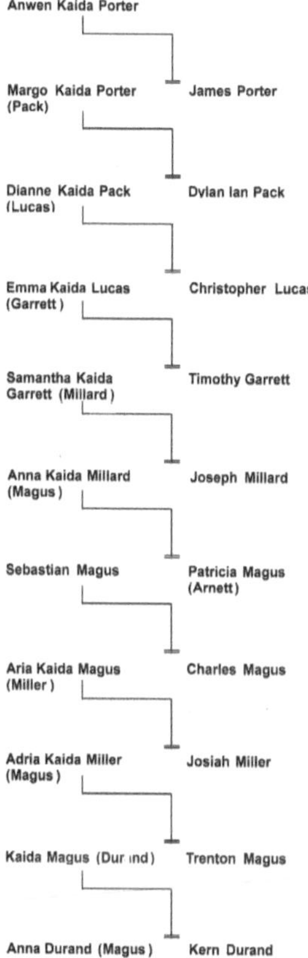

ABOUT THE AUTHOR

Karlie Lucas is a member of the Society for Children's Writers and Illustrators, as well as the American Night Writer Association. A graduate of Southern Utah University, Karlie received a Bachelor of Arts in Creative Writing. She is a member of Sigma Tau Delta, The International English Honor Society. She is interested in all things magical and mysterious, especially elves and dragons. She currently resides in the Dallas, Texas area with her husband.

Check out her blog and website at:
http://www.karlielucas.com

www.ingramcontent.com/pod-product-compliance
Lightning Source LLC
Chambersburg PA
CBHW050506190726
48284CB00003B/710